HOLLOW MAN

ALSO BY MARK PRYOR

The Bookseller

The Crypt Thief

The Blood Promise

The Button Man

The Reluctant Matador

HOLLOW MAN
MARK PRYOR

SEVENTH STREET BOOKS®

AN IMPRINT OF PROMETHEUS BOOKS

59 JOHN GLENN DRIVE • AMHERST, NY 14228

www.seventhstreetbooks.com

Published 2015 by Seventh Street Books®, an imprint of Prometheus Books

Cover image © Matthew Heptinstall
Cover design by Jacqueline Nasso Cooke

This is a work of fiction. Characters, organizations, products, locales, and events portrayed in this novel either are products of the author's imagination or are used fictitiously.

Inquiries should be addressed to
Seventh Street Books
59 John Glenn Drive
Amherst, New York 14228
VOICE: 716–691–0133
FAX: 716–691–0137
WWW.SEVENTHSTREETBOOKS.COM

19 18 17 16 15   5 4 3 2 1

Library of Congress Cataloging-in-Publication Data

Pryor, Mark, 1967-
 Hollow man / by Mark Pryor.
  pages ; cm
 ISBN 978-1-63388-086-3 (pbk.) — ISBN 978-1-63388-087-0 (e-book)
 1. Psychological fiction. I. Title.

PS3616.R976H65 2015
813'.6—dc23

2015011552

Printed in the United States of America

To my brother, Richard.
I will always be grateful for your belief in me
and your support all these years.
I love you very much.
And, sooner rather than later,
I shall see you on the slopes . . .

CONTENTS

"Those who have crossed
With direct eyes, to death's other kingdom
Remember us—if at all—not as lost
Violent souls, but only
As the hollow men . . ."

—"The Hollow Men" by T. S. Eliot

CHAPTER ONE

CACTUS LAND

My parents' lawyer called with the news as I climbed out of my car, our conversation a hesitant hopscotch of words until we caught up to the slight delay that comes with international calls. His voice seemed thinned out by the distance between us, me in a downtown garage in Austin, Texas, him in his small village in England.

Or perhaps the quaver in his voice came from what he had to tell me. The news, of course, wasn't good. People don't make long-distance calls to strangers for anything but the bad, and so he cleared his plummy little throat and told me that my parents were dead. Killed yesterday, on the family farm.

"I'm frightfully sorry," he said.

I thought at first he must be joking, or mistaken. But English solicitors don't play cruel practical jokes, and they certainly don't make mistakes like this. Which meant that my mum and dad, both of them, were really dead and had been since yesterday. Dead when I went to bed last night, dead when I got up this morning, dead when I was deciding how many tacos I wanted for breakfast. I didn't know what to say, and when I tried to speak, nothing but a croaking came out, so I stayed silent.

"There was a big storm," he explained. "The next morning your parents went for a walk to see if there was any damage, trees blown over, that sort of thing. Your father stepped on a downed power line." My mum, he said, raced over to help without realizing what had happened, and reached for her husband's hand one last time.

"I'm sorry," he said again, "I'm sure this is quite a . . ." He couldn't very well say *shock*, but it was the right word.

"Thank you for letting me know," I said. I closed my car door behind me and kept the phone to my ear.

"You're probably wondering about . . . the farm, all the practical stuff."

I wasn't, of course. I was struggling to bring up a clear picture of my parents. It's a funny thing that when you've not seen people for a decade, even people you love and who love you, their faces seem to quiver in your mind, blurring in and out. I stood there in the garage, a block of sunlight creeping toward my toes, and I simply couldn't bring up a clear image of them.

But Craig Whitfield, Esquire, didn't know that. He was like so many English people of his generation and class: welcoming the busy necessities so they could blanket those awkward emotions that one was supposed to experience weakly, and express not at all.

"Not the best news there, either, I'm afraid," he was saying. "You see, farming isn't what it was twenty years ago. The new, open Europe has been good for everyone except farmers—can't compete, and the subsidies are a fraction of what they used to be. As a result, I'm afraid your father picked up a spot of debt along the way. More than a spot, quite frankly. The land is worth something, but some of the larger fields he'd already sold off and was leasing back."

"Oh, I didn't know that." I didn't know that because I hadn't spoken to my parents in many years.

"I'm the executor of the will, so I'll have more information in a week or so, once everything's tallied up."

"What about the funeral arrangements?"

"They didn't want one. You know them—they weren't religious in any way and didn't believe in making a fuss over the dead. They have identical wills, which say they want to be cremated and their ashes spread in the back meadow. No service, no memorial."

Just gone.

My mind held a picture of them now, a little fuzzy but safely created and tucked away, high on a shelf but visible for when I wanted to see it. My father thin and weathered, an unruly flop of hair his only departure from a life of order and logic. My mother just as wiry, a pretty lady when she made the effort, but a woman of the country, just as hardy and ready to work as her husband.

I struggled for something to say, wondering what I *ought* to say to a stuffy English solicitor bearing bad tidings. I didn't really know even though my mind was working overtime, processing all he'd told me, but I knew that I didn't want this call to end, not yet. It couldn't end because then I'd be left holding a phone in the gathering heat of a Texas summer morning, and everything would be the same as yesterday, except my parents would be dead. This moment, this call, it was too brief to herald the obliteration of the people who'd conceived, raised, and eventually exiled me.

But I had nothing to ask. I knew how they'd died, and I knew the farm would disappear into the debt hole they'd created; and with them and it gone, all connections were severed. Just a final "tally up" from Craig Whitfield, Esquire, probably no more than an e-mail letting me know precisely how worthless my inheritance was.

"Right," I said. "No funeral. That makes sense for them, I guess. Do I need to come over there for anything?"

"No," he said, a little too hurriedly. "I'll spread their ashes, it's what they wanted. I'll take care of all the paperwork, the legal mumbo-jumbo, and send you a copy of the wills. Like I said, I don't know that there'll be much—we'll have to have an estate sale to take care of the bills. There's a guitar, though, your dad's old one that he wanted you to have. You play?"

"I do. Prosecutor by day, musician by night."

"Splendid. You'll appreciate the guitar, then."

"Absolutely. Thanks again." I stood there in the shadows of the garage, the stale smell of urine and dust coming into focus as Mr. Whitfield's presence receded.

"Yes, you're very welcome." His voice softened, as if emotion was allowed after all, or a measure of sympathy anyway. "And my condolences, Dominic, it's all quite a shame."

Indeed. My parents had been electrocuted to death, and even though I'd not seen them in a long time, they'd finally abandoned me permanently, irrevocably, taking into oblivion with them the house I'd been born in, the fields I'd played in, and the woods I'd explored for my most formative years. So yes, at that moment I tended to agree with Craig Whitfield, Esquire, that it was all quite a shame.

O

I put the phone in my pocket and stared out into the sunlight, perched on the hood of my car, wondering whether to go home, go to England, or do what my parents would have done: carry on with a stiff upper lip. They'd done that after I left, got on with their lives while allowing for the occasional parental exploit, a Christmas or birthday card. Eventually, like the missives from a senile grandparent, the cards stopped arriving. I didn't mind as much as I ought to have, just because I knew what my parents were like and I knew that day would come. It wasn't born of callousness, either, just practicality. Logic. What would an estranged son want with a birthday card from someone he's not seen in years? Exiling me wasn't an act of callousness, either, though it's easy to see it that way, pitch it as one. As much as anything, it was a way of saving me from something I'd done, something that could have had much worse consequences than a new life in America.

It happened when I was sixteen years old, on a foggy morning in the English village of Weston, when I mistook the florid features of a local man for a rising pheasant and shot him in the face.

The man died the next day, and as usual I thought I could atone for my misdeed by writing a song. My family called me cold-blooded, and when I tried to explain some of the things the man had done, they wouldn't listen, they didn't care, as if death erased the man's own misdeeds. It wasn't the first time they'd failed to believe me, but it was the most serious, and the last. Instead of writing my song, I was shipped to wealthy and disinterested relatives in Texas. There, I lived out my youth in a military school where I hung on to my accent for dear life and carried a guitar everywhere I went. I stayed in Texas when I graduated and my most prized possession remained my guitar, but I quickly bought a gun and loved it enough to make my guitar sing with jealousy. It was a semiautomatic Smith & Wesson, sexy but not as beautiful as the antique Purdey shotguns I'd left behind in England. The shotguns. When I was on the phone with the lawyer, I'd wanted to ask for them, ask him what would become of them. But the thought seemed crass. Hell, maybe my father already sold them, after what happened.

In all other ways, and as I've done ever since I came to America and came to know myself, I donned the local camouflage and learned to fit in: I kicked my car door closed with a cowboy boot every day and strolled into work with a breakfast taco in each hand. After a few years, I thought I was free and clear of my tragic past but, as they say, accidents happen in threes.

The first one came with that pull of a trigger and exiled me to Texas. The second one was a slower kind of disaster that hid itself inside a normal Thursday, a day that started out like any other. A slow-burn disaster that, step by step, twisted my future out of trajectory. Not as quickly as the blast of a gun but in a way that, much later, made me think I should have seen it coming.

A car passed me, adding its fumes to the rancid air in the garage, and I wanted out of there. Not to go home, I didn't need to spend the day in maudlin reverie. Nor was I needed in England. I'd do what I could to honor my parents and behave the way they'd hope for, the way they'd behave and expect me to. I'd go to work.

I opened the front door and retrieved my 9mm from the glove compartment and tucked it into its cloth bag. A second wave of oil and piss hit me, and I held my breath while I locked my gun and guitar in the trunk, as I did every day. This garage was for county employees only, but defendants at the neighboring courthouse used it without compunction, which should have surprised no one, but seemed to. As a result, I threw furtive looks over my shoulder as I stashed the guitar case and felt that daily twinge of hope it'd be there when I finished work. I'd asked to have cameras put up in the garage (I had a thing for cameras and surveillance, having won some of my biggest trials because critical moments were caught on tape), but neither the county nor the city wanted to pay for them.

They went everywhere with me, the gun and the guitar, everywhere except the office. Even though I prosecuted murderers and rapists for a living, my boss had seen fit to ban us from packing heat while at work. Our offices were in the same building as the courts, so he was right that the place was stuffed to the gills with cops and sheriffs but, for an Englishman living in Texas, not being allowed to carry my sidearm was a grave disappointment.

I took the stairs to exit the parking deck, having learned my lesson about the unreliable lift on two separate occasions. To my right sat a small park, a hollow of dead grass and bare earth with a surrounding ribbon of sidewalk that guided men and women in suits toward the criminal courthouse. Sitting catty-corner to the courts, the park was littered with the unmoving bodies of the homeless, a dozen or more lying still in the gathering heat. It was the first of July, and soon these men, and a few women, would rise like zombies to begin the daily ritual of plodding across the worn, brown grass to their favorite tree to bag space for the day. As the sun rose and normal people sought shelter in air-conditioned offices and malls, these people shuffled their packs and ragged bodies, creeping in tiny circles like the shadows of a sundial in their attempts to stay cool.

I stood in the shade of the parking lot and watched, something I often did. Had always done. My best friend back home had once come across me—I think I was about nine years old—sitting in a tree in the school playground. My back to the trunk, legs dangling as I watched my classmates roam around beneath me. He'd likened me to a leopard, alert, solitary, a cat of prey sitting high on my branch while the world passed by.

A chorus of voices drew my attention to a row of colorful media trucks that lined the curb around the courthouse plaza, their engines humming in anticipation of action, antennas spiking from their roofs and wires spilling from their sides. The reporters, called *talent* for no reason I could figure out, were getting ready for the morning's live broadcast, coiffing their hair and powdering their noses. A quick scan showed they were all male.

I moved toward the news vans, and when I got close, I spotted Patrick Stephens. He'd covered my last murder trial and given me some airtime when the jury came back with a guilty verdict. I liked him more than the other reporters who, with their serious faces and fake importance, were like car salesmen always looking for an angle. Not Patrick. He was like a friendly Irishman who'd buy you pints at the pub and expect nothing in return except a joke or two. He was red-haired, roly-poly, twinkly-eyed, and the only person I knew who looked ten pounds lighter on camera.

"Hey, it's Dominic, the musical British prosecutor," he said. "You look frowny, what's wrong?"

"You know, the usual. Shitty news arrives early in the morning just so it can screw up your whole day."

"That's why we have a morning show," he grinned. "Care to unload on a friend?"

"When I find one, I will." My smile was supposed to be friendly, to show I was joking, but I expect it looked as insincere as it felt. "Also, I'm a musician, not musical. And I'm English, not British. How would you like me to call you Canadian?"

"Just fine. I'm from Ottawa."

"I feel like I should know that. Eh?"

"Hilarious. But I've been in Texas ten years, so don't sweat it."

He interrupted a stroke of his comb to look over at the growing crowd.

"Why are you chaps here?" I asked.

"Covering the Wilbert trial," he said. "Closing arguments today. Should be good."

"Yeah, any time a kid gets stabbed it's awesome."

The Wilbert trial. The man looked like a librarian but had stabbed his ex-girlfriend thirty-six times with a knife he took from her kitchen. When her five-year-old ran screaming to his momma's side, Wilbert stabbed him four times. Momma died at the scene, but the boy lived, which, if nothing else, seemed like poor planning. Leaving a witness, and all.

"You know what I mean." He poked me in the chest with his comb. "And don't act all high and mighty—we both make money from other people's tragedies."

"Except I do something positive about them, whereas you guys turn them into gossip."

"I'll remember that next time you ask for some airtime."

"*Touché.*" I looked toward the courthouse but the main entrance was out of view. The building was U-shaped, the left wing being the jail, the right wing housing the admin buildings, and the entrance at the end of a walkway that ran between them. The protestors filled the walkway that led to the main doors. "So, not here to report on the protest?"

"We'll cover it," he said. "Your office rarely seeks the death penalty, so this lot doesn't usually come out."

"Well, have fun. I have a boss waiting for me."

Before I could move off, a chorus of shouts exploded from the courthouse entrance. We couldn't see what was happening, but the shouting got louder and several deputies dropped their cigarettes and started running toward the noise. The reporters finished patting their noses in double-time, and the cameramen hoisted their equipment onto their shoulders and headed into battle.

By the time I got there a line of brown-shirted sheriff's deputies had blocked the passageway to the front doors. Behind them, eight more deputies knelt on the wriggling bodies of four men. The TV cameras were trained on the melee but it wasn't the subdued protestors that had their attention.

The glass front of the courthouse, including its two enormous doors, dripped red, the crimson liquid pooling on the sidewalk and creeping out toward the crowd. On the ground, a dozen Mason jars lay cracked or broken, glinting on the white concrete like busted teeth lying amid unfurling tongues of red.

I walked up to the line of officers, aiming for one I recognized from the courtroom. I covertly checked the tag on his chest.

"Hey, Bateman, what the hell's going on?"

"Protestors," he said.

"No shit. I hope that's paint."

"Nope, it's blood."

"Delightful. Cow or pig?"

"I wish." He looked over his shoulder at the mess. "Theirs."

"The protestors'?"

"Yep." Bateman nodded. "One of the assholes said they've been storing it up since the beginning of the trial, about twenty of them. Taking a pint here and there, sticking it in the fridge. They showed up with jars of it, just started flinging the stuff all over the front."

"Jesus. That's disgusting."

"It's a friggin' health hazard, is what it is. We got the ones who did the actual throwing, though." He grinned and thumbed toward the four in custody. "The stupid fuckers were too weak to run."

More bad planning. "Anti–death penalty nuts?"

"Right." He mimicked them while pulling a pouty face. "If the state can spill blood in our name, we can spill our own."

I could smell it now, a metallic odor that clung to the air and started to coat the inside of my nostrils. It was 9:15 a.m. on the first day of July, and every day of June had been over ninety degrees. I could almost hear the flies swarming toward us, rising up from the dumpsters and roadkill, passing word to each other about the delicacy that soaked the courthouse like gravy, human blood ready to simmer and bake in the heat, a once-in-a-lifetime treat not to be missed.

"Who's cleaning that mess up?" I asked.

"They're sending a hazmat team. Who knows how many of those fuckers have HIV or hep-C or some shit."

"So the courthouse is shut down?" My voice rose with hope.

"Closed to the public. They're letting the lawyers in through the judge's entrance. No day off for you."

"Great. Any chance some others will come back and splatter the judge's entrance before I get there?"

Bateman laughed, the cracking sound in his throat telling me he was due for his morning cigarette. "They're guarding it pretty good, so I'm guessing you're out of luck."

I moved away, pushing through the crowd. As I reached its outer edge, I noticed several people looking back and forth from the scene to the bus stop across the street. Two women stood there, apparently disinterested in the chaos and confusion, which told me they were probably involved. One of them was Hispanic, and she'd squeezed herself into jeans and a T-shirt several sizes too small, giving her a bulge of fat that surrounded her waist like a ship's life preserver.

The other girl turned to face me, and my throat closed up. She was strikingly pale, with wide-spaced eyes that returned my gaze without blinking. She wore no makeup that I could see, but her brown hair tumbled onto her shoulders with perfect Lauren Bacall elegance. Best of all, she wore a tight, lime-green dress that shimmered as it hugged her figure, catching the light and my eye like a hypnotist's crystal. China-white legs curved out from the hem of her dress, down to delicate ankles and a pair of red heels that were brighter, and even more startling, than the pools of blood she'd just left behind.

With everything that had happened that morning, she was something glorious to hold on to, a beautiful flash of lightning in a doom-laden sky, and I couldn't tear my eyes away. I stood and stared until a bus came between us, breaking the spell and taking her away in a roar of hot diesel fumes. I couldn't see her through the tinted windows of the bus, but I stared at each one just in case, and I hoped like a teenager that she was peering back at me.

When the bus had gone, I stood in the quiet street for a full minute, wondering what had just happened. Not love at first sight, I wasn't capable of that, but nonetheless a childlike rush of excitement that I waited to analyze, that I let myself enjoy before dissecting it into rationalities that made sense to me, labeling it with worlds like *curiosity, surprise, interest,* and the more carnal and justifiable *lust.*

CHAPTER TWO

THE PRICKLY PEAR

Puzzled and oddly chastened, I made my way to the judge's entrance, punching numbers and swiping my way through three security doors. As they thumped shut behind me, they pushed the girl in green from my mind and I made mental adjustments to begin the routine of the day.

My job at the DA's office wasn't always the most exhilarating, but the pay was decent and at least kept my head and budget above water, though barely. Today I was going to cross swords with a recalcitrant witness, the kind of thug I took great pleasure in putting behind bars. Normally this idiot would be the one holding the gun, but for this case he'd been one of the victims. He was recalcitrant in that he didn't want to testify in the upcoming trial, and I needed him to.

That was the one part of my job I did relish, the part that fed the performer in me and made my day-to-day acting a benefit, not a burden: the theater of a jury trial. It began with the drama of opening statements, when the story of the crime was first revealed to the jurors, twelve men and women twitchy with anticipation, eager to soak up my words. Then came the witness examinations, the orchestrated reinforcement of my opening statements, when the jurors would nod along and think to themselves, *Yes, the prosecutor said it happened that way, we should believe him.*

Occasionally there would be cross-examination, when a half-witted defendant would take the stand and try to lie his way out of a conviction, and those moments, not just for me but for any prosecutor, could be sublime. The gentle questions that would begin to unravel his story, without him even knowing, then the flourish of a question, asked with eyes on the jury, not the dirtbag defendant, and a slow turn to watch him squirm in his seat as he realized the game was over. A game for me, of course, not so much for him.

And finally, the closing arguments. Most lawyers claim that jurors are decided on a verdict by the time we stand to close. But I never believed that, and anyway I had more than persuasion in mind when I argued my case. I was handing those who agreed with me the tools, weapons even, to challenge any jurors who wanted to acquit. In Austin at least, criminal juries were more than willing to set free an obviously-guilty man on some meaningless, mindless argument made by a desperate defense attorney. So I shot those down the first chance I got, and always reminded the jury that a victim, as well as a defendant, awaited their verdict. *Remember the victim*, echoing in my softest, most heartfelt voice, the moment when, if I could cry, tears would prick at my eyes and spread to the weakest, most feeling of the jurors. It was a badge of honor to make a juror cry, and I did it whenever I could.

Ah, yes, each trial was a play in three acts, with the requisite tears and histrionics, and just occasionally a courtroom fistfight. Usually an unhappy defendant punching out his lawyer, and no one much minded that.

The sight of Michael Cherry standing outside my office captured and clarified my drifting mind, the look on his face hauling me into the present and telling me all was not well.

I called the man "Cherry," everyone here did, and I suspected his mother had done the same. Each of the seven courts had four prosecutors assigned, and he was the most experienced attorney in ours, which made him our chief and my immediate boss. He was a longtime prosecutor who dressed like a 1950s model, tailored in his tweeds and double-breasted worsted suits. He was about four inches

taller than the next tallest prosecutor, which was me at six feet, and
he had the stooping, stalking gait of a giant heron. Everyone liked
the guy, me included. He was unfailingly polite to all of us, and when
you talked to him, his hooded eyes would settle patiently on your
face, absorbing everything, following your logic with gentle nods,
his tongue flicking his lips when he spotted a flaw in your thinking.
With me, he knew there was something a little off but he couldn't
quite figure out what, and so, as some sort of coping mechanism, he
liked to practice his sarcasm.

"Good of you to show up," he said.

"You're welcome. How's Vicky this morning?"

He'd been talking to our secretary, Vicky, when I came in. We all
did it, despite the fact that she was a one-armed and entirely legless
mannequin taped to a swivel chair. Our previous secretary, Adri-
anna, quit in a huff about something, and because we work for a
governmental agency we got tired of waiting for a replacement to
be hired. Truthfully, Vicky's attitude was something of an improve-
ment on the chair's previous occupant, as was her productivity level.
Some joker had covered her mouth in bright-red lipstick and then
drawn a thick red line from her nostril, bleeding it artistically down
her chin and into her blouse. She was, after all, originally purchased
as a prop for our trials, the poor girl having been raped, robbed,
and murdered more often than the gypsies under Stalin. Hence her
missing limbs and her name, which was short for Victim.

"She's fine, I think. No complaints from her, anyway."

"Good. Where's our hero?"

Maurice Darrell Griffiths, aka "Stuttering Mo," was an eyewit-
ness to a murder. Not one of the cool ones you see on TV, no, this
was one of the classics we get in this business, a killing that warranted
news coverage until someone figured out that drugs and gangs were
involved. At that point it all seemed rather seedy, and pretty quickly
no one gave a shit anymore. Except the family and friends of the dead
guy, of course.

So it was with this case. Mo and a few other worthless members of his crowd were drinking and smoking PCP on a quiet street in East Austin when a rival moron drove up and shot one of them. I'd brought Mo in to interview him here because when I went to his house he slammed the door in my face. I figured that was for show and he might actually want to help, as long as the prying eyes of his neighbors weren't watching.

"He's not here. Let's talk in your office," Cherry said.

"That doesn't sound good. Someone bump him off overnight?"

I followed him into my office and sat behind my desk. Cherry sat opposite me in one of the chairs usually reserved for files.

"Some bad news, I'm afraid. I've had to reassign the case."

Something told me that wasn't the extent of the bad news. "Why?"

"Because someone reassigned you."

"Seriously?"

"Yes." Cherry held up a warning finger. "Now remember, you've been in this court more than three years, which is very unusual. Hardly anyone gets to stay in the same spot that long."

"Where am I going?"

"Juvenile."

"Fuck."

"Yes, I thought you'd say that."

"Did you stick up for me? Try to get me out of it?" I was annoyed, not just because of the transfer but because he didn't seem bothered enough.

"Sure. But what can I do?"

"Jesus, Cherry, I just won a friggin' cold case. One of the hardest cases we've had here for years." And by "hard" I meant a twenty-five-year-old murder case with no forensic evidence or eyewitnesses, just strands of circumstantial evidence that I connected tightly enough to get a conviction. Some in the office weren't convinced the guy was even guilty, the case was that weak. I didn't much care either way, but as I said to them, *How good am I if I can convict an innocent man with shitty evidence?* Of course, they laughed and walked off as if I was joking.

"Yes, you did." The way he said it switched on a light in my head.

"Shit, does that trial have something to do with my reassignment?"

Cherry held up a placating hand. "Not that I know of. It's true that you've been in the news and on the TV more in the last month than our dear leader has in a year, and I'm sure he doesn't like that, but I'm also pretty sure he doesn't do revenge reassignments."

"Bullshit." I felt my hackles rising.

"Look, you think you're immune from the way this place works? You think your floppy hair and pretty accent mean you can stay wherever you like for as long as you like?"

"No, Cherry, I think I'm one of the better trial lawyers in this office, and I think that it makes no fucking sense to take me away from prosecuting murder, rape, and robbery so I can give probation to wannabe gangbangers who smoke weed and steal sneakers from Wal-Mart."

"Hey, corporations are people, too. Apparently."

"Shut up, Cherry, it's not funny. I'm better than that, I don't want to be doing that."

"My, we do have a high opinion of ourselves."

"And I deserve to, don't you think?"

"As I keep explaining, my opinion doesn't matter."

I knew he was right, and I liked him enough not to cuss him out anyway. "When does this move happen?" It being Thursday, I had a pretty good idea of the answer.

"Monday. Maureen Barcinski is the chief down there. I told her you'd stop by this afternoon to say hello, meet some people, and then move over by Monday."

"Can't wait."

"Hey, you'll be sharing an office with Brian McNulty. He's a musician like you, so take your guitar."

"OK, stop right there. First of all, Brian illegally downloads music off the Internet and burns CDs for people. That makes him a thief, not a musician. Second, I'm *sharing* an office?"

"Yes, everyone does except the chief. They don't have much room down there." Cherry shifted in his seat, like he wanted out of there. "One more thing, too. You're not going to like it."

"That surprises me. So far it's been nothing but good news."

"Yeah, well. Part of your docket will be handling drug cases, where the kids are sent to in-patient treatment here from other counties. Sort of an inter-county liaison."

"Sounds awesome."

"Thing is, that's a state position." He sucked in his cheeks, clearly uncomfortable. "Paid for with a state grant, rather than a regular county position like you have now."

I sat up. "Oh, no. No. Don't tell me—"

"Yes, I'm afraid so."

"A fucking pay cut?"

"A little less of the green stuff, yes."

A vision of the girl in green popped into my head, but right then I wanted to be annoyed and didn't appreciate the comfort, or distraction, she offered. With the stress of this conversation, of her, I barely noticed the hum that set into my hands, the twitch that on weekends made me grab my guitar just to feel the strings against my fingertips. I'd written a song about that feeling, comparing it to the shivering skin of a "cutter" or to the cold gasp of a drug user's desperate veins. I needed the sweet relief of my guitar, but instead Cherry was still talking.

"You'll keep your current benefit package," he said, "including healthcare and retirement. Vacations and sick time will remain as is, too."

"Cherry, look. I know every prosecutor has to do their bit, and these moves happen." I leaned forward over the desk. I wanted him to know that the joking was over, that this mattered to me. "But I just moved into a new apartment, with a roommate no less, but I have more than forty grand in school loans. I have credit-card debt and a car lease I can't get out of."

He held up placating hands. "It not that much of a pay cut. Couple hundred a month."

I clenched my fists and worked hard not to punch the desk, the wall, him. "I'm on the edge as it is. I don't have leeway to give up a couple hundred a month."

"You have your music gigs. Don't they pay?"

"No, Cherry, they don't. The going rate is a couple of free beers and a waitress passing around the tip jar."

Austin, the Live Music Capital of the world, was chock-full of musicians like me, part-timers who could play well enough but who competed for time at the smaller joints and had no hope playing at the big ones, except as an opening act. Which took luck and a crapload more exposure than a part-time soloist like me could manage. Meanwhile, the pubs and small clubs gave us stage time for tips while they cleaned up with the sale of booze. Win-win for the bars and customers, not so much for the free help, the hopeful, the dreamers like me.

"Ah, I didn't realize," Cherry said. "I'm sorry about the money thing—all of it really—but there's nothing I can do at this point."

I sat back and loosened my tie, wondering whether it was for moments like this we weren't allowed guns in the building. It crossed my mind to tell him about the phone call this morning, make him feel like a weasel for doing this to me on the day I heard my parents were dead, but I knew it wouldn't make any difference. He and I were cogs in the machine, and the machine had been pre-programmed to spit me out into juvie and didn't have the capacity to care.

"How long is this for?" I asked.

"They're trying to keep these rotations to a year, give or take a few months. A year is the goal, though." He scratched the back of his head and squinted. "I'm not being facetious, but technically this is a promotion. As far as your résumé goes, that is. You'll be second in command over there, under Maureen but senior to the three other juvenile prosecutors."

"A promotion." I needed deep breaths to stop myself from throttling the messenger. "I'll be handling shoplifting, weed-smoking, car-breaking little punks instead of real criminals. I'll get a pay cut and will share an office with a dork. How the fuck do I apply for a demotion?"

"Yeah, I know. Sorry." He looked up, like a hopeful child. "I gather the workload is much lighter. Less stress and all."

"I know this isn't your fault, Cherry, but that won't stop me plotting your miserable death as I stare out of my window on those interminable, but low-stress, days."

"Yes, well." He stood and smoothed down his trousers, a tiny smile tugging at one corner of his mouth. "I suppose my demise is far from imminent then."

"Meaning?"

"Funny thing, really. They're all interior offices down there. You won't have a window."

O

There's a coldness that settles around my heart when my life starts to slide in the wrong direction. It's a physical sensation, not an emotional one. I don't really do emotions, you see, not like most people. I can feel some of them, ones like anger, disappointment, and lust. Emotions that begin and end with me, those I can feel, but my life is generally governed by logic, reason, and manipulation. Emotions that tie me to others, like compassion, love, or even fear, those I don't feel. I pretend to, of course, I've been pretending since I was a kid, and my success in life depends on me wearing the right mask at the right time.

So when Cherry walked out of my office, I wore the hangdog, poor-me face that he expected, lowering my eyes so he couldn't see the dead space in them that held visions of a knife slicing through the wrinkled skin in his neck, covering his crisp, white shirt with blood, and severing his exposed windpipe. I wanted to release that inner demon that I kept locked up and hidden away, to look the other way and feel nothing as he sought revenge for trashing the one part of my life I'd made something of, my job.

I wanted to be, just for once, the psychopath that I am.

CHAPTER THREE

SHAPE WITHOUT FORM

J ust to be clear, and despite the occasional white-hot flash of temper, I'm not one of *those* psychopaths. I don't have any desire to hurt or kill people. I see no gain or benefit there, so my inclinations are not of your TV slasher, world-domination, sexual-sadist types. The urge to hurt people bubbles up sometimes, and I'd feel essentially nothing if I acted on it, but I only feel the desire to hurt when someone has ignited my anger. Even then, I don't act out. My lack of impulse-control has gotten me in trouble before, and I know that psychopaths have a habit of repeating the same mistakes, so I've made a powerful effort to blend in and live as normally as possible. I don't hide in the bushes looking to do harm. I camouflage myself alongside the CEOs, politicians, and lawyers who pretend every day, like me, to be empaths (that's the term I use), faking it in social situations while taking advantage every which way in business.

I also prefer the term "sociopath" because it has fewer connotations of evil and violence.

If it helps, picture a huge parade in your hometown, a procession of bands and floats and fun, all colors and music. It'll be made up of happy people, sad people, funny people, and fools. They're experiencing the joy of community, a shared celebration made more meaningful by being together.

I'm not in the parade. I'm one of a handful of people looking out of a window as you go by, watching, learning. Trying to understand. Some of the people in the overlooking windows are ready to do you harm, but I'm not. I could if I wanted, but I want to fit in, not go to prison. I'm a leopard, yes, and while I'll happily sit in my tree and watch people with cold, dispassionate eyes, I don't kill. I just don't.

O

I followed Cherry's orders and drove down to my new digs midafternoon, heading south over the Congress Avenue Bridge to the part of town that was the center of my after-hours world. The tourists would be along in a little while, leaning over the balustrade like gargoyles to wait for the nightly display: a million bats in search of food, an epic swirling, switching cloud of black that funneled low along the river into the dusk for forty minutes or more.

After the bat show, the tourists would either head north into downtown or walk south onto South Congress Avenue proper. Known as SoCo, it was Austin's hippest street. Its cafés and boutique stores, its food trailers and western-wear shops, all kept the sidewalks hopping during the day. The bars, restaurants, and clubs brought crowds in by night. I'd played several gigs at the Continental Club, an Austin institution that sat near the bridge and right where everyone wanted to be. I was just the opener for other acts but loved the club's mix of customers, especially the girls—the pretty students from the University of Texas who mingled with the tattooed Austin originals, the lean chicks who were there for the music first and the hookups second. They were the ones who didn't mind buying their own beer or sharing their weed, not that I dared partake of the latter. Self-control issues and drugs don't mix well, and no one approves of a dope-smoking prosecutor. The perky UT girls were quicker to go home with the musicians but quicker to move on, too, once they'd figured out where you were on the talent pecking order. There was always someone else above you, prompting apologetic texts and awkward moments at some crowded club a week later. Awkward for them and not me, of course, their discomfort being my own form of post-coital revenge, something I enjoyed watching but never felt. If only they knew that I rather admired such cold-blooded calculation.

It wasn't just the girls I enjoyed. The almost-palpable energy was why I loved SoCo, all of Austin really, the rat race of the music business with its club owners, promoters, and self-appointed agents, all trying to rip us off and make us play with the same breath. Even the fans were ruthless, clapping and hollering their support but looking into their beer bottles and margarita glasses when the tip jar appeared. It wasn't glamorous, not like it should have been, but when you were in the middle of it, playing your songs and making music for strangers, the grubby and superficial elements of the music business faded away and left you with the energy of the moment, that pounding, strumming rush of time that swept over and intoxicated those pouring out the music, as well as those drinking it in.

That may sound odd coming from a sociopath, a little emotional, perhaps. But don't make the mistake of thinking that we don't feel things, because we do. And we're not all the same, either. Music happens to be one of those things, maybe the only thing, ever to have reached through and touched me. Not in a traditionally emotional way—songs have never made me cry, but they can provoke a visceral reaction that is as emotional as physical. Imagine standing beside a speaker at an AC/DC concert. Sure, you'd go deaf, but before that, every physical sensation imaginable would seize and shake your body. You wouldn't respond to the music with normal emotions but with ones battered out of you in a physical way. For me, music can do that without the need for massive volume. It's the thin, knifelike feel of a guitar string under my fingertips or the repetitive, sexual thump of a drum beat. Classical music, too, allows me a soothing escape into a symphony, a forest of sound where each note or instrument is a tree I can hide behind. And just because I don't cry at a Celine Dion song, don't think I can't appreciate her technical range or the mathematical precision of her chorus. Music, as you might have gathered, is what makes me most human. It may not take me all the way there but, on the nights I get to play or lose myself in listening, it's a bridge into your world and is perhaps the only real connection we'll ever have.

But it wasn't just the music end of SoCo that drew me.

Farther south from the bridge, a mile or so away, SoCo's original character began to show, where the boutiques and bistros made way for burrito stands and barred-up liquor stores. Two years before, I'd been on a ride-along with the cops down there, a two-night prostitution sting. The first night, undercovers posed as Johns to clear the yellow-skinned, scrawny whores from the area. The second night, the female cops dressed the part and wandered the streets, luring in slack-jawed punters without having to compete with the skanks they purported to be. It was an old-school, north–south divide, and in the name of progress the battered flop houses were being bulldozed and the scrub-patch junkies were being picked on by the cops and shunted slowly but surely away from downtown. No way in hell you'd see the crack whores from that end anywhere near the Congress Avenue bridge, not unless they had a bat fetish or, more likely, were broke and broken, looking to jump.

My new home, the Juvenile Justice Center, or JJC, was located on a side street at the crease where SoCo started to blur, where hip turned to hapless and the few tourists who wandered this far down started to clutch their purses and look nervously at passers-by.

The building itself was modern, a large and well-lit atrium with rows of bolted-down, plastic chairs where the juveniles and their families waited to go into court and receive, so I'd been told, a stern finger-wagging and a gentle slap on the wrist. I didn't know the number code to get into the secure side of the building, which housed the DA's offices and the probation officers, so I waited by the reception desk for Maureen to come and get me.

Maureen was Indian by birth, with light-brown skin and very black hair. She was petite, wore a lot of dark purple, and spoke in a clipped accent that sometimes sounded English, sometimes not. I'd been told she was industrious, plain-spoken, and didn't micro-manage her lawyers. I approved of all three qualities, especially the last two. Unfortunately, no one had mentioned to me her lack of humor.

She shook my hand, hers a tiny little thing that I didn't want to break.

"Welcome, Dominic, I've heard a lot of good things about you."

"That's unlikely," I said cheerily. She shot me a sideways glance that lingered too long. It may have been a cultural thing, or maybe she was generally curious about her new colleague. But there are some people who see past the mask, people who are immune to the charm and wit, at least to some degree. I don't know if it's because they are like me or if it's because they are so empathetic that they sense my lack of it somehow. It's like I'm hollow. I can hide that from most people, but some seem able to hear the emptiness. I don't know if that's true, really, because I've always done my best to stay away from those people, just to be safe. Of those I'd worked with so far, I suspect Cherry came the closest to seeing the gap in my soul, but I don't think he ever considered the possibility that I am what I am. The few people in my life who've figured it out have told me it's a frightening realization to come to, so maybe people like Cherry stop themselves before getting there.

Maureen led me through the security door, saying, "The number is four digits and changes every time someone comes or goes from the DA's office or probation. One-six-seven-five, right now."

"Got it."

Immediately inside, she waved a hand to her right. "My office."

"Ah, yes, nice window." It looked out over the parking lot, good to know if I was planning an early escape or late arrival.

A conference room was next to her office. "We use this to meet victims and witnesses or have them wait here during trials."

"So you do have trials, then."

"Bench trials only. The judges are lenient here and so no one ever wants a jury trial. Hasn't been one in fifteen years."

That's what I'd heard, and I was unhappy to confirm the rumor. Theater closed.

My office was around the corner on the left, a narrow space about the size of a walk-in closet. And no windows. Inside to the left was Brian McNulty's desk. He wasn't at it, and in the far right corner was mine, apparently. The walls were cream-colored and bare, sporting an occasional black dot that told me someone had once pinned up a picture or print. I briefly wondered whether anyone would mind if I put the classic prisoner's slash marks on the walls, crossing off each day that I survived down there.

"Small but functional, and you'll have Brian to talk to."

"I was afraid of that."

"I see." She turned and looked at me. "This can go one of two ways. You can spend a year down here sulking and moaning like a baby, in which case it'll seem like two years and everyone will hate you. Or you can appreciate the lighter workload, the reduction in stress, and the proximity to good lunch places."

"Can I take a day to decide?"

Another blank look, then she said, "Brian has a trial tomorrow. He's interviewing a witness at her house right now, so if you don't mind helping out, I'd like you to prep one of his other witnesses."

"Happy to. Where and when?"

"Our conference room, and now." She nodded at the bookcase carrying notepads and pens. "I'll see if he's here and bring him to the conference room. It's a simple assault case, one kid punched another and the officer, our witness, pulled surveillance tape and recognized the kid who started it."

She didn't wait for an answer, so I picked out a notepad and a pen and wandered back to the conference room next to her office. It wasn't a real conference room. No large table dominated the space. Instead, sofas and chairs backed up against the walls, and two coffee tables sat in the middle. A television was bolted to the wall, its remote nowhere in sight.

My phone rang, showing a local number I didn't recognize. I always answered those, in case it was a club or bar requesting my services, though it rarely was. I recognized the voice on the other end before he said his name.

"Hey, what's up, Dom? Brian McNulty here."

"Brian, how're you?"

"Great. Welcome to the team. Hey, I'm interviewing the victim at her house. Did Maureen tell you about the cop?"

"Yeah, I'm waiting for him now."

"Cool. Just make sure he's okay testifying. It's a simple case but I don't want him fucking it up."

"Why would he fuck it up?"

"Because he's an Austin Independent School District cop. Rent-a-cop. Most of them are idiots."

"What do you mean, 'rent-a-cop'? They're certified peace officers just like the sheriffs and every Austin PD cop."

"Hey, I figure if you're good enough to be a real policeman, then that's who you work for, APD. If not, you wind up sitting behind some desk on your fat ass, shuffling paper and keeping a bunch of jackass kids on the straight and narrow."

"You just described your own job, Brian."

"Yeah, well, yours too. Anyway, just checking in. You have my number now in case you need it."

"Great," I said, and rang off. I looked up as a uniformed officer walked in, glancing about hesitantly until he saw me.

"Holy shit," I said, standing. "Otto, what are you doing here?"

"I'm your witness, I guess." He smiled and shook my hand. Right there, I should have known it, should have figured out that seeing him in that place, something bad was brewing. But Otto Bland lived up to his name, too nondescript to be any kind of omen I might recognize.

He used to work at the DA's office. He'd started his career as a patrol officer and worked his way up to detective with the Travis County Sheriff's Office. After a couple of decades, he'd resigned or retired, and had come to work for us as an investigator. Each court had one and, while the work wasn't exciting or glamorous, it was safe and it paid well. Investigators located recalcitrant witnesses, served subpoenas, and ferried evidence from the police lockers to court. He'd been fired about two years ago and, depending on who you believed, it had been for laziness, sloppy work, or losing evidence. Specifically, two four-ounce bags of weed.

"Working for AISD, huh?"

"Yeah." He sat on the green sofa, his bulk pressing into the foam and his gun belt cutting into his belly. The groan might have been for that, or for the sheer pleasure of being off his feet. He was larger than ever, and his skin had an unhealthy, gray tinge to it, only slightly lighter than the bags under his eyes. Brian was a jackass, but it looked like even a jackass could be right once in a while.

"So how's life?" I closed the door to the room and sat opposite him, dropping my feet onto the nearest coffee table.

"Honestly?" He shrugged. "It sucks. Remember when we met? I was a freakin' detective."

"The Salinas robberies, right?"

"Nailed those fuckers to the wall."

"Technically," I smiled, "you caught them, and I nailed them."

An uncomfortable silence sat between us. Otto Bland shifted and the leather of his gun belt squeaked. I wanted to ask what happened at the DA's office but didn't feel like I could. I'd learned that when it comes to potentially embarrassing personal matters, empaths will usually squirm a little and then tell you the truth, hoping you understand. I never did understand, mostly because I wanted people to think highly of me, so it was my practice to lie about such things.

"How do you like being a cop with AISD?"

Doleful eyes turned to me, and his shoulders seemed to slump even farther. "Do you know what they make me do? Do you know how I start my job every day?"

I shook my head.

"I'm not at any of the regular schools, you see. They figured with my experience I could handle being at ALC. You know what that is?"

"I just started here, didn't look through my acronym dictionary yet."

"Alternative Learning Center. It's where the kids get sent when they fuck up at school. When they fight or bring in shit they shouldn't. It's one stop short of juvenile court, and pretty much every kid you see here will either be at ALC already, or will go there once you've finished with him. It's basically a school for all the little shits in Austin."

"Sounds delightful."

"You know what my job is every morning?" he asked again. "They make me sniff their fingers."

"What?" I genuinely didn't understand. "Who makes you sniff whose fingers?"

"That's my job. To sniff the fingers of the little assholes when they come to school every morning, and sometimes after lunch. It's to see if they've been smoking weed."

"That's . . . unpleasant."

"It's worse than that, it's disgusting. They're the punks and I'm the one being humiliated. They know it, too."

"And what if you smell weed on them?"

"That gives me probable cause to search their stuff. Backpacks, pockets, whatever."

"I can't believe they make you do that. Can you refuse? Tell them to buy a dog, or something?"

"No." He heaved a sigh and looked up at me. "Truth is, I can't lose this job, Dom. It's part-time as it is. I'm hoping to live like a beggar for a year or two, cash in my retirement, and go buy out half of my brother's business, a bar on the beach in Tampa. Twenty grand, and I can spend my days wearing flowered shirts and serving drinks to chicks in bikinis. I'm looking to start a new security gig soon, some fancy new apartment complex off Seventh Street, all co-eds and cheerleaders, I'm hoping."

"That doesn't sound too bad."

"Yeah, if it happens. Meanwhile, I gotta hold on a little while longer, and I sure as hell can't afford to lose this job, no matter what they make me do."

"Jeez, I'm sorry." I wasn't, I didn't care in the slightest, but I also didn't know what else to say. Every thought that popped into my head made the humiliation worse, and I saw no point in that right now. The guy wasn't wallowing in his misery. He'd all but given up the struggle, like a man neck-deep in quicksand, hoping against hope that by staying still he'd make it. But I also didn't have the mental energy to steer us back toward a polite and meaningless con-versation, so I just asked him about the case, the reason he was there. We looked over his written report of the incident, going through the motions, pretending he needed to be prepped.

He left after about twenty minutes, offering a handshake that my father would have described as "wet-fish"—cold, clammy, and weak. I walked out into the atrium with him and watched as he trudged down the stairs into the parking lot. I half expected him to climb onto an AISD bicycle, complete with pink ribbons and basket, but I remembered his weight and figured he'd not seen a bicycle in a few years. An image of donkey transportation popped into my head, but I held my smile until I was sure he wouldn't see me. I scanned the lot, looking for a police vehicle, wondering if they'd given him that much, but it was his own car he clambered into, a battered white Chevy with one working brake light and a rear license plate screwed on not quite straight.

I turned back toward the security door, but a flash of color to my left caught my eye. She stood against the side wall, her hands behind her back, her eyes on me and her head tilted to one side, just a fraction. My pale, thin girl wearing the same lime-green dress that she had on this morning, the same bright-red shoes telling everyone to look her way so she could look right back.

I knew I was staring, but she was, too, so I didn't stop. I couldn't understand why she was there and I wondered if she'd tracked me down, but that made no sense. Women, relationships, have always been the hardest things for me to figure out. It can begin with a sort of childish infatuation, and it's needy and possessive. No matter her wonderful qualities, we don't appreciate a woman unless those qualities are of some benefit to us, and if so, we horde and exploit them. Not maliciously, not always anyway, but the way a child will charm his mother into buying him a toy, then thank her with kisses and hugs until the next crushing need arises. And like a child, I will lie to impress.

I took a step toward the girl and noticed the lanyard around her neck. It struck me that she might work there, too. "Hello," I said.

"Hello again." Her voice was soft but flat, leaving me with no idea if she was being polite or shy.

"You're a fugitive from the law, aren't you?" I said it to be funny, to break some of the ice, but something flickered in her eyes and she didn't smile.

"No."

"I was kidding. After this morning."

She nodded and finally looked away, down to the floor. I followed her gaze, and my eyes locked onto her red shoes, her thin ankles, the hard muscle of her calves. I forced myself to look at her, but when I opened my mouth I didn't know what to say. I cleared my throat, hoping it would clear my mind, and it restarted my brain at a fundamental level.

"Do you work here?" I asked.

"No."

I looked at the lanyard around her neck and saw that it wasn't a badge after all, but a visitor's pass.

"I'm here for my brother, Bobby. He was picked up last night for drugs. Hoping I can take him home."

"Really? I guess I shouldn't be talking to you, then."

"Why?"

"I'm a prosecutor here. First day on the job."

"Oh." I'd expected suspicion or distaste, but she seemed disinterested, and it crossed my mind that she might be on something herself. But when she looked at me again, those wide, brown eyes were clear, stunningly clear, and I was unable to look away, let alone walk away. The only question I could come up with drew me further toward forbidden territory.

"How old is your brother?"

"Twelve." She glanced over my shoulder, but when I checked, no one was there.

"You don't talk much, do you?"

"You said we shouldn't be talking at all."

"True. We probably shouldn't."

She turned her eyes back on me, and I know what it felt like to be a rabbit in headlights. What I couldn't be sure of was whether she was doing it on purpose, whether she knew that each time she looked at me full-on like that, my mouth dried up and my blood fizzed.

"Where are you from?" she asked.

"England, originally." I wanted to tell her the story, how I got here and why I stayed, but I didn't want to do it here, and she didn't press.

I heard voices behind me and we both looked over to see a teenage boy walking alongside an adult.

"That's my brother. And his probation officer."

"He has one already?"

"We've been here before," she explained, her voice still flat, quiet.

She started to move away from the wall toward them, and I tried to give her room but froze when she paused and put a hand on my forearm. She was looking at me, touching me, with the simplicity and innocence of a teenager, and I didn't know what to do or feel.

Her eyes locked mine in place, and she gave her first smile, just a gentle tilt of her lips.

"I hope your gig goes well tonight," she said. "If I can, maybe I'll come watch."

She drifted away, leaving me with the lingering touch of her hand and the soft smell of baby powder. Confusion spun inside me and for a moment I just stared at the wall, wondering. But no answer made sense; I simply couldn't fathom how she knew I was a musician.

And then I smiled because the part that mattered right there and then was simply that she *did* know. She knew I was a musician. And that mattered not just because girls like musicians but because the fact that she'd found that out meant she was interested in me *before* she knew.

And if there's one thing I like, it's having a beautiful girl chase me.

CHAPTER FOUR

THE TWINKLE OF
A FADING STAR

I made it to the Norman Pub that evening, thirty minutes before I was due to play and planning on my usual routine of an orange juice and tonic water over ice while sitting on the front deck. I used to drink, but it's one of the things I gave up, like violence, because even a calm and rational man can find his mask slipping when he's had a few. Because I'm hardwired to lie, exaggerate, and act impulsively, alcohol was a risk I'd stopped taking.

I was also there to hang out with perhaps my best friend, and the night's main act, Gus Cronstedt. Gus was a Costa Rican–Swede who'd inherited the best physical characteristics of each culture, leaving him tall, dark, and handsome, with the iciest blue eyes I'd ever seen.

We'd known each other for several years, having met in court. He was an immigration lawyer who found himself out of his depth in criminal court one morning. I'd enjoyed watching him flail, but after a few minutes I figured I could get some traction, an edge of sorts, by offering to help. The solicitous prosecutor, I'd held his hand and shown him which forms to fill out and helped him get a good deal for his client. Not because I cared, of course, but because I wanted him in my debt, and, as usual, I was right about the favor: he'd been overly grateful ever since.

He was an odd duck, though, one of those guys who'd sit around and watch everyone else talk, occasionally offering comment in a deadpan delivery, whether it was a political statement or a joke. Like when he told people about his cousin, Thor Einarss, he'd repeat the name until they got he was saying "sore anus." Although that one actually made him laugh. But generally he was quiet and introverted, which is why he preferred the solitude of his office to the stage. He was good, though, his voice and songs powerful and hypnotic, and he was one of the few part-time Austin musicians whom the clubs willingly paid to play. The fact that he had to be dragged kicking and screaming made him all the more attractive. I should've minded, been jealous, but even I loved hearing him play, and he always insisted that I open for him so any resentment on my part would have been counterproductive.

He was already at the wooden picnic table when I arrived, and he had bought my drink. All around us, outdoor fans wafted at the evening heat. Each one was armed with a tiny spray pump, and together they set a mist all over the patio, like a foggy heath from my homeland. Despite them, it was baking hot.

"So what's going on?" I sat down and nodded at my waiting drink. "That for a reason?"

"They changed the lineup," Gus said, not looking me in the eye.

"Changed it how?"

He shrugged. "Don't know all the details, Marley wouldn't say." Marley Jensen, the owner of the pub. He was one of those older, balding guys who managed a ponytail. His was white, plus a few yellow patches from the haze of cigarette smoke he'd lived in for the past fifty years. His voice was scratchy, his eyes watery, but he was generally an honest guy and loved his music.

"Are you trying to tell me I'm not playing tonight?" Lineups changed, of course, but not last-minute, and whoever was in charge of booking usually had the decency to call the affected musician. Even if it was just a guy playing for tips.

"That's what he said."

"Seriously?" I felt a hot flash of anger that chilled immediately, like the end of a fuse that flares for a second, then settles in for its slow, lethal burn. "Is he inside?"

"No. Went out for the pizzas."

The Norman Pub was small enough that it didn't serve food, but Marley would buy a dozen pizzas from the little place next door and sell them at the bar, good and hot around 7 p.m., cold and stringy by midnight. He was a lush and brought in the pizzas early, as opposed to in shifts, because pretty soon after the music started he began knocking back bourbon, and by the middle of the evening he'd have tripped over his feet or gotten lost on the short trip to the pizza place.

We sat in silence for a minute as my mind ticked over and I wondered what might have happened, and how I should handle it. I put my anger on hold until I could get some answers from Marley, not wanting to think about revenge until I knew it was required. In the meantime, I didn't want Gus to think it was a big deal, that I was overly upset, so I talked as if all was normal.

"Any new material?" I asked.

"Yeah. Couple of songs. Been slow at work, so I've had more time to write."

"Slow? I thought Mexicans were pouring across the border just to come to your office."

"Whatever. Plenty of them in Austin, but those who do show up want the advice but don't want to pay for it. Fuckers." I wasn't sure if he meant that, if his disgruntlement was real or for show. "What about you?"

"Same set," I said. "Six songs, then I'll slide out the way and get drunk while the chicks throw their panties at you."

They did, pretty much. Gus was married, though, and I'd barely seen him look at another woman. He tried to steer them my way, and sometimes it worked. Another reason I didn't resent opening for him.

"Yeah, well, I like your stuff," he said, looking over my shoulder.

I turned to watch Marley walk across the parking lot between the pub and the pizza shop, pie boxes piled high and balanced with both hands. I wanted to trip him.

"Be right there," he said as he went past and shouldered his way into the pub, the tower of pizzas leaning dangerously as he disappeared inside. We sat in silence until he reappeared two minutes later. He stopped halfway between us and the door.

"Talk to you?" he said.

"Over here, sure." I didn't see any reason to get up or conceal the conversation from Gus.

"Sure." Marley came over and sat down. "Dude. I'm sorry, but I've got bad news."

"So I gather. You're really not letting me play?"

He ran a hand over his head, adjusting his ponytail. "Yeah, a problem came up. Don't really know how to say it, honestly. Kinda fucked-up, really."

"Spit it out."

"Someone said you'd stolen a song. Copied, I guess."

My mouth fell open, but I was speechless. Not that stealing a song was beyond me, I just hadn't. I'd only do that if I could be sure of getting away with it, and if I actually needed to. I enjoyed the process of writing songs, creating my own little worlds with each one. And, as I said, the fact was I *hadn't* stolen anyone's song.

"Now, I know that's a helluva accusation, bub, and I'm not the one making it. You need to know that straight up."

"Then who the fuck—?"

"Just hold on, we need to take this slow and easy."

"The fuck we do." The fuse was lit and I was looking for a direction to explode. "This is bullshit. I've never stolen a thing." Not even close to true, but I'd not stolen anything for a long, long time. "Marley, I've never copied anyone's music or lyrics. Ever." Quite true.

He held up his hands, but in defense, not surrender. "I have no idea what the fuck's going on, but the person who called me also plays here sometimes, and so I can't let you on stage tonight. Just tonight, okay?"

"What 'person'? Who?" I demanded. I felt like a sniper, swinging my scope across an empty battlefield, looking for a target.

"I don't want to say, don't want to start a feud." He held up his hands again, this time to calm me down. "I have your music, and his, on tape. I'll just listen and decide. Seriously, Dom, it's an easy fix."

"Bullshit. Even if they're similar, how do you know he didn't copy mine, whoever this mysterious fuckface is."

"If they're similar, we'll worry about it then, okay?"

"No, not okay. This is bullshit, seriously bullshit."

"I know, I know. It's upsetting to be accused of something you didn't do. Happened to me once." His eyes flickered at me, as if he meant something by that. As a prosecutor, I'd heard the line before from various people, and it was usually used as a justification for shafting me. He turned to Gus. "Change your mind?"

"Nope, sorry."

A silence descended, and I looked between them. "About what?"

"He said that if you weren't allowed to play, he wasn't going to." Marley said it matter-of-factly, as if a striking musician was to be expected.

"Why?" As soon as I said it, I knew this was one of those empathy things that I didn't get but needed to be on the lookout for.

"Why do you think?" Gus said, maintaining eye contact with his drink.

"That's sweet, Gus, but stupid," I said, meaning it. "What good does this do you?"

As much time as I'd spent trying to understand empaths, mimic them, *become* one, this kind of thing bamboozled me. To act in a way that benefited no one and annoyed the people who funded you, to make a meaningless gesture in support of someone who was not only indifferent and would never do the same for you (the latter he couldn't know, of course) . . . it was bizarre. I argued with him. Not to change his mind, because I didn't much care, but to understand. "You want out of the office rat race as much as I do, and people actually pay to hear you play. Why would you risk pissing off your fans and your employers?" Again, true, and as I said, I certainly wouldn't have done the same for him.

The other thing at play here was that I didn't like people doing me favors I couldn't return. A fundamental principle of controlling the people around you is gaining power over them, having them in your debt. It didn't matter that I wouldn't pay him back; it was that reversal of the power balance I didn't like. And, truthfully, I didn't like not understanding his motivations and subsequent actions. Solidarity and friendship, sure, whatever, but how strong could those things be, even for empaths (and Gus had always struck me as something of a lone wolf, not the do-gooder type)? The musical ladder was slippery enough without taking voluntary nosedives on principle, even for friends. I was obviously missing something because Marley seemed pretty phlegmatic about it when he should have been angry.

"Yeah, solidarity, friendship, and all that shit," Gus said, reading my mind.

Marley started toward the door. "I got another act on the way, I need to check on them. As I said, I'll listen closely to both songs and call you. Tomorrow, I promise."

Tomorrow.

Depending on what he said tomorrow, and it was physically painful to have to wait for someone else's judgment like that, my music career in Austin could be over. Such an irony, too, because I'd manipulated and cheated to do well in law school, not much but enough, and more than a few defendants had enhanced my reputation with long prison sentences that resulted from missing or tampered-with evidence. But music, that was the one area I'd played it fair, the only place I'd never felt inclined to cheat. And not because of some moral compunction but because there'd been no need. I simply had the skills and the talent to satisfy myself in that arena, to be confident that my stuff was good and different enough from everyone else's that we weren't really in competition. I'd really believed that one day I could leave the law behind and soak myself in writing and singing, leave behind the daily toil of manipulating my colleagues and my opponents for the life I felt I deserved, the one that was easier and more fulfilling.

I nursed my drink, staring at the sliver of ice on top of the piss-colored liquid, and I thought about what I'd do to the lunatic who'd accused me. I hadn't committed an intentional act of violence since I was a teenager, and I'd fought every urge to do so since. Like a snake sheds his skin, I had to shed parts of me if I wanted to function well in society, and violence was one of the first impulses that needed sloughing.

Make no mistake, I arrange my life so that I come out on top. Sometimes innocents get trampled, but I, for one, don't go out of my way to undermine the lives of most empaths. (Criminal defendants, yes, but research shows about a quarter of them are psychopaths, and the rest aren't exactly innocents, are they?) But our disguise is a thin one indeed when it comes to revenge because righting a wrong committed against us is the only real sense of justice we have. And when the rage is triggered, it burns white-hot until the proper balance of things has been restored. It didn't much matter who'd pitted themselves against me, it only mattered that they had, and that I'd win.

"You okay?" Gus asked.

"Yep, fine," I said. "It'll be cool, he'll phone tomorrow and apologize."

"Yeah, for sure."

In a way, I was fine. For the first time in a while I was going to let myself off the leash and use the disability of having no conscience to get my world back on track. It didn't matter what Marley said on the phone tomorrow. Whoever had called me a thief was finished in Austin. How I would finish him, well, figuring that out was part of the game.

I felt a kick from Gus under the table, and I looked up to see the only good thing that had happened to me that day. I hadn't seen a bus or a car drop her off, but there she was, a vision in green, gliding across the cracked pavement toward the patio. Gus's foot had let me know she was there, and he seemed to be entranced, a rarity in itself. She sat with a nod to him, and then turned to smile at me.

"Told you I'd come."

I smiled back, knowing I'd have to explain why I wasn't playing tonight. But that's another advantage of my condition: the lie comes as easily to the tongue as the truth, and in this case, it came much, much more easily.

CHAPTER FIVE

EYES I DARE NOT MEET

"Double-booked?" she asked when I'd finished explaining.

"It happens," I said. "Too many musicians in Austin. If you don't confirm straight away, it takes them about nine seconds to get someone else."

"You too?" she said to Gus.

He shrugged. "That's how it goes."

"Are you a full-time musician?" she asked him. "I saw you play at the Lakeside Club a few months ago. My girlfriend has a crush on you."

"And you don't?" Gus asked.

"I'm a lesbian," she said, throwing me a look that meant one of two things: *I'm a lesbian, aren't you an idiot?* or *I'm not a lesbian, and you're in luck.* I'm pretty good at faces and knew which one I would go with.

"Huh," was all Gus could muster, adding, "No, I'm not a full-time musician. An immigration lawyer."

"You make much money doing that?" she cocked her head. "I figure, either you do and you exploit immigrants, or you don't and you help them."

Gus looked at her for a second, and I could see she confused him like she confused me. Difference was, I wanted to possess her and wasn't flustered by her. "I do okay. Not great, but . . . you know."

I knew. He didn't do great. He and his wife, Michelle, joked about packing it all in and buying a shack on a beach in Costa Rica, where he was born. Instead, they'd bought the kind of house a lawyer was supposed to live in and the kind of car a lawyer was supposed to drive. Every month, he squeezed the last penny from his bank account to stay afloat, money pulled from the dust-lined pockets of day laborers and from envelopes handed over by Central American grandparents hoping their kids and grand-kids would find a better life north of the border. Bottom line: he made a living, but they used up pretty much every penny that came in.

"Are they all poor, your clients?" It seemed to me that she was picking at a scab, trying to provoke a reaction, just the way I like to. I wondered for the first time whether I'd bumped into one of my kind. A kindred soul.

Without the soul, of course.

"Mostly." He swirled his drink. "Except a couple of them."

"Tell me," she pushed.

Gus sighed. "One guy. Ambrosio Silva. He's of Portuguese descent but is from Mexico, came over about eight years ago. Tall, good-looking dude, used to be a pro soccer player, or that's what he told me. He bought a trailer, mobile home, a used one. He's real good with his hands, so he fixed it up and rented it out while he stayed with friends. Two months later, he used the cash from that trailer to buy two more. He rented those as well. First year, he had seven trailers. Second year, he bought about eleven more. By year five, he had over a hundred. Now he has between one fifty and two hundred."

"Who rents them?" she asked. She seemed genuinely curious, but what I noticed was the sheen of sweat worn by me and Gus, where her pale skin looked crisp and cool.

"Illegals, mostly. Some people fresh out of prison who can't get apartments elsewhere. Sex offenders. It's a good deal for both sides of the equation. They get low rent and an even lower profile; he gets to declare however much money he wants to the IRS. When he pays me, it's in cash that I count wearing surgical gloves."

"Oh?" She raised an eyebrow.

"It's the story of the illegal immigrant," Gus said. "Blood, cocaine, and honest sweat." He allowed himself a small smile. "None of which I need to be touching."

Sometimes a man in the desert sees an oasis that isn't there. Sometimes, it's there and he's not sure. But mirage or reality, the thrill is the same, the hope and relief he feels are very real. His feet pick up, his spirit soars, and his focus narrows. He sees a possibility and it becomes all he sees, whether that's reasonable, real, imaginary, or ridiculous. And when he's spent the day being stung by scorpions, hissed at by snakes, and scorched by the sun, a streak of self-preservation narrows it even further.

"How does he collect his rent?" I asked.

Gus was drinking and swallowed loudly. "That's what I was getting to. It's funny how he comes from this dangerous place yet conducts his cash business like Austin's trailer parks are the safest place in the world."

"Meaning?"

"Meaning, he drives around on the last day of every month in his Ford Transit van. He spends eighteen hours knocking on doors, collecting envelopes of cash." Gus spread his hands. "I told him it's insane, but compared to where he used to live, it really is relatively safe. Plus he's under the impression that everyone out there knows him, owes him, and has nothing to gain by boosting him." He took another sip. "Which is true. I mean think about it, if he starts insisting on cashier's checks or having armed guards escort him, then the rent goes up and a lot of people lose their homes. His tenants probably don't love him, but they do have an incentive to look out for him, or at least maintain the status quo."

We sat in silence for a minute. I couldn't vouch for the others, but my mind was on a crappy van full of cash, and I had more questions.

"Does the guy have tinted windows or something?" I asked.

"Seems like wads of cash rolling around in the back of his van would eventually attract attention."

Gus wagged a finger admonishingly. "Funny you should say that. He did the first year, but got a ticket for too much tint. That's where we met. One of the things I've helped him do is understand all the traffic laws so he doesn't get pulled over. That and get his relatives into the country on visas."

"So if no tint, then what?" I asked.

Gus shrugged again. "He bought a couple camouflage bags from a hunting store. Cabela's, I think. He thought it was funny, using camo bags to hide his money, and he loved it when I told him they were tax deductible."

"How much do those trailers rent for?" I asked.

"No clue," Gus said.

"No, I mean like two hundred a month or a grand a month. Ballpark me."

"Look at you with the baseball references," Gus said.

"You don't like baseball?" she asked. It seemed to amuse her.

"He hates it." Gus perked up because he, on the other hand, loved baseball and found my distaste for the sport inexplicable and ripe ground for provoking me.

"Why do you hate baseball?" Those wide eyes looked at me intently, and I felt a flash of anger that she might side with Gus against me, even on something stupid like a sport. I explained it, calmly, careful to keep some light alive in my eyes.

"It's not a sport if its most famous player, its best-ever player, was fatter than a walrus. It's not a sport when it takes five hours to complete a game and both teams spend most of that time sitting on their arses. It's not a sport when players can consume tobacco products while playing. And it's not much of a sport when every play is called from the sidelines, by some old man with yellow teeth and an anger problem."

"Isn't that like cricket?" she asked, with that head tilt again. "Except doesn't that take days to finish?"

"No and sometimes." I turned back to Gus. "Anyway, the trailers. How much?"

"About five hundred," the girl said. "I used to be an addict, and I bought from people who lived in them." She said it so matter-of-factly. *I used to be an addict.*

"Five hundred then."

I suspect we were each doing the math because we all fell silent. I got there quickly because, well, I'm me, and that day of all days I had an incentive.

So yes, the math came easy: by the end of the eighteen hours, Señor Ambrosio Silva would be driving around East Austin, carrying between seventy-five and a hundred grand, all in cash. Maybe more.

"He does carry a gun, of course," said Gus.

"Of course," I said. *Ah, Texas.*

CHAPTER SIX

HERE ARE THE STONE IMAGES

"Fords and Hondas are the easiest to steal," she said, eventually breaking the silence. "Late nineties models in particular, and my little brother tells me that kids these days seem to prefer Accords to the other models."

She was right. About a year ago, our office worked with Austin PD to bust a group of teenagers and young adults who couldn't keep their hands off other people's cars. Patrol officers were told to stop every late '90s or early 2000s model Honda or Ford in East Austin if the person behind the wheel looked to be under twenty. The kids liked those cars because there were so many of them, and a screwdriver jammed into the ignition was as good as a key. The little punks didn't even have to figure out how to hot-wire them.

"You know what'd be fun?" she said, holding my eye.

"What's that?" asked Gus, looking back and forth between us.

She shrugged, a delicate movement. "He's nuts to drive around with all that money." She looked at me. "And you're a prosecutor, right?"

"Right. So?"

"So you need to make him understand that it's not safe, what he's doing. It's not just unsafe, it's crazy."

"And?" I knew where she was going, but I wanted her to hold my hand all the way there.

"You should teach him a lesson."

"By stealing his money?" I smiled because I'd thought of it, of course, several sentences into Gus's story.

"No, silly, by hiding his car. You'd be doing a public service. Doing him a service, at least. One day someone's going to hit him over the head, or maybe even shoot him, for all that money."

"Seems like they wouldn't need to," I said. "Just steal his car when he's collecting his last payment."

"That's my point. You should steal his car and hide it for an hour. For ten minutes. Then he'll realize what he's doing isn't smart."

"Or I could just tell him," I said.

Gus snorted. "You could, but you won't. First of all, if you do, he'll know I told you about it. Second of all, as I said, I already told him. Several times. He's the only client I have who pays in full and on time—trust me when I say I've tried to persuade him."

She shouldn't have suggested it. Not then, anyway, not even as a joke. It was like a perfect storm for me. I was looking at a pay cut, my musical career was on the line, and the eight-year-old in me had been dared to do something impulsive and exciting. By a beautiful girl. I felt like a drug addict trying to resist the needle, a thirsty drunk saying no to a glass of cold beer.

But I did resist. I had to. It's one thing being unable to get off the slide once you begin; it's quite another to step onto that slippery slope with your eyes wide open. I'd trained myself that being a functional human being meant, for me, recognizing dangerous situations and steering around them. Not resisting the temptations, but avoiding them in the first place. I was the serial adulterer hiring an ugly secretary, or the booze-hound driving the long way home to avoid his local liquor store.

"Prosecutors don't steal cars," I said. "Not this one, anyway."

"It's not stealing," she said, "if you give it back. It's not even borrowing. It's teaching him a lesson."

"Technically, it's the offense of unlawful use of a motor vehicle, which is a felony in this state, and one that would have me out of a job, if not behind bars." I raised my drink and held her eye. "So no thanks."

Gus laughed. "I don't think she was seriously considering doing it, Dom. She doesn't strike me as the car-thieving type."

She put a hand on his arm, and cold fingers clutched at my chest, the childish jealousy I'd not felt in a while, the one that made my jaw tighten and my blood seethe. But she smiled at me as she replied.

"Oh, Gus, you'd be surprised."

O

We stayed for two hours, talking about other things. Music leaked out of the club to the patio, but I tuned in to the hum of the fans instead. I did more listening than talking, for a handful of reasons. First, girls like it when you're distant and mysterious. Second, I was half annoyed and half amused by Gus's fawning over the girl. I was already angry at Marley, and I didn't want to show either of them how I was feeling, so keeping my mouth shut seemed best. Third, when I meet new people, I have a tendency to talk about myself too much and, shall we say, exaggerate, which is fine until I'm hanging out with someone like Gus, who might catch me in a lie. He'd probably assume I was doing it to bed the lady in question and not mind, but needless lying is something I'd been trying to cut back on.

There's actually a list of things we do, one used by shrinks to figure out whether we're soulless monsters or just ordinary folks who can't behave. It's called the Hare Psychopathy Checklist—Revised (aka Hare PCL-R). Twenty questions, two points for a "yes," and if you score more than twenty-five out of a maximum forty (although the passing score is thirty in the United States, which tells you how scientific it is), then you're in the club. You're not supposed to be evaluated until you're eighteen years old because so many of the factors run consistent with the behaviors of regular juvenile delinquents, and even "normal" teenagers, who are selfish, willful, and judgment-free. I was evaluated at age sixteen, after the pheasant incident, thanks to a private shrink and my parents' money. Lucky for me they had some then, before farming in England went to the dogs, and lucky for me I could be marked and graded as a sociopath—I passed the test with flying colors. One of the early questions deals with "Pathological Lying" and to no one's surprise I scored full marks on that one.

Even though I did lie, a lot, I never liked the word *pathological* because it implied some sort of disease and suggested a compulsivity that over the years I managed to tamp down. Still, lying was undoubtedly a trait of mine, usually a strength but occasionally a weakness. It irritated me to be caught out and have to invent a covering lie, especially with Gus around, who seemed oddly gifted when it came to remembering things about me.

My mysterious act at the club may have worked a little too well, prompting one from our companion. Or maybe she got sick of Gus leering at her. Either way, she disappeared on us. She drifted off to use the bathroom and never came back. Gus was worried, then outraged, then worried again, but I assumed it was a game and I liked it. What I liked best of all, for some reason, was that she'd taken Gus's phone number and not mine, but had given neither of us hers. As we walked toward our cars, I decided on some minor revenge.

"Never seen you drool like that over a girl."

"I wasn't drooling," Gus said. "If I ever did, though, it'd be over her. But you were quiet."

"No choice, you wouldn't keep your yap shut."

"Yeah, well, I think she liked me, kept asking me questions."

"You know who else likes you?"

"Who?"

"Your fucking wife."

"I was just talking to the girl, dude. Michelle doesn't mind me talking to girls. You know I've never cheated on her."

"You would have tonight though."

"Bullshit. Flirting, that's all it was."

"Right. Ever given your number to a girl before?"

"I didn't give her my number." He stopped, a goofy grin on his face. "Oh, shit, I did."

I patted him on the back and circled the front of my car. "When it rings, make sure you get to it first. I think she liked you, so who knows what she might say."

I knew she didn't really like him. I knew it was me she was interested in and that she was using him as a foil. My evaluating psychiatrist, Evelyn, would have raised an eyebrow at such confidence and no doubt patted herself on the back that she'd scored me right on another PCL-R topic: "Grandiose Sense of Self-Worth," two out of two points.

I would have pointed out to Evelyn, a stout lady with the kind of penetrating, beady eyes an empath isn't supposed to have, that judging me like that was unfair. After all, I'd also maxed out on the very reason I knew Gus was my runner-up for the evening, the first rating on the list that scored me full marks for "Glibness and Superficial Charm." Evelyn joked that there should have been a "Hell Yes" response for that one. She was right, I think, and I knew that even if I didn't have her number, my new friend would be in contact soon enough.

It took sixteen days and she called Gus, not me, which pissed me off. She called at 9:30 on a Saturday night, while Gus was in the shower. His wife answered the phone, which made me laugh.

When Gus got on the line, she claimed to have a gun in her hand, pointed at a bad guy, which is why Gus ignored his angry wife and called me immediately, and why I decided to give her another chance.

CHAPTER SEVEN

OUR DRIED VOICES

Gus barely contained the panic in his voice, his words falling fast and jumbled.

"She's terrified, she doesn't know what to do." He was almost panting down the phone he was so breathless. "Dom, shit, you have to help."

Fear can be contagious, I know that and have seen it, but I am immune. My fear response is almost nonexistent. If someone close to me is in danger, or even if I am, it's as stressful as a game of chess. My chief response to Gus gabbling down the phone like a rooster with his arse feather plucked was impatience.

"Just call the police," I said. "What else does she expect *you* to do?"

"She said something about having drugs, being there to rescue her brother and so no cops. I think I'm going out there."

"Good plan. But first, check with your wife that it's okay for you to go out and rescue a super-sexy woman who you have a massive crush on, and who's covered in bags of heroin while holding a gun on someone. If she says you can go, I'll join you."

Gus's voice hardened. "This is serious, Dom. She needs help."

"Maybe she does. But not ours. You're being ridiculous." He was, of course. And the tickle of interest I felt was equally idiotic. But I couldn't help feeling that way—it was a part of me just like the other bricks that built the wall between me and everyone else. It was the part of me that I fought and repressed the most, actually. And

I knew that, like magma beneath the earth's crust, it bubbled ferociously hot, looking for a crack that would allow it to burst free and scorch everything in its way. "Impulsivity": number fourteen on the checklist, and two more points for me.

Gus wouldn't give up. "You're in law enforcement, aren't you obliged to help?"

"I'm a lawyer, Gus. I file motions and show up to court with polished shoes. Boots, to be precise. I don't have tactical training and I don't wear a cape under my suit. In fact, as I see it, my only obligation is to call the police."

"And a nice girl gets arrested for trying to save her brother."

"How do you know she's a nice girl? She's pointing a gun at someone." A moment of silence echoed through the phone, and, given Gus's panic, I knew he wasn't telling me something. "Gus, what the fuck is going on?"

"She is a nice girl." He'd lowered his voice, almost to a whisper. "We've talked on the phone a couple of times. She told me about her family. Her dad is in prison and has been since she was a baby. Her mother is a drug user, and she's raising her brother by herself. So yeah, Dom, she's a nice person who's living in a shitty situation, one where the involvement of the police won't help."

I gritted my teeth and felt a growl in my throat, low and primal. Gus was an idiot, a goat tied to a stake in the ground, waiting to be devoured. Worse, he'd tied himself to the stake. She wasn't a nice girl, she was toying with him to get to me. She was letting Gus think that he'd won her over, and she wanted me to know it. The problem was, if I didn't play along right now, then I'd lose for sure. Not that Gus would ever have her, no, either she'd cut him loose or his moral compass would flicker straight and true. But I'd lose and I didn't like to lose, especially not to a demure, unexciting, married man.

"Fuck it," I said. "Give me the address."

○

The east side of Austin used to be where all the rookie cops wanted to work, the sector known as Charlie where the gung-ho boys in blue were guaranteed nightly encounters with drug dealers and gangbangers. In the rundown shopping centers and broken parking lots, there was the promise of nabbing a local politician getting his knob polished by a crack whore. I'd done ride-alongs in Charlie and had seen for myself the change that came with nightfall. The potholed alleys that were deserted in the day's heat became busy with shifty buyers and sellers who would lounge with practiced innocence every time a black-and-white rolled past. The car washes, too, filled in the daytime with pimps scrubbing their Cadillacs, were even busier at night as their girls steered a procession of Johns into the car stalls for, well, knob polishing. The place used to make SoCo look like Mayfair.

Lately, though, economics had succeeded where the cops had failed to crack down on crime. The worst parts of East Austin were too close to downtown for the developers to ignore, and the slum landlords developed dollar signs in their eyes, unable to resist the hefty sacks of cash being dangled in front of their greedy, sniffing noses. This meant a slow death to the excitement of Charlie Sector as eco-friendly homes popped up alongside crack houses, and solar-powered town houses nudged aside crumbling, cinder-block duplexes. The yuppies moving in needed organic-food stores and coffee shops, not crack and hookers, and they didn't hesitate to call the cops about the hoodlums lurking on the street corners.

As I drove, I spotted several clubs I'd heard about but not played in, new and hip and cool places to see, be seen, and pick up chicks. I felt acid in my stomach, that flash of anger as I realized that I may not get to play in those clubs, ever, and reminded myself that my extracurricular time needed to be spent tracking down the snake who'd lied about me stealing his music, rather than risking life and limb for Gus and his crush.

The violence and discord moved farther east, away from down-

town and into the ramshackle apartment complexes and trailer parks
already inhabited by the poorest people who moved to the outskirts
of Austin, the Mexicans and Hondurans who felt unwelcome and
didn't much want to be seen unless it came to their lawn-care business. Or the gaggles of day laborers who gathered early in the morning
hoping to feed their family that day and maybe pay some rent.

The address Gus gave me was in this new war zone, a patch of
unused land that lay between East Austin's jugular, Ed Bluestein
Boulevard, beside a sprawling mobile-home park. About the size of
a football field, it was all rock, dust, and broken beer bottles. If I'd
looked closely, or perhaps remembered to bring a flashlight, I knew
I'd have seen a sprinkling of used condoms and needles, too. Sometimes it's better to stay in the dark.

It was 11 p.m. when I pulled up behind Gus's car. I doused my
headlights and sat looking into the darkness for signs of the mayhem
I'd been expecting. All was quiet. I opened my car door, and the
ding-ding from the dashboard startled me until I whipped the key
from the ignition.

I got out and walked slowly toward Gus's car, reassured by the
weight of my gun in the small of my back. The day's heat seemed to
have settled on this place, pressing down on me and provoking the
millions of cicadas, setting them to a cacophony of noise that blan-
keted the field. The moon fed down its light intermittently, wisps of
cloud fanning across it like fingers playing Guess Who?

I followed a dirt track that curved to my right, and stopped
when I saw another car, a van. Two people stood watching me, and
I knew who they were. I looked past them, and then down at their
feet to see if they stood over a body, and when I didn't see anything
I wondered if there was already one in the van. All seemed calm,
normal. Safe for me to leave.

That moment, I think, was my last chance to walk away, to turn
and set my boots on the path back to my car before the dust settled
behind me. I didn't do that. I couldn't because in a life so repressed, so

controlled and so unnatural to me, I found myself presented with an adventure. Not just a theoretical one, either, but one that lay not more than twenty yards away in a dark field, an adventure that pitted me both with and against the closest thing I'd had to a best friend in years, and over a girl who intrigued me beyond any other. It felt like a black hole was drawing me in, and I crossed that dusty gap as the fragile safety of my life crumbled under my feet, disappearing with every step of those twenty yards. Tunnel vision blocked out the tedium that waited behind me, kept me from seeing the safety of my carefully contrived world, and the glimpses of my life that I did get were of a job demotion and a decision from Marley, a forever ban from playing music at the Norman Pub. So right there, at the edge of a moonlit field in the wrong part of town, with a gun for comfort and a mystery unfolding before me, my involvement had ceased to be a choice.

When I got close, she moved forward, the pale skin of her face glowing like platinum in the moonlight, but her eyes were narrow, as though she wasn't happy to see me.

"Gus said you'd come," she said. "I wasn't sure."

I didn't know what to say. The spell was almost broken by her flat tone, her unwelcoming face, as if I'd misread her, misread this evening. But this was a mystery in itself, part of her game perhaps. While I figured it out, as tricksters and liars will do, I refrained from committing myself to an emotional position and instead turned the focus outward, away from her and away from me.

"What's going on?" I asked Gus. "Whose car is that?"

Gus looked over his shoulder as if he didn't know it was there, then back at me. "I don't know."

I looked at her standing beside him. Her face softened and she smiled suddenly, a coy and teasing look. "You don't recognize it?"

"A Ford van near a trailer park, I'd guess it belongs to Gus's client. But I can't imagine either of you would be stupid enough to *actually* steal it."

"Wrong on both counts," she said. "The first count. For now."

"Meaning?"

"It's a 1995 Ford Transit van," she said. "Same make and model, different color. I wanted to show Gus that it was easy to steal."

"Borrow," Gus said hurriedly.

"Why would Gus care that it's easy to steal? Or borrow?"

"Ask him." She shrugged. "It was his story, after all. And the point of his story, unless I'm mistaken, was that some guy rides around with sacks of cash in a car that's easy to . . ." She shrugged again.

It was true, of course, it *was* the point of his story. But she'd taken a story that you shake your head at and made it into a game that could land someone in jail. Also, I wasn't sure who was supposed to be in this game, or what the rules were. All I could think was that she'd recognized three people who needed money, including herself, and that was reason enough to roll the dice. But she was mistaken if she thought I needed money badly enough to steal.

I started as the rear doors of the van opened behind her. A boy stuck his head out and looked at me, the same boy I'd seen at the JJC. Her brother.

"Can we go?" he said. "My iPod battery is dying."

"Wait, he stole the van?" I asked.

"I told you," she said. "He has experience in matters criminal."

"And how nice of you to encourage him."

"I'm his sister, not his mother." Her voice was soft. "Maybe we'll do a shift at the soup kitchen tomorrow. You ever help out at the soup kitchen?"

"No," I said. "What exactly do you want from us?"

"Oh, Dom, don't be so suspicious," she said. "So judgmental. Gus told a story, and we all wondered how easy it would be to steal that man's car."

"I didn't wonder that."

"Yes, you did." It was the first hard note I'd heard in her voice, and again, she was right.

"Fine," I said. "I also wonder what it'd be like to drive at a hundred and twenty on I-35, but I'm not going to do it." *I also wonder what it'd be like to fuck you, but I'm not going to rape you.*

"Really? If you had a fast-enough car and were sure no one would catch you?"

Gus gave a gentle laugh. "Even if you got caught, this is liberal Travis County. You'd get a slap on the wrist, if that."

They were actually being logical, persuasive, but it was still a road I didn't need to go down. "Then it's done. We know how easy it is to steal a 1995 Ford Transit van, so we can all go home."

No one moved. That vein of curiosity still pulsed in me, and I moved past them both to the car where the boy sat slumped in the front seat, plugged into his tunes. I looked to the ignition and saw the yellow handle of a screwdriver jammed into the key slot. He glanced up at me, then looked away as if he didn't want to be seen, didn't want to be there.

I knew how he felt. I was at a crime scene that I wasn't going to report, standing next to a juvenile delinquent who'd stolen a car and broken curfew to do it. I was, legally speaking, at the sharp end of a conspiracy to commit a felony, which I also was not planning to report. I looked over my shoulder and found myself the hub of this little prank, two pairs of eyes on me as if the next move were mine, and mine alone. Normally I would want to take the lead so I could manipulate the situation to make sure my own ends were met. As it was, I just stood there staring back at them. And wondering.

Could it really be that easy?

My job had taught me many things, but that night the two that came to mind were the facts that criminals got away scot-free a lot more than they got caught, and that as a general rule, even the ones who got away were pretty stupid. I'd also been wayward enough as a youth to know that it wasn't necessarily the criminal act itself that determined whether or not you got caught, it was the planning. That was my bypass mechanism, the route I took to avoid my own nature.

Because if I planned carefully enough, I could follow the rails of my own logic like a train and not be sidetracked by impulse.

I watched as she climbed into the minivan with her brother, and it struck me that I didn't even know her name. I couldn't imagine what it would be, either, because ever since we'd met I'd thought about her as one would a dream. Or maybe a ghost in a nightmare—real enough to make me react, to entice and intrigue me, but in the end not a real person, and not with a real name.

She drove without turning on the headlights, the van's tires spitting out dust and pebbles as it rocked and bounced along the dark track away from us.

"So who lied about the gun to the head, you or her?" I asked.

"Her," he said, still staring down the track. "I wouldn't make that up."

"Figures." We were silent for a moment, then I looked at him. "So what's her name?"

"I have no idea," he whispered.

CHAPTER EIGHT

THOSE WHO HAVE CROSSED

Sixteen days after my gig was canceled, that was also how long it took Marley to call. He phoned midmorning, as I was scribbling some lyrics on a notepad, and I wanted to ignore him. The words were flowing, soft and manipulative verses that girls would swoon over. Words that my sweet little sadist would fucking hate. And yet I wanted to sing them in a crowded bar with her right there in front of me, so I could watch the irritation on her face, watch her roll her eyes at the sap I was singing, and have her see all the other girls lap it up.

I answered, though, as the name on my phone's screen told me who it was, and I listened as he hedged and stammered, the quiver in his voice giving me advance notice of what he was going to say. He apologized for taking so long and got halfway through firing me permanently before his spine kicked in and he switched to mild outrage that I'd try to deceive him and my audience.

"I'd like to think this was accidental, Dom, but that's not possible. Parts of it are a carbon copy—chords, rhythm, even some of the damn lyrics are the same."

"Who says I stole their music?"

"You did steal it, man, but if you don't know who complained then maybe you did it more than once. Maybe several people have complained to me about it, and I ain't telling. Come on, get real, Dom, you can't do that shit." He started up again, talking about ethics and trust, as if he didn't screw every musician who came into his shitty little bar, making them play for tips and be grateful for the chance. As he rambled on, I tuned him out and thought about what to say in reply. I could go with the apologetic, *So sorry, it won't happen again, please forgive me*, or maybe try, *I must have absorbed it without knowing, I'm just so embarrassed*, both attempts to save my musical career in Austin. Manipulation is my strong point, especially making myself the victim, but in the end I chose door number three. I waited until he was midflow to interrupt. "Hey, Marley. Fuck you." I hung up.

At moments like that, when events conspired and turned against me, I could always set them straight by tweaking someone else. Usually, I'd find a girl to sleep with, make some impressionable, dumpy chick do something she didn't want to do in bed by feeding her hope for the future. I'd lie about a pending record deal and ask if she'd want to go on the road with me, did she like hotels and breakfast in bed? Then I'd not call her, or call her and ask for another girl and act like I couldn't really remember her. It sounds cruel and maybe it is. Cruelty is pretty abstract to me, a concept I get on an intellectual level but don't experience. After all, cruelty requires empathy, and that bucket is empty.

And remember what I'm saying, the *reason* I toyed with these girls. It wasn't to be cruel—it wasn't about them at all. It was to build myself up, and their hurt feelings were a mere by-product. Something more, too, these excursions acted as scientific endeavors because incisions into a person's soul gave me a chance to see emotions I didn't have, to experience things vicariously that most other people experienced all the time. And I benefited from that vicarious experience by studying it in a detached way, learning a little more about my fellow man. Or woman. If I saw an emotion, heard it, then I could mimic it.

The drunk girls in Austin were safe, though, that night at least. I just wanted my music. My lovely guitar, the gentle hum of words in my throat, perfect accompaniments to an idea floating like a song in my mind. It was a song about the unthinkable, and yet I couldn't stop thinking about it.

O

I took two more weeks to decide, but in the way a starving man sits before a meal and decides to eat it. Some things become inevitable. I'd surrounded myself with a force field of reasons to keep on the straight and narrow, to stay invisible behind my one-way mirror: personal safety, financial security, avoiding the stigma of my condition. Those reasons were still there, but the force field had weakened thanks to a pay cut, an unwanted transfer, and accusations of musical fraud. And on the other side of the mirror, out in the real world, a beautiful woman beckoned like a proverbial siren. I wasn't planning on shipwrecking my life, of course, but given the circumstances, a careful tack in her direction seemed, at the time, reasonable enough. And, of course, there was the money.

Money meant freedom. And pleasure. It meant that to everyone, of course, but to me it meant I could live more like myself, not worry so much about the people around me finding out who, or what, I was. And as question nine on the Hare PCL-R indicates, living off other people was just another part of me, one of the internal cogs that worked in synchronicity with the other elements of sociopathy. Which is to say that money wasn't just alluring, getting my hands on it was a biological imperative.

After a morning docket at the JJC, I took off my tie and drove across town to buy a disposable cell phone, what the bad guys call a "burner." Gus didn't answer when I called, perhaps he didn't recognize the number, so I left a message for him. Deciding which number to leave gave me pause, because my regular cell phone was issued by the county. We were allowed to make personal calls—they didn't expect us to lug two phones everywhere—but using them to foment criminal conspiracies would no doubt be frowned upon.

He called my burner two hours later. "Get a new phone?"

"Borrowed one. You have plans tonight?"

"I'm guessing I do now."

O

I looked at him over my grapefruit and tonic. We'd not talked about the van in the field, other than that night when we'd watched our co-conspirators drive away. Gus had said, "What the fuck are we doing?"

I'd just patted him on the back, and said, "Nothing. Yet."

I took a sip and asked him the same question, kind of. "Why did you go out there that night?"

He shrugged. "I don't know. It seems so stupid now."

"Daylight can do that," I said. "I'm wondering if you really think stealing your client's car is a good idea."

"This might surprise you, Dom, but I do. I mean, look how easy it was, a frigging twelve-year-old managed it."

"A twelve-year-old with plenty of practice."

"That's what the Internet is for," he said. "You can figure out anything nowadays."

"True. You need the money that badly?"

"Things aren't good. Seems like every kid out of law school is jumping on the immigration bandwagon, and they're using daddy's start-up money to undercut my prices. In business, or even criminal law, clients care if you're experienced, if you're actually good. In my line of work, not so much. The clients are all poor as hell, and frankly I don't do much more than fill out the paperwork for them. If they can get some recent grad to do that for half the price, why wouldn't they?"

"And if you get caught?"

"I've thought about that, yeah. But like you've said a million times, idiots get away with crime every day. We're not idiots, so . . ." He drank some of his beer. "Plus, he's my client. I could say I was out there looking for him. I'll have some paperwork in the car for him, something like that."

"Sneaky."

"And you also said that no one ever goes to prison for a first-time offense, right?"

I nodded. "Unless it's murder or something like that, true. If you just steal a car, you'd get probation for that, absolutely. But you'd also lose your law license."

Gus waved a dismissive hand. "And not be allowed to fill in forms for the rest of my life? Poor me. Maybe I could play music full-time. How cool would that be? And I'd have a bad-boy reputation, too. That'd help with the crowds. Or just move to Costa Rica and play my guitar on the beach."

He was good enough to play full-time, for sure, but we both knew the romance of doing so wasn't the same as the reality, though he seemed to be ignoring that fact. With no job to fall back on, with a wife to support and kids to plan for . . .

"And Michelle, how does she feel about all this felonious activity?"

"You think I haven't told her?"

"Yes, I do."

Gus smiled. "I did kind of bring it up last week. No specifics, just how she'd feel about me being a secret master-criminal and showing up with wads of cash."

"And?"

"Made her horny."

Fucking Gus, and his perfect wife.

"Okay, Mr. Master-criminal, how would it work? Seriously, if you think it can be done, tell me the details."

Gus chewed his lip for a moment. "We watch him. Follow him on a day he's collecting rent, see how he does it and when he leaves his car."

"Stupid plan," I said.

"Why?"

"Still speaking hypothetically, of course, there's no point stealing the car before he's collected any money, it only makes sense to do it at the end of the evening. So I don't see any point in following him all day and risking being seen."

"Ah, right. Didn't think about it that way."

"Plus, it's summer and we should probably do this in the dark, later at night." I smiled. "Maybe you can leave the master-criminal thing to me."

"Fine, how would *you* do it?"

"It'd be like preparing a case for trial, except in reverse. When I get ready for trial, I go through the police report and pick out the witnesses and evidence I can use, make a list of both. And I make a note, too, of the evidence that likely won't be admissible, and a list of flaws in the case. The trick in planning a crime, I think, would be to make sure that second list is nice and full, and that there's as little as possible on the first."

"The perfect crime?"

"No such thing."

"I disagree. I talked about that with Michelle, actually. She thinks the perfect crime is one where no one even knows a crime's been committed. That way, the perpetrator gets away with it, keeps the money or whatever, and never has to worry about looking over his shoulder. Makes sense to me."

It didn't to me. I couldn't fathom doing that much work and planning, putting my neck on the line and taking potentially deadly risks, only for no one to know about any of it. My narcissistic streak, perhaps, but it would be like that tree in the woods, falling without anyone hearing. I would want my crime to make a noise, a crash, I would want people to know that it had been committed and then have to suffer the torture of not knowing who did it. But Gus was right about one thing, I certainly wouldn't want to live my life looking over my shoulder, not any more than I already did.

As I sat there nursing my drink, I had an idea how to address that particular issue. Then I tucked it away for future use and went back to the subject at hand. "Michelle's perfect crime makes me wonder," I said, "if maybe your client might be a little hesitant to call the cops and report all that money missing."

Gus's eyes lit up. "That's a great point. If he reports it, all of it, there's a good chance the IRS would come poking around. The immigration people too."

"Precisely. It's possible that he's better off losing a month's takings than losing his business altogether. So maybe the perfect crime is one that the victim doesn't dare report."

Gus painted trails in the condensation on his beer glass. He looked up at me. "You really serious about doing this?"

"I guess you can say that I'm serious about exploring it. You?"

"Seems crazy, but . . . yeah."

"Cool," I said. "Although I would have one condition."

"What's that?"

"Our new lady friend is kept out of it."

Gus thought for a moment, then asked, "Are you being sweet and protecting her, or . . . ?"

"The other. I don't trust her."

"That so?" He smirked. "I thought you wanted to—"

"We both want to do that. And I'm happy to, I just can't tell what she's up to, and I don't like that. Have you talked to her since last weekend?"

He shifted in his seat. "No."

"But you've tried."

"Once. I called and left a message."

"Do me a favor and leave it alone, will you? Just for a while."

"Sure." Gus cleared his throat, then looked me in the eye. "Are we really going to do this?"

We were, because the elements of my true nature had already collided, a rolling snowball of sociopathy gathering momentum.

Impulsiveness picking up on my need for risk, rolling onto my lack of fear and the deceptiveness and sense of self-worth that convinced me I could get away with it. And on top of it all, I got to manipulate another human being into playing soldier under my command. Not to mention all that cold, hard cash.

"Let me plan it out, check out the end of his route. I'll take lead and let you know, okay? We're just stealing a car, not even really stealing it for long. *Borrowing*, like you said."

"Right," he said. "And I have a condition, too."

"Oh?"

"No guns. I know how you like to carry everywhere you go, but on this, no guns."

"Yeah, okay. No guns is fine with me. You said before that he carries, though."

"I think so. . . ." He snapped his fingers. "Come to think of it, he might not. He picked up a DWI a year ago, which means he has to wait another four years to get a concealed carry license. He's not allowed to carry a gun."

"Which means he *shouldn't*, not that he doesn't."

"True. But if he's trying to fly under the radar, he'd be stupid to take the risk."

"On the other hand, he'd be stupid *not* to carry. He's more likely to get jacked by a civilian than by the police. Anyway, just do your thing and I'll let you know if it's feasible."

He left me there in the bar, to go home to his wife and work on those kids. Truth be told, I didn't trust him much, either. For a decent, conscientious, loving man to commit a serious crime and jeopardize his future and his family . . . well, there was a lot about empaths I didn't get, and this went on the list.

I thought about going home and beginning the feasibility analysis, but I wanted to start then, that very second. I also didn't want the distraction of my new roommate, Tristan Bell.

I'd recently rented a room in a condo that Tristan owned, to save money. He was the IT guy in the main DA's office downtown and had posted a note saying he wanted a roommate. I asked around about him, and people told me he was quiet and would be easy to live with. So far that had been true, excessively true almost. The name "Tristan" reminded me of the dorky vet of the same name in the English show from when I was a kid, called *All Creatures Great and Small*, and this Tristan fit the mold. A modern version, he was a classic computer nerd, complete with glasses and reclusive streak. He spent almost all his time in his bedroom, and when he wasn't there he kept his bedroom locked. It seemed odd at first, paranoid even, but I figured that we didn't know each other that well and, if he had expensive gadgets or porn in there, I could see why he wouldn't risk a stranger nosing around in his room.

The best thing was that he didn't bug me, ask me questions, or want to be my friend. He left me alone the same way he liked to be left alone. I'd worried about my guitar playing, but he told me he liked the muffled strum coming from my room. "And I do have headphones," he said, "if I don't like the song you're playing."

So I probably could have gone home and thought about this little caper, but I wanted some immediate answers. Or if not answers, some decent lines of inquiry and maybe a list of supplies. I borrowed a pen from the waitress, reached for a paper napkin, and opened it up.

Let the planning begin.

CHAPTER NINE

A TREE SWINGING

Three weeks later, I walked into my office to find Tristan sitting at my desk, his nose in my laptop. I stood in the doorway until he noticed me, eyes blinking in surprise.

"Something wrong with my computer?"

"Doing some updates. Security stuff and new software that allows downloads straight from the APD servers to your computer. You'll be able to watch in-car videos minutes after they're shot. Assuming the officer downloads them properly."

"You couldn't do that remotely?" I wasn't tech savvy by any means but, in the past, the folks in IT had been able to help me with problems from where they sat, taking over my computer somehow and doing what they needed to do.

"Almost done." He typed for a second, then stood up. "Sorry, but you should be good to go. If you have any problems just let me know."

"Thanks."

He ducked out and nodded to Brian McNulty, who was on his way in from court. McNulty dumped his briefcase on his desk and sank into his chair with a groan. "Be thankful you don't have my judge for your dockets. He's an asshole." McNulty suddenly leaned forward and looked both ways through the door. "And speaking of assholes, you just met a prize one."

"Oh? Being a computer nerd makes you an asshole?"

"He's a nosy fucker, is what he is. And not above a little blackmail. Threatened to report me for using my work computer for my music."

"You mean your illegal downloading of music."

"I don't illegally download, I sample songs and create my own mixes. Just because I don't pluck at a guitar and croon to the ladies, doesn't mean I don't make music."

I didn't have the energy to argue. "Whatever. You were saying Bell threatened to report you?"

"Yeah, like I said, he's nosy. I'm pretty sure he peruses our Internet history, looking for dirt to use against people. He made me write him a letter of recommendation for a job application."

"He's leaving?"

"The county's letting a few people go in that department. I guess he might be one of them. This was only two weeks ago, so I don't really know."

"Huh, I had no idea," I said. "Which is weird, when you think about it."

"Why?"

"The chap's my roommate. He's never mentioned anything about that."

"Wait, he's your roommate?"

"That's what I said."

"Seriously? How did that happen?"

"Long story. Anyway, he's fine, keeps to himself."

McNulty snickered. "That's what they say about serial killers."

He might have been right about Tristan but I doubted it, even though my roommate and I still barely spoke. Not through any animosity but because of our schedules. I was either at work, playing music, or chasing women. Even when I was at the apartment, I barely saw him. He was an odd duck, still locking himself in his room most hours of the day and subsisting on Cheerios in the morning, delivered pizza the rest of the time. Once, I brought him back a salad plate from Whole Foods. Not because I cared about his diet but because I wanted to see what he'd do. Like feeding a monkey couscous instead of bananas. And he did what I'd expect a monkey to do: eye it warily for a moment, eye me warily for another moment, then disappear into his room with it. Only difference was, Tristan grunted a thank you. He was odd enough that I'd gotten interested in him, wanted to understand him.

When McNulty turned away, I sat down and looked over my computer, noting a new icon on the desktop but nothing else to worry me. I double-clicked it, and APD's Versadex system opened on the screen, asking me for log-in information. It seemed to be exactly what Tristan had said it was. And truthfully, I didn't care whether Tristan was a nosy bastard as I hadn't been doing my private research on my work computer. I knew enough about technology to avoid that trap. Every morning at work we logged in using individual usernames and passwords, so I figured our online activity could be tracked. As a prosecutor, I probably could have explained away most of it as job-related, but I went in the opposite direction. Call it paranoia, but I'd bought a cheap laptop that I used solely for researching the theft. And once it was done, the computer would find itself at the bottom of a lake or . . . somewhere that wasn't my apartment. And I'd double-deleted the early searches I'd done on my work computer weeks ago.

Gus had been right, of course, the Internet was invaluable. Within days, I knew how to break into a car in seconds, using a small ball-peen hammer to punch out the lock. I also knew how to start it with just a screwdriver, jamming it into the ignition the way twelve-year-olds apparently knew how to do. As a backup plan, and in case we had time, I also knew the theory behind hot-wiring a car. Just for fun, I studied the art of lock picking, researching the theory online and ordering a pick and tension wrench.

Gus and I had swapped a couple of e-mails before he read that a politician cheating on his wife had devised a safer communication method: sharing an e-mail account and leaving messages in the "drafts" folder. Apparently, or so he said, if e-mails never actually got sent, they left no trail. So we both cleared our earlier e-mail exchanges as best we could, and we did that, instead. Safe for work, even, Gus said, and he knew more about those things than I did.

Toward the end of the month, I spent a couple of hours on a Thursday evening following our intended victim, Ambrosio Silva. Gus had given me a list of parks where several of his mobile homes were located, as well as his address. I figured he'd either start nearest his home and work his way out, or start farthest away and pick up his rents on the route home. I exercised my love of surveillance cameras and researched battery-powered ones, finding a nice line in camouflaged cameras.

The day before Silva made his rounds, I put one at the entrance of the park nearest his home and one at the park farthest away, testing my theory. I forced myself out of bed at dawn and spent a boring two hours in front of my computer, but eventually I spotted him at the park closest to his home. I knew he'd be there for thirty minutes at least, which gave me time to drive out there. I did what I told Gus I wouldn't: I followed Silva. I'd realized that knowing his route was vital. Not every minute, not every twist and turn, but to know basically which trailer parks he went to in rough order. So I followed him, at a distance, for two hours, making sure my supposition about his route was correct, and by the time I turned back toward central Austin, I was sure it was. The final piece of the puzzle fell into place when he turned into what I'd assumed to be his final destination at ten o'clock that evening. As I'd suspected, it was the rundown heap of a place that sat right next to the deserted field where I'd last set my eyes on a stolen Transit van. Which is precisely where I figured the getaway car would wait.

I had a date in mind and a plan well formed in my head. Like a video game, I was able to put the players in position and watch the clock ticking down, execute an escape from the grimy and appropriately named Crooked Creek Mobile Home Park with another man's car and another man's cash.

That plan, however, went to shit on a Thursday morning when I opened our communication system and saw a message from Gus.

CHAPTER TEN

THE TUMID RIVER

A light rain fell as I left my parents' farmhouse, both of them watching from the back door. My father had given me one brief shooting lesson in the back meadow, standing beside me and throwing a plastic bucket high and away from us, gentle encouragement when I hit it, muttered never-minds when I missed. After twenty minutes, the barrels started to get hot, so we quit and sat at the large table in his study as he showed me how to clean my new Holland & Holland .410 shotgun. I was thirteen.

At that point, they'd lost a degree of contact with me. I'd spent three years at boarding school, and I think they watched me a little warily that morning, hoping that school and a measure of maturity had wiped away the dark edges they'd glimpsed during my childhood. The gun was another rite of passage, like boarding school, only one I'd been looking forward to since I was seven.

In an English drizzle that morning, I walked down the gravel track and away from the farmhouse, my coat pockets bulging with Eley cartridges and a wool scarf itching my neck. My father had bought me a flat cap to go with the gun, and it, as much as the weapon itself, was a marker of adulthood. The little peak kept the rain from my eyes, but I wouldn't have minded a downpour as I set out on my first hunt, rabbits and pigeons my quarry. The prospect of my first pheasant shoot was still a month away, the time when I'd stand side to side with my father's friends, the noblest of the Hertfordshire gentry, as a long thin line of farm workers pressed slowly toward us through the undergrowth to flush wave after wave of pheasants over our heads, our waiting guns. It wasn't a slaughter, though, not like the animal-rights people claim. In fact, it was deemed too easy and unsporting to shoot the low-flying pheasants, and the guns either side of you would take a dim view if you did. No, the challenge was to shoot the high, fast ones and, even better, to "wipe the eye" of your neighbor, take out the bird that he just missed.

But that chilly October morning I was by myself. I had to get used to the feel of the gun, my father said, the weight and the sound of it when I fired. Get used to killing something by myself, so I knew that I could. And that's what I wanted, too.

I carried the gun under my arm the way I'd been taught, with the barrels pointing safely at the ground. A half mile from the house, I cut left along the edge of a field and headed toward the narrow end of a wood we called Arrow Wood, for its triangular shape. When I got there, I started slowly down the right-hand side, in between the edge of the trees and the strip of mustard that our gamekeeper had put down as game cover. That thin belt of mud and patchy grass was where I thought I'd find rabbits.

And maybe my first kill.

Up to then it'd been a few insects and fish. Same as any other boy, though perhaps my curiosity levels were a little higher. Once I'd done it, though, and seen and felt nothing, there was no great desire to harm other creatures. Not the way you read about when it comes to people like me. The question in my mind that morning was whether killing warm-blooded creatures would feel any different. I suspected not, if only because the killing itself would be more remote—the fish had been hauled in from the farm's three ponds, wriggling on the end of a line and dispatched in various ways that included a rock, a knife, and ten minutes of me staring at it flapping on the ground. Drowning, I suppose you'd call it.

But out there by the woods, death would come at a distance. A rabbit bowled over at fifteen or twenty yards, a pigeon knocked from the sky and thumping onto the ground even farther away. I wasn't expecting much from the killing. And it wasn't just the killing that drew me there, brimming with suppressed excitement and anticipation. No, to suggest that would be a sore misrepresentation of my motivations. A huge part was the power, not just of the gun but of the trust my parents placed in me, the freedom to look like a child but act like a grown-up. I didn't want to disappoint them, either, by missing or not finding anything.

Nor did I want to lie about what I'd shot just to impress my father. The rule was: All dead animals were brought back to the bothy, the out-building where we hung the pheasants after a shoot. Even rabbits and pigeons were supposed to hang for a day or two, to loosen the meat and improve the flavor, and my father would no doubt be waiting for my return to see how I'd done. I could lie and claim to have shot a few things, but one other rule of his was: no animal was to be left out there, either dead or wounded. If you killed it, you brought it home; and if you just wounded it, then you stayed out there until you found and killed it. He didn't miss often, my father, but when he clipped a bird, he made sure it was tracked down and its neck was wrung before he moved on. I'd seen him beating through brambles to get to a wounded pheasant, hands and legs torn up by thorns just to make sure the bird didn't suffer a slow, lingering death. I didn't care about that, but I knew enough to follow my dad's rules to the letter if I wanted to keep my new shotgun. It was a beauty, too. Double-barreled with two triggers, a forward one for the right barrel, and the back trigger firing the left barrel, which was itself choked a hair's breadth tighter to keep the shot pattern more compact for an extra yard or two.

I walked as quietly as I could beside Arrow Wood, cursing silently as a pair of sharp-eyed pigeons popped out of the trees sixty yards in front of me. They flitted and dipped as they flew away, as if expecting a blast of pellets from behind. I looked back toward the track, and my eye caught a sudden movement ahead and to the right, on the verges of the mustard growth. I stopped to stare and listen. The mustard grass rustled, but it could have been the wind. I lifted the gun and tucked the stock into my shoulder, watching the ground where I'd seen movement. I could hear myself breathing and feel tiny drops of rain tickling the top of my nose.

The grass rustled again, closer to the edge this time, and I shifted my feet to get a better stance, sure the rabbit would bolt for the woods. I stood like that until my shoulders ached, but I didn't want to blink first, to lower my gun and give the creature a free pass. Be outwitted by a rabbit. I sidled forward, still aiming. Ten yards away, nine, eight . . . then a flash of movement farther out, twenty yards at least, a ball of fur leaping out of the mustard grass onto the track of green and closing the gap to the trees in a heartbeat. I didn't aim—didn't have time to—I just jerked the gun up and swung it in the direction of the rabbit, pulling the forward trigger as its head came level with the first line of trees, letting the second barrel go a split second later, lead shot spattering into the woods with a blast of frustration and hope.

The moment I fired, a dozen or more pigeons took off from the trees, the flap of their wings startling as they swirled over and around me before spotting the source of the noise and spiraling away, some scything the ground as others soared upward toward the low, gray, clouds. In seconds a silence fell over the woods, leaving me with just the gentle patter of a slightly harder rain, a soft *thunk* when I dropped two new cartridges into the gun, and the sound of my feet on the ground as I walked toward the rabbit's point of entry.

A thin path led into the woods where the rabbit had disappeared, just in inch or two wide, and I wondered if animals had habits like us, stuck to routines and routes the way we did. Useful information for a hunter, I thought, and filed it away as something to ask my father about when I got home.

I stood there, peering into the trees, letting my eyes adjust. I could smell moss and wet bark, and the trees reached over me to

keep the rain away as I looked for signs of movement, of life. Barely
six feet away, I saw the rabbit, crouching under a fallen log. At first
I thought there might be two under there, but I realized why it was
hiding, not running: the back leg poking out beside the blinking
eyes and twitching nose belonged to the same creature. My shot had
disabled it, broken it. I moved slowly into the woods, and the rabbit
tried to shrink further, its small body rippling against the dark and
crumbling bark of the log. But it had nowhere to go.

I crouched down barely three feet from it and saw the blood on
its hind leg. My father hadn't told me what to do if I injured a rabbit
or hare. How to kill one off. Pheasants and pigeons, you just wrung
their necks, I'd seen the shooters on a pheasant hunt do that with a
quick flick and jolt of the wrist. But I didn't know if you could do that
to a rabbit, and I didn't want to get bitten finding out. I stayed there
looking at it for a moment, watching its tiny, black eyeballs swiveling
back and forth, as if by not seeing me it would be safe. Then I pointed
the end of my gun at its little head and pulled the trigger.

O

I stepped into the woods just after three in the morning. A full
moon cast an odd silvery light onto the path ahead of me, making
me feel like I was in a photo from the 1800s. This wasn't the woods
of my childhood, green and lush, with rabbits hopping into muddy
burrows and the outraged calls of disturbed pheasants rising from
the undergrowth. No, this was a monochrome spinney of leafless,
sunbaked trees and browned grass, where dust and cicadas rose up
around me as I walked. This was a place to be careful, where snakes
lived and the poor Mexicans from the Crooked Creek Mobile Home
Park came to have illicit sex with their neighbors or sell their drugs
to children. I'd had to wait in my car while several groups wandered
out of the trees, wait for them to get clear, and make sure others
weren't in their wake.

The flashlight in my backpack jostled against the camera, secure in its bubble wrap, and I was about to pull the light out when I found the perfect spot about forty yards into the woods. The tree was U-shaped, off the trail to my right, at the edge of a ditch and with its lowest branch too high for kids to climb but within reach for me. I scrambled up with a little difficulty and sat, fifteen feet above the ground in the *U*, catching my breath and scanning the trees for movement.

All seemed quiet, so I pulled the camera from my backpack and got to work. It was a beautiful little device, half the size of a shoe box and could take pictures or record video. Best of all, most important of all, I could operate it remotely from my laptop, download or watch images from the comfort of my bedroom. Two hundred bucks was a small price to pay for such a beautiful little device.

Secured in the *V* of two smaller branches, I lay my head beside it, making sure it had a clear view of where Silva would park his van. The final touch was to wipe the camera down with gentle strokes of my handkerchief, just in case things went sideways. If there was one thing juries loved and defendants hated, it was fingerprints. Hard to explain away innocently, and in my case, impossible.

Happy all was safe and secure, I dangled from the branch for a few seconds, enjoying the stretch in my shoulders, feeling the pain gather after a minute, and dropping myself to the ground before it seared me, feet landing as gently as possible in the crackle of brown leaves. I looked up and had to squint to make out the camera, not even sure I was seeing it then. I took one more look around me, then made my way toward the car. On three trees I put inch-long strips of white tape, markers to my camera but haphazard enough that it wasn't obvious which tree they led to. Then, as the night lifted slowly around me, I drove away from the mobile-home park, content that my prized piece of equipment was in place, that no one had seen me, and that my plan was as close to perfect as it could be.

O

The message Gus had left made my blood boil. I picked up my phone and called him.

"Gus, what the hell are you doing?"

"Not on the phone, Dom, jeez. I guess you got my message."

I got up from my desk and stuck my head out into the hallway, looking for McNulty. No sign of him, so I shut my office door. "Yeah, I got your damn message. And I want you to look me in the eye and tell me."

"Fine, I will."

"Meet me now."

"Dude, I've got clients coming in thirty minutes and a bunch of paperwork needs to be ready for them."

"Right, because that's more important than abandoning your friend."

"Fine, fine. Where?"

"My place." I left the building, checking the parking lot, hoping to see Tristan's car because this was a conversation I didn't need him hearing. He'd parked in a different spot than usual, which I'm sure irritated such a creature of habit, but it was there nonetheless, shining in the sun like he'd just washed it. I'd told Gus to meet me at my place, and he was waiting in his car in the large parking lot when I got there. He followed me up the stairs and down the hall in silence. When we got inside, I went to the fridge and poured myself a glass of milk.

"Tristan is at work, so go ahead."

He stared at the floor. "I'm sorry, Dom."

"I'm not understanding this. The whole thing was your idea. You came up with the guy as a potential target, you're the one who persuaded me it was realistic, this is your deal."

"I don't want it to be. Not anymore."

"Why?"

"Because I'm not a criminal."

"Oh, for fuck's sake." I took three deep breaths to calm myself. "We went through all this, we talked about it. First of all, you're a goddamned immigration lawyer, Gus. That's a criminal with a license. Every dollar you earn, pretty much, is covered in cocaine or weed, or was made illegally some other way."

"Dom, I know you're trying really hard to be offensive, and I get it, you're mad, but—"

"I'm not done being mad. Second of all, as I already said, we talked about this. What's changed?"

"I don't know. I just thought about it more."

"You told Michelle, didn't you? You fucking told Michelle."

"No! I did not. I absolutely did not. I promise, Dom, I really didn't."

I looked in those doelike eyes and believed him. One of the reasons I liked having him as a friend was his inability to lie to me. "Then what changed?"

"I just thought about it. I've done nothing but think about it, and while I know it's supposed to be easy, and in some ways it'd be pretty exciting, I'm just not sure the risk is worth the reward."

"And do you think maybe those are some things you might have mentioned earlier?"

"I'm not changing my mind, Dom."

"It's a theft. Simple, piddly theft. Burglary of a vehicle, a misdemeanor. And you know me well enough to know that I have no plans to be caught. I'm a smart fellow, Gus, and you know I'll plan this down to the last detail. The only thing that can go wrong is that we end up with less money than we hoped." I shrugged. "Of course, we could end up with more and your little Costa Rica shack can be a mansion."

"I don't need a mansion."

"Then don't fucking build one." I took him by the shoulders. "Gus. You may not need the money, but I do. The guy we're taking it from doesn't even . . . he's a slum lord."

"And that's worse than a thief?"

I smiled. "Now you're judging me? For wanting to go through with *your* plan?"

"You're right, it was my plan. But it's not anymore. Dom, the truth is I don't want to steal the damn money, and I'm afraid something will go wrong. Someone will get hurt, or killed."

"How's anyone going to get killed? I told you I wouldn't take my gun. And if we steal the car when he's not there, how the hell does anyone get hurt?"

"I don't know, I just—"

"Maybe we'll run over an orphan on the way out. Is that what you're afraid of?"

"Very funny."

"I'm not trying to be funny, Gus, I'm trying to understand."

"No." Gus was silent for a few seconds. "No, you're not trying to understand. You're trying to change my mind. I'm sorry, like I said, I really am. And you can go ahead with it and I'll never breathe a word to anyone. But I'm out, Dom, I'm one hundred percent out."

He turned and went to the front door, paused as if he had more to say, then opened it and walked out without looking back.

I sat there quietly for a moment, wondering what had just happened. I knew he had a conscience, and I didn't mind that about him. What I didn't get was how it could come and go, how theft can be a great idea one minute, *his* idea no less, and then become something too wrong to contemplate doing. That was what made me angry, that he would bring me in to a simple, straightforward act like this and suddenly turn and walk away. I was wondering whether I could somehow talk him around when I heard a sound that snapped me to attention. At first I thought it was Gus returning, but it came from the wrong end of the apartment.

I stood and moved into the center of the room, listening intently.

With a gentle swish, Tristan's door opened, and he stood there staring at me. His eyes were wide open and his mouth agape, telling me he'd heard everything.

CHAPTER ELEVEN

OF MEETING PLACES

W e stared at each other for a moment. "When did you get here?" I asked, my voice flat.

"I've been here all day. I didn't go in this morning, didn't feel good."

"I saw your car in the parking lot at work."

"No. You can't have . . ." He shook his head, then understanding dawned. "That's Susan Walton's new car. Same as mine, just . . . newer."

Which explained the different parking spot and its shininess. I silently cursed myself.

"Dom, what the hell's going on? What are you planning on doing?"

"Nothing. Mind your own business."

"Dude, I heard most of it."

"Again, mind your own business."

"You know, you're in my apartment, discussing committing a crime. And I heard everything. That makes it my business."

"Did you hear most of it, or everything? Either way, no, it doesn't make it your business."

"I have to report this to the police."

I laughed, unable to help myself. "Report what, exactly?"

"You and your friend Gus. You're planning to steal someone's car and there's money in it. I may not be a prosecutor, but I'm pretty sure that constitutes a crime."

"Talking about it doesn't. Sorry, matey, there's no crime unless something happens, and nothing's happening."

"Talking about it, planning it, that's a conspiracy, isn't it?"

"Oh, for fuck's sake, we're talking about it like people talk about winning the lottery or doing away with their mother-in-law. Wishful thinking."

"Right, so Gus was just backing out of some wishful thinking."

"Leave it alone, Tristan. I'm serious."

He shifted in the doorway to his room, a sly smile on his face. "You don't know much about clearing your Internet history, do you?"

My heart thumped in my chest but I said nothing.

"I heard you guys talking so I jumped online. I can access my stuff at work from here in about twelve seconds, look at whatever I need to. That thing you guys do, where you use a draft folder for messages? That's only mildly clever. I mean, the reason you do it that way, know about that method, is because that politician got found out, right? A military general or something, wasn't he?"

"You're starting to irritate me, Tristan."

He moved into the living room and leaned against the wall. "Look, we both know I'm not calling the cops. But I need money."

"Everyone needs money."

"Do you know what I do in there when the door's closed?"

"I can guess."

"Yeah, but you'd guess wrong. I gamble a lot. And I mean *a lot*. Not many gamblers make money."

I stood. "Then my advice to you is simple. Stop gambling."

We locked eyes as I moved past him into my room, and the urge to hit him surprised me. I resisted it but slammed my door a little too forcefully. I stood in front of my desk and stared at the laptop I'd bought for this venture. Whatever Tristan had seen, it wasn't on this. I was sure he couldn't get in without the password—he wasn't that good, else he wouldn't be working for a county salary, he'd be in the private sector. Then again . . . how well did I know him? Not very, and certainly not as well as I thought. He'd been able to uncover my deleted messages, maybe some Internet searches I'd done early on. I tried to remember how much I'd done, what he might have seen. The location, possibly, and maybe even the amount of money. One, maybe both. Maybe neither. The first day or so after Gus had mentioned the idea of a heist, I'd been characteristically impulsive and reckless, but only because I'd never really thought it would happen. As it become more possible, more likely, I'd been more careful. And, of course, I thought I'd deleted all that stuff.

I put my anger toward Tristan to one side and thought about my position. He was right on the law; I was technically guilty of conspiring to commit a crime. I didn't think he'd call the cops on me, though—he had nothing to gain from that.

In the corner, my guitar case beckoned to me. I flipped it open and took out my guitar, then sat on my bed, strumming idly. I played random chords, ten in a row and quickly, and then tried to remember the order of them, playing them again. It was a way to clear my mind, focus on my fingers and familiar sounds to the exclusion of everything else. I messed up, though, and found myself hitting the strings too hard, squeezing the neck of the guitar too tightly, and I almost threw the instrument down in frustration. I stayed there, on my bed, my head in my hands until my eyes caught sight of the box holding my second-favorite instrument. I kept it in a small safe by the bed, and I leaned over and punched in the four-digit code. The door popped open, and I took out my Colt .45 revolver.

I didn't carry it with me, ever, it was too valuable, too beautiful. And too heavy. My fingers still stung from the guitar strings, but as I turned it over in my hands, the weight and coolness of the gun felt soothing. That something so lethal could also be so beautiful was not new to me. The Holland & Holland I'd learned to shoot with was a work of art, and worth tens of thousands of pounds. Had I stayed in England, I would have taken possession of my father's pair of Purdey shotguns, handmade and worth even more. No, it seemed right to me that if life was imbued with value, that which took life away should be more than a cheap hunk of metal churned out by a factory in China or Siberia.

The cylinder click-click-clicked under my fingers, and my eyes feasted on the gun's meticulous finish, Colt's trademark royal-blue steel barrel and cylinder, and its hand-fitted walnut stock inlaid with a gold Colt medallion.

I couldn't afford this gun when I bought it, but I bought it anyway. Or sort of bought it. I played on an indoor soccer team for one season, three years previously. Our goalkeeper had been a gun dealer. He'd also been a drunkard, which was fine for day games but if we played any time after seven in the evening, he either showed up swaying or didn't show at all. For one game, though, a five o'clock game, he didn't show up. He called the captain of the team the next day to say that he'd been arrested for drunk driving, his third time, which made it a felony. He hadn't known what I did for a living, but when he found out, he coyly asked if I could give some advice. I went to his shop and browsed while he served another customer. Which is when I saw the Colt.

He came over as I was looking at it, entranced by it the way a magpie is drawn to something shiny, and as we talked, my eyes kept dropping to the glass case between us, the beautiful, almost-liquid quality of the steel. I didn't even notice the price, I didn't care. Same for whatever he was telling me, I couldn't care less whether or not he went to prison except for the fact he was a decent goalkeeper, when sober. I just wanted that gun.

He must have seen that, my lust for it. It's not like we made any kind of deal because I didn't know who was handling his case—it could have been me or one of the other thirty trial-court prosecutors. I did promise to put a good word in for him, and that seemed to be all he wanted. I walked out of the shop with my bones humming with excitement, a thrill that was almost sexual, and that gun in a triangular, plastic case that I threw away as soon as I got home.

On reflection, it wasn't the best way for me to acquire a gun. Or anything else. But I never regretted getting my hands on it, because the few times I'd given in to powerful urges like that one, worse things had happened than me acquiring a new toy.

The bullets were loose in my little safe, and I collected a few in my hand. I didn't keep the gun loaded because it was more like a piece of art than a weapon. And the process of loading and unloading it was a part of the art, performance art perhaps. Slipping the bullets into each slot, the almost-imperceptible hiss of brass on steel, the reassuring sound of the rim clinking into place, the click of the cylinder revolving to accept another bullet, and another, and another. As I filled each chamber, I thought about my options. If Gus was well and truly out, there were just three things I could do.

The first was to abandon the plan altogether, forget about it and move on. I rejected that immediately because I needed the money. More than the money, I had released the impulse to steal the money and I knew myself well enough to know that I couldn't put it back in the bottle. I was standing over the counter, staring at the Colt all over again, and listening to reason was like listening to that guy talking about his life, his case, his fears. Empty words that meant nothing, other than opening the door to me getting what I wanted.

The second option was to go it alone. That would allow me to keep all the money for myself. But it meant that two people would hear about the heist and know I'd done it. They'd know about the money. They might just want some, and since they hadn't taken part in the theft, they would have leverage over me and no liability. And as a practical matter, I didn't know how I'd pull it off alone. My idea was for one person to drive us both there, for me to steal the van and drive it away to a nearby location, where we'd unload the cash and either torch the van or just wipe it down very carefully. That was a two-man operation and I was down to one.

Which meant that the third option was to bring Tristan in, just as he wanted. If I did, he'd be as liable as me and therefore keep his trap shut. I could do all the planning, keep control of the operation, and just have him drive me there. I'd have to share the cash, but then I'd always expected to have to do that.

The problem was that I didn't know Tristan the way I knew Gus. I didn't know how he'd react under pressure or whether he'd chicken out at the last minute. I told myself that knowing someone didn't make a difference, which Gus had proved by backing out on me.

The other problem was that I didn't like being forced into this position. What I really wanted to do was scare the daylights out of Tristan so that he'd leave me alone, leave the plan alone, and give me time to work on getting Gus back on board.

I caressed the barrel with my fingers and felt my breathing slow and deepen. I pictured the end of it against Tristan's forehead, then imagined him waking up to find the gun between his eyes. I wondered what he'd say or do and whether his eyes would dart about like that little rabbit's, whether his body would press back into the sheets as if to make himself disappear. And, just for the slightest of moments, I pictured my finger on the trigger, the pads of my forefinger lying on that little blue tongue of steel, squeezing it slowly but surely until my nosy, meddling, and dangerous roommate's eyes stopped moving and his body settled into his bed, no longer trying to wriggle its way into invisibility.

I stood up with the gun in my hand, appreciating the delicate difference in the weight when it was loaded. I walked to my door and went out into the living room, the pistol down at my side. A rectangle of light surrounded his door, and I walked slowly toward it, drawn not by the light but by my own impulses, some inner power that possessed me.

Two feet from his room, I paused. I raised the gun and held it straight out in front of me. I tapped the barrel against his door, three hard taps, and kept the gun raised, point-blank to the door.

I heard a rustling from his room, and a moment later Tristan flung the door open. I caught a glimpse of his expression, dark and angry like he'd been practicing his self-righteous speech, but the blood drained from his face in an instant when he saw the gun, blue-black and lethal, pointed straight at his nose.

CHAPTER TWELVE

TREMBLING WITH TENDERNESS

Tristan's jaw worked silently and he stepped back. I followed him into his room, the gun still pointed in his face.

"Dom, please," he stammered. "What are you doing?" His hands had risen in surrender, in supplication, and the terror in his eyes was magnetic to me, drawing out some kind of primordial need to exert power, to relish in dominance over another human being. I liked it, a lot.

"Dom, please," Tristan said again, his voice a whisper. "Please, put the gun down. You're being crazy, Dom, put the gun down." His head dipped, another moment of supplication, I thought, and he was no longer looking me in the eye.

I lowered the gun, slowly, inch by inch, and he stayed frozen in front of me, as if by moving I'd raise it up again and shoot. When the gun was hanging by my side, I spoke in a soft, calm voice.

"Why do you think I did that?"

"I don't know . . . I don't fucking know." His voice cracked like he was going to cry.

"You want in, right?"

"In?"

"You want to be my new partner in this little venture I'm thinking about undertaking."

He nodded.

"It's a theft, nothing more. Taking money from an arsehole who exploits other people."

"Okay." He still hadn't moved.

"But the thing is, Tristan, I needed to know how you act under pressure. I'm not expecting anything to go wrong, but no one ever is, right?"

"Right," he whispered.

"Look at me." He lifted his head and I saw a spark of defiance in his eyes. "You didn't faint or collapse or wet yourself, so that's good."

A tiny smile twitched the corners of his mouth. "How do you know I didn't wet myself?"

There was, I realized, more to this computer geek than met the eye. "Change your underwear and we'll talk."

O

We'd not eaten a meal together once, and I wanted to see if I could make him uncomfortable by taking him to a fancy restaurant. Actually, what I managed to do was convince him to take me. I phrased it as a buy-in, an investment, a commitment that would be richly rewarded. He was so keen to get his hands on Silva's dough that a hundred bucks on a couple of steaks seemed like a small price. As usual, though, he wasn't privy to the big picture, the real reason we were going to dinner. I'd serve up that juicy tidbit later.

"Where do you want to go?" he asked.

"What's that place on Fourth Street, I always call it Smith & Wollensky but it isn't."

"Simon and something. Kinda pricey."

"I don't drink. What you lose on the food, you gain by me drinking water."

"Yeah, fuck it. Been a while since I splurged, and this is a celebration." He wagged a finger. "But if we take less from that slumlord than I spend tonight, I want my money back."

"Deal."

He went into his room for his wallet but came out shaking his head. "Can't find the damn thing."

"I've got cash," I said. "Write me a check when we get home. Better yet, write me a check now." I pulled ten bills from my own wallet, all twenties, and handed them to him.

"I don't get it."

"So sue me. I like the idea of you pulling out a wad of cash and buying my dinner. Now write me a check."

"Okay." He shrugged and went back into his room, coming out with his checkbook. He scribbled the amount and his signature, then paused. "What should I write on the memo line? 'Pre-heist dinner'? 'Celebration of conspiracy'?"

"Yeah, very funny. Since we can't remember the restaurant's name, put Smith & Wollensky."

"Sure. You know, I can spell 'Smith,'" he said while writing, "but—"

"No clue," I interrupted, "just put 'W', I'll figure it out." He handed me the check and stuffed the cash into his pocket.

"Let's go eat."

I drove, and on the way I filled him in on some details. He was acting giddy, and I didn't want to talk about it in a crowded restaurant.

"I already set up a camera at the place it'll happen, to watch him once or twice and also keep an eye on the place on the day we do it."

"Okay," he said. "Makes sense. What if someone finds the camera?"

"They won't. I have a camouflage one, which I can control and view remotely. There's a decent-sized wood very close to where he parks. It's about fifteen feet up, and I found a spot that's inside the wood but looks out through a patch where there aren't any branches."

"It's in place already?"

"It is."

"And the rest of the plan?"

"We watch through the camera during the day of the theft. Just to make sure all's cool, we can take turns. In the evening, we'll head out there. Around nine. Check again on the camera when we arrive." As we turned onto Fourth Street, I reached into the glove compartment and pulled out a pencil and a pad of paper, handing them straight to Tristan. "I'll describe the place, you draw it. Something my dad used to do with the rabbit and hare trails on the farm—you'll remember it better if you draw it yourself."

"Okay, sure." He took the pencil and paper.

"The main road is quiet and leads past the front entrance to the park, put that down here. We ignore that and go on about a hundred yards or so to a track which runs alongside a field, bordering the park. When the track meets the wood, it doglegs to the right. About twenty yards after it bends is where Silva leaves his car. Right before it bends, there's a blind spot, invisible from the main road, from the mobile homes, even from where Silva parks. It's a cutout, so we'll pull off the track there."

I glanced over as Tristan put finishing touches to the map. He'd noted the location of the camera in the woods, the place where Silva left his car, and the other important points on our treasure map.

"So how does it go down?" he asked.

"With as little fuss as possible. When he's in one of the trailers collecting his money, we'll break into his van and drive it to a secondary location. Then, we'll have a set of bolt cutters and plenty of time to get into the steel cage he's built into the back of the van."

"How do you know about the cage?"

"Surveillance."

"OK, then what?"

"Then maybe we let the air out of his tires and drive the hell away from there."

Tristan chewed his lip, then asked, "How much money are we talking?"

"No way to know." My first instinct was to lie, to try and shave a larger portion off for myself, but I'd read enough novels and seen enough movies to know where greed led you. And in this case, he'd see the money for himself when we got it, be there for the accounting. And, of course, I really didn't know exactly how much there would be. "Gus said tens of thousands, and if we hit him at the end of his run, that could be right."

He let out a low whistle.

"So how much do you owe?" I asked.

"Not tens of thousands. But not too far off."

"That's a lot of gambling."

"Yeah, I'm aware of that."

"Maybe pay off your debts, then use some of the money for treatment or counseling," I suggested. He shot me a look, like he wasn't sure if I was serious or kidding. We sat in silence for a moment.

As we pulled into a parking spot, Tristan turned toward me. "Hey, Dom. Can I ask one thing?"

"Yeah, of course."

"No guns. I know you like your guns," he smiled to acknowledge what had just happened. "But seriously, if the guy shows up while we're, you know, taking his van, let's just split. Leave. No fighting, no guns, just split."

He reminded me of Gus, of course, as if by somehow having a gun present it'd automatically get used, death and destruction raining down of its own accord. And yes, I suffered from impulsiveness and "Poor Behavioral Controls," but the one thing about sociopaths—our strongest instinct is self-preservation. And I knew that pulling a six-shooter on a sweaty, overweight Mexican ran second best to, well, running.

I killed the engine. "I wasn't planning on taking my gun, don't worry. Don't make this into more than it is, just five minutes of taking someone's car and we're done."

"And their money," Tristan grinned.

"Yeah, that is the point," I agreed.

"Is there a risk of getting stopped by the cops on the way home? Have you checked the route back?"

"Yeah, of course. Plus," I said, "I have a badge. I've been stopped three times for speeding, and as soon as cops see the badge, they pat the top of the car and wish me a happy day."

"That's good. Awesome even." He sat back and furrowed his brow. "One other thing. I don't know the guy at all, but you're sure Gus won't be a problem?"

"A problem how?"

"Do you think he'll change his mind and want to do it?"

"No. And I have no desire to take all that risk to split the money three ways. At some point, it becomes not worth it, and for me, that's splitting it three ways. Even if he wants back in, it's not happening."

"Cool. What about afterward?"

"What do you mean?"

"Do you think he'll hear about it and, you know, want a piece of the action?"

"Blackmail?"

"I guess."

"No. I can absolutely, definitively, tell you he won't do that. And," I added cheerily, "if he does, then I have my little friend Mr. Colt in there, don't I?"

He shot me that look again, the one that told me he didn't know whether I was serious or kidding. I was pretty sure I was kidding.

"So when are you thinking this happens?" Tristan asked.

"I have the camera in place and I know what his route is. Next week is the end of the month and, according to the trusty Internet, it'll be dark by ten p.m. Which is also when he'll be there for his last collection."

"Next week?"

"Yep." I smiled. "Any reason why not?"

OVER BROKEN GLASS

I wanted to practice. I couldn't do a run-through of the theft itself. It had too many moving parts and was also a matter of planning, not practice. No, I wanted to test myself so I'd know how it felt to be a criminal. After so many years resisting that very temptation, I needed to break the seal, give up my virginity, phrase it how you will.

Or maybe that's what I told myself so that I could break into the pub and find out who'd screwed me over.

The Monday before the theft, I played it safe and made a trip to the suburbs to buy a black hoodie and a pair of gloves. I thought about getting a balaclava, but I wasn't planning on being seen, and somehow it felt too theatrical, too silly.

The Norman Pub was closed Monday nights, like a lot of clubs in Austin, which left a good number of people strolling the sidewalks, looking for a piece of music to listen to or a drink to buy. And wandering people meant more cover for me.

By 8 p.m., dusk had settled over the city, in that perfect-crime light that makes strangers hard to see but not yet suspicious. I parked two side streets away and ambled casually toward the pub. It was still baking hot, so I held my hoodie in one hand, sweat prickling my forearms. I cut down an alley that ran behind the pizza place and the pub. It was a dead-end alley, no use for anything but drug deals and paid-for hookups, and as long as I got there first, its users would about-face the moment they saw me. The rancid smell of rotting food coming from the three garbage cans was also encouraging, repellent to even the most desperate drug or sex addicts.

I'd been to the pub the night before and left a window to the bathroom unlocked. Not the most sophisticated entry technique, but it was predicated on the assumption that by closing time Marley Jensen would be drunk and make no more than a cursory check of the restrooms. Standing by the window, I pulled the gloves from the pocket of my hoodie, but they were new and stiff, and when I put my hand to the glass and pulled on the lip of the frame, I couldn't get any real purchase. I took the gloves off and levered the tips of my fingers under the edge and pulled once, twice. My assumption had been wrong.

Even unsophisticated plans need a backup, and this one involved a small rock and a fervent hope that it sounded louder to me than anyone else who might be around. I listened for a moment as I pulled my gloves back on, then reached through the broken pane and unlatched the window. All seemed quiet inside and out, so I hoisted myself up and wriggled into one of the grimiest and most graffiti-infested bathrooms in South Austin. Its darkness felt like a sanctuary.

I crouched on the floor and waited for my eyes to adjust. I had a flashlight in my pocket, but I wanted to operate without it as far as possible, as nothing screamed "intruder" quite like a small light bobbing around inside a closed premises.

After a minute, I moved to the bathroom door and peered down the hallway. At the far end was Marley's office. The door to it was closed, but a weak, yellow light bled into the corridor, and it somehow irked me that he'd locked the bathroom window but left his office light on. I wasn't worried about him being there, though; his car hadn't been out front when I drove past, and Monday nights he drank in his buddy's bar on Sixth Street.

I crept down the hallway, my eyes glued to the office door, my ears alert for any sound. The place smelled musty, the stale beer and unwashed carpet odor that all pubs had, a smell that made me a little queasy at the best of times. Which this obviously wasn't.

I reached Marley's office and listened at the door. No sound, so I turned the knob and pushed it open. A banker's lamp spilled light onto the desk, but I saw no other signs of life. Time pressed in, its edges sharpened by the fact that I didn't really know what I was looking for. Maybe an e-mail chain on his computer or perhaps a couple of CDs bearing my name and the name of the lying bastard about to endure a campaign of harassment.

Marley's desk was surprisingly tidy, three stacks of papers, a dozen CDs, and a closed laptop computer. I sat in his chair and sifted through his papers, mostly bills and flyers for upcoming bands. No telling notes bearing my name or listing my songs. Same with the CDs. All looked to be from solo musicians or bands wanting to play at the pub. I recognized a couple of the names, but none seemed like candidates for treachery—either their sound was totally different from mine or they were so new, Marley never would have taken allegations by them seriously. Plus, I imagined my CD would be clipped to the one belonging to the deceitful wanker I was after.

I opened Marley's laptop but stopped moving when I heard a sound from the hallway. I sat perfectly still, wondering if my ears were playing tricks on me. But there it was again, a shuffling sound.

I put my hands on the desk to rise, but froze in position as a burly figure swung through the doorway, his gun pointed at my chest.

"Let me see your hands!" the man snapped.

I held them up, my eyes glued to the little black hole in the end of his gun. Weapon focus, it's called, and it's the reason eyewitnesses tend to be hopeless when their assailant has them at gunpoint. I dragged my eyes away from the barrel and looked at the face of the man, recognizing him a fraction after he recognized me.

"Dominic," he said. "What the fuck?"

"Nice to see you, too. Do you mind lowering that thing?"

Otto Bland was sweating, far more scared than I was. Wet patches sat under his armpits, and for no apparent reason I wondered where he'd been hiding and what he'd been doing in the dark as I broke in. One thing I was sure of: I didn't want his greasy finger on the trigger. He complied with my request, but hesitantly, as if I might actually be there to do him harm.

"What are you . . . ? Jesus, Dom, I could've shot you." He stared at me like I was an alien. "Fuck, did you break in here?"

"No comment."

"You did, man, I heard glass break in the bathroom." He shook his head in confusion. "Why?"

"Long story, but believe it or not, I'm still one of the good guys."

"I'm pleased to hear that, I really am." He holstered his gun and pulled out his cell phone.

"Whoa, what the fuck are you doing?" I stood up, my hands extended, telling him to slow down.

"Dude, I gotta call this in."

"The police? No, no you don't."

"Yeah, I do." He sounded apologetic, but resolute. "I'm sorry man, but you can give your explanation to the cops; if it's all good they'll let you go."

"Jesus, Otto, I broke a window and crept into the fucking bathroom, they're not going to let me go. This is burglary, which means I spend tonight in jail and, assuming I bond out, I spend tomorrow clearing out my desk."

"That's harsh, man, and I'm sorry, I really am. But it's either you or me."

"No, it's not." You fucking moron. "Look, I came here for a good reason, a legitimate reason, and if we stop talking I'll be out of here in about eight minutes. No one needs to know."

"Not that simple."

"Why not?" I masked my frustration. It wouldn't help to get mad at the guy.

"Marley has cameras. Digital ones. They'd have caught you in the hallway." His face changed as a thought occurred to him. "And they'll catch me coming in here and finding you. Sorry dude, like I said, it's you or me."

Cameras were supposed to be my friends. Fuck. My mind went into overdrive. I knew there was a way out of this, it was just a matter of finding it.

"Delete the footage," I said.

"I can't. The software he has puts a little red mark when something's deleted. How do I explain that?"

"So what happens if we do nothing? Just ignore it. He's not going to scroll through twenty hours of video tape on a hunch you're keeping secrets."

"He will when he sees the broken window."

"So explain it. Kids, or vandals."

"That alley is used by hookers and dopers, everyone knows that. And anyone with half a brain will know the window was busted to break in here, so I'll get fired either for not noticing or for not calling the cops. And like I said the other week, I can't afford to get fired." He looked at his phone. "I'm really sorry."

I sat down. One thought loomed in my mind, pressing into my consciousness like a knife: he needed money, I needed out of there. And I had just one thing to bargain with, and given how he was looking at his phone, very little time.

"Wait." I held up a hand. "Just so we're clear, you're worried about your job and don't give a crap that I broke in. This isn't a morals thing."

"I don't . . ." He looked confused. "No, I don't care why you're here. I don't care that you're here. I just need to do my job."

"Right. Because you need the money."

"Yeah, of course, I told you that before. Why the fuck else would I be here?"

"Shooting for that bar in Florida, I remember."

"Right. That bar. Meanwhile, I have no money, I keep losing jobs, and I'm sick and tired of . . . pretty much everything."

Perfect. "Then I think we can help each other."

"What do you mean?" The phone stayed in his hand, more lethal to me than his gun.

"Sit down, I'll explain."

With that same confused expression on his face, Otto pulled a chair to the desk and sat, leaning forward as he listened. I didn't want him in on the theft; I knew better than anyone that the more people involved in an illegal scheme, the more people there were to squeal. But I wasn't bargaining from a position of strength, and I was confident that the lure of tens of thousands of dollars would be too much for a man like Otto to ignore. I didn't think about what I'd do if he didn't go along with it. I plan well and think quickly on my feet, but I'm not infallible. I suppose that a part of my conceit was the presumption that I could convince him. Luckily, the idiot stayed quiet as I laid out the rough edges of the plan, and his eyes stretched wide when I gave him the numbers.

"Shit, thirty grand each? That much?"

"Yes," I lied. "Conservative estimate."

"Why would he carry all that? It doesn't make sense."

"Habit, mostly. He started doing it when he collected a few hundred, kept doing it when he was collecting thousands, and saw no reason to change a successful business practice. He doesn't see it as a risk—he sees it as a monthly chore and a way to avoid paying taxes."

"A hundred grand." He was like a junkie eying a syringe after a long, dry spell.

"You in?"

"Sure. Hell yes, I'm in. What do you need me to do?"

"First things first. We need to get rid of any camera footage of me."

"He'll know I was playing around with it and fire me."

"We've already established that, Otto. But we're taking the money this weekend, so I can spot you a couple of hundred until then, okay?"

"No, I'm fine until the weekend." His shoulders slumped, and he finally tucked away his cell phone. "I guess I'm just sick of being fired."

This is where I was supposed to feel sorry for him, so I made an effort and pulled the right face. His weakness, though, his pathetic, beaten-down spirit, was good for me because I knew that he'd be malleable and do what I told him. And his natural sense of self-preservation would mean he'd keep his trap shut afterward, head to Florida, and be out of the way entirely. Also, he'd snuck up on me pretty well, and he knew how to hold a gun, two assets that might come in handy along the way.

"The video?" I prompted.

"I can do it on the computer."

I slid the laptop to him and watched as he switched it on.

"You know the password?" I asked.

"Isn't one. His staff uses it for communicating with and researching bands, that kind of stuff. He has another one for accounting, or so he told me." He tapped on a few keys. "There's the cameras. Now let me see . . ." He sucked on his lower lip as I battled my impatience. Finally he spoke. "Right. I deleted footage from the one that would have caught you and shut it down for the next thirty minutes. If he notices, and I'm sure he will, I'll tell him I heard some-thing and was checking, accidentally deleted it."

"Great, thanks. Wait, let me use that for a minute, will you?"

"Why?"

"Because that's why I came here. Some bastard is screwing with me, using Marley, and I want to know who."

"Sure." Otto passed the laptop back to me. He stood but hovered in the small office, so I shot him a look. "I'll wait out here," he said, "but don't mess anything else up on his computer, okay?"

"I'm not planning on deleting or changing anything. Just looking."

Otto mumbled something and shuffled out of the office. A moment later, I thought I heard the clink of a bottle neck on a glass, but he might have just been moving an ashtray. The way his life had gone, I wouldn't have blamed him for drinking on the job.

I spent five minutes looking through Marley's e-mails but didn't see anything related to me stealing music, so I switched to the folders on his desktop. The second one I opened was called "No Play List" and a sub-folder inside read "Dominic." I took a deep breath, double-clicked on the file, and started on the three listed documents. The first was the lyrics from my song, with my name on top. The second contained the lyrics from his song, with his name on top.

The chair squeaked as I sat back and stared. The smell of the pub rose up again, dank and stale, and I felt dirty. I knew the guy, of course. Austin's a busy but incestuous community of musicians, and I'd rightly figured I'd know the guy.

And now that his identity was established, I was left with one simple question: what to do to him.

CHAPTER FOURTEEN

FROM PRAYERS
TO BROKEN STONE

When the day came, Tristan and I took turns in the late afternoon watching the surveillance computer in one-hour shifts. Lucky we did, because we spotted a potential hazard I'd not seen before: a security guard. He was barely more than a shadow in the corner of the screen, but given his size and where he was working, I wagered he was one of those sloppy cop wannabes who were weeded out at the first round by the police academy and whose only connections to law enforcement were a desire to exercise power and a love of donuts. Underpaid, disinterested, and trying to stay out of the heat, he or she bumped past the other corner of the computer screen an hour later in a golf cart. In search of, I assumed, a shady tree and a breeze. Certainly not looking for trouble.

The next most exciting thing we saw was a squirrel checking out the camera. Its rodent face loomed on the screen like a giant rat, looking in on us for a few seconds before it lost interest.

At 9 p.m. I left Tristan in front of the computer and carried three blankets to the trunk of my Honda, to use as bedding for the surveillance camera that we needed to retrieve and to cover the two camouflage bags we'd be taking from Señor Silva.

We left at 9:30. We both wore dark cargo pants and black T-shirts. I wore my old Doc Martens, and Tristan clumped to the car in his new sand-colored Timberland work boots.

He seemed calm when we left, but he fidgeted beside me all

the way to the trailer park. He began by picking at his seatbelt like it was a guitar string and moved on to twiddling his shirt buttons, clutching the edges of his seat, and finally, as we got within a mile of the park, tying and retying his shoelaces. I wanted to laugh but instead wondered whether I should feign nervousness, too. I didn't bother in the end because my mind was occupied with what we were about to do, and also because he was too antsy to notice my demeanor. He'd gone from calm to anxious in twelve miles, and I didn't like it. I'd worried about holding Gus's hand, and once he'd gone I figured I had a useful partner next to me. I didn't want to hold Tristan's hand, if only because I didn't know where it'd been.

By the time I turned into the trailer park, the sky had darkened, if not to black then at least a long way from the scalding steel-blue it had been all day. A breeze had picked up and leaves, and a few pieces of trash, scuttled in front of the car. I turned left inside the rusted, metal gate poles, bumping slowly along the dirt track. I could see in the distance a few men standing beside their grills, poking at coals with crooked sticks and holding beer cans, either oblivious or studiously ignoring us.

I stopped the car in the blind spot, lowered the front windows, and killed the engine. Tristan opened the laptop and tapped a few keys.

"Connected to the Internet," he said. "Camera coming up now."

"Which means the cops didn't take it," I said, provoking him on purpose.

"Doesn't mean they didn't find it."

"Hey, if they roll up lights and sirens, we're just a couple of lovers pitching woo."

"I'm not gay," he said, "and I'm not pretending to be."

"Right, God forbid. Much better to go to jail, you're right."

He shot me a look, then his eyes went back to the screen. "He's here. Early, fuck."

"Stay cool, little friend." I leaned over and watched Silva park in the same spot he'd used the previous month. We sat in silence as the landlord moved across the screen, climbing out of his van with his shoulder bag bumping against his hip. He looked tired, his feet shuffling in the dust and his head down. Even better.

He moved out of sight and we waited the agreed sixty seconds, then Tristan closed the laptop, put his hand on my leg, and pulled a knife from his boot.

"Change of plans," he said.

I stared at the silver blade, wondering if it was the kind of hefty but blunt toy that juvenile punks waved at each other to look tough. But it looked new, shiny, and very sharp, the five-inch blade curving up into the kind of tip that would disappear through clothing and flesh with ease. With pleasure, even. Someone else had visited Cabela's hunting store to prepare for this outing. This would explain why he'd suddenly become so nervous, wrestling with himself as to whether he'd go through with it. Whatever *it* was, in his mind.

"What's your plan, then?" I asked. "Stab me to death, and keep the money?"

"No. Look, we need to forget stealing the car. It's too complicated, too risky. Way too much can go wrong. Much easier to just threaten him, take the money, and go."

"Much easier how? Done this before, have you?"

"You know I haven't. But think about it, he's not going to want to fight two guys and a knife."

"Unless he has a gun, then I'm sure he'll be happy to. Now put that away before you cut yourself, or me, and we leave a nice red trail of evidence."

"Dude, I'm serious—"

"So am I," I snapped. "Original plan or we leave right now." He didn't respond, so I turned the car back on and made a show of checking my mirrors, like my biggest concern was flattening some Mexican's crappy grill.

Tristan swore and leaned forward, sliding the knife back into the ankle sheath I'd not noticed.

Fucking idiot, I thought. I was happy he'd just done as he was told, but much less happy that he was showing signs of being a wild card. I'd explained to him, oh, about a million times, that the only way we pulled this off and stayed out of trouble was to formulate a good plan and stick to it.

"Thank you." I killed the engine and opened my door, screwdriver and ball-peen hammer in hand. "You just wasted two minutes of our time, so how about we get on with this?"

"Sure." His voice was flat and I couldn't tell whether he was recalcitrant or pissed. But he followed me out of the car and we strolled, as casually as we were able, around the slight bend to Silva's van. I breathed a sigh of relief when I saw it but froze when I saw someone walking to our right, a man acting like he hadn't seen us. His hands were deep in his pockets, and he looked like he fit in, a fat dude ambling his way toward a case of beer somewhere: my other partner in crime, Otto Bland.

I'd not told Tristan about him, about his involvement. For many reasons. Mostly I didn't want him bitching about the cut in his share, or asking fifty questions about Otto that I couldn't answer. They'd crossed paths at the DA's office, but not very often, and I was certain that Tristan knew more about Otto's reputation than about the man himself. As a result, he had no reason in the world to trust Otto, and telling him about the man's inclusion wouldn't have helped his nerves one jot. That was why I'd made it a condition of Otto's involvement that he act like he'd just come across us, ham it up a little. I didn't figure him for much of a George Clooney, but given that we'd be in the middle of a crime, it seemed unlikely that Tristan would pay much attention to his theatrical deficits. Otto had even taken the initiative and gotten himself a security job with the management company running four mobile-home parks, one of them being Crooked Creek. I was impressed.

At that moment, Otto was forty yards away and acting oblivious to the world around him. He shuffled through the dust, then stepped off the track and squatted under a tree, facing away from us and toward the mobile homes that Silva was visiting for his monthly scoop.

"He hasn't seen us," Tristan whispered. "And we're not bailing now."

I nodded my agreement and was at the driver's door of the van in a few seconds, focusing on the job at hand. I tried the handle and it was locked, as I'd expected. I used the round end of the hammer and gave the lock a hefty whack. The lock popped inward like it was greased, and a quick tug had the car door open. I slid behind the wheel and looked up in time to see Otto rise to his feet, looking around. He'd heard the whack but wasn't sure what it was, and I was low, so he shouldn't be able to see me.

I put the tip of the screwdriver into the ignition slot. Holding it there with my left hand, I used the business side of the hammer to tap and then whack it deep into the steering column. I gave it a twist, but nothing happened.

"What the fuck," Tristan hissed. "Hurry up."

"I'm hurrying, it's not working," I said. I tapped the screwdriver again with the hammer, then turned it. This time it felt like it would go with a little more effort, so I gripped the handle of the screwdriver until the ridges bit into my hand, then turned it with all my strength. The engine sparked and turned over with a short growl, shaking the van into life for a brief second before falling silent. I twisted the screwdriver again, harder, my wrist shaking with the effort, and the engine ground its teeth for three seconds, but it was a protest, not acquiescence, and I yanked the screwdriver out of the ignition slot with a curse.

"Oh, fuck." Tristan was backing away from the Transit van, and I looked through the windshield to see two people running toward us. On the edge of the track, Otto gaped like a fish as Ambrosio Silva and the sloppy security guard jogged toward us, dust kicking up around them. I considered one more attempt at starting the van and speeding away with the jackass's money right in front of him, but they were closing fast and, even if I got it started, speeding away would necessarily involve running them over. And I was still trying to avoid bloodshed.

I jumped out of the van and looked to see if either had a weapon. The security guard had lost his cap on his run, and I suddenly didn't like the look of him. A buzz cut suggested he was former military, and despite his bulk he moved with the kind of grace and power that indicated more-than-grunt military. He was several steps ahead of Silva and making a beeline for me, a walkie-talkie in one hand, a wooden baton in the other.

He stopped twenty feet from me, puffing but attentive. Behind him, Ambrosio Silva skidded to a halt in the dust and shouted, "What the fuck you doing in my car?"

I held out my hands, all open and innocent, knowing I didn't look the part of a car thief. Didn't look like I belonged in this part of town at all.

"Relax, the car was open, I was just curious about—"

"Hands where I can see them." The security guard looked even meaner and more capable up close than when charging up the track. And it was him I watched, because whereas Silva was a criminal and barely legal, which meant he was careful around confident, white strangers, the security guard was all attitude. Like he already had us in handcuffs.

"Dude, I said relax. I'm with the DA's office, we're out here on a case." I had my badge with me, in my wallet as ever, though I was not happy about having to use my ace so soon. My right hand drifted toward my back pocket.

"Don't fuckin' move," the guard said. I didn't see where his gun came from, had no idea he was carrying. But he was, a nice shiny piece with a silver barrel pointed right at my chest. I would've invited him to get my wallet himself, but my gun was tucked in my belt, and that would take a little explaining. From my perspective, this was all turning shitty. We'd gone from a quick, anonymous, and unarmed car-grab to a standoff involving, it has to be said, at least one Mexican.

And then Otto appeared.

Apparently, he'd ducked into the tree line when Silva and the security guard passed him, making his way up to us quiet and unseen. Impressive for a lump like him. He came out of the bushes, slightly behind Silva and the security guard, his gun leveled and his voice firm.

"Austin Police. Put the gun down, *now*."

The security guard stiffened but didn't turn around or lower his gun. "What's your badge number?"

It was a smart question because it told us he knew cops, and it tested whether Otto knew how many digits APD gave their officers. Otto knew. "Six-three-four-nine."

The security guard looked slowly over his shoulder at Otto, his gun still pointing at me.

"I said drop it," Otto repeated.

"You're not APD," the guard said. "You're with these assholes." He didn't wait for a response, shifting his weight to his left foot and pivoting, the gun swinging away from me and toward Otto. Two loud bangs made me jump, and for a moment, the few seconds it took my ears to stop ringing, I couldn't tell who'd fired. Then the security guard staggered backward, his arms cradling his midriff, his gun dropping into the dust. He stood still for a moment, rocking gently in the evening heat, then fell face down into the dirt.

Otto moved forward, his gun trained on the fallen man, and then a movement by Ambrosio Silva caught my eye. He'd sidled away so we couldn't see his back, and he was reaching into his waistband. I glanced at Otto, but his eyes were on the motionless security guard, so I took care of it myself. I pulled my gun and aimed at Silva, a twenty-foot shot that I nailed. The first bullet hit his shoulder, spinning him to face me, a stunned look in his eyes.

A look that turned to dead when I shot him in the chest.

○

Tristan was as white as a sheet and almost hyperventilating. "Jesus. Fuck. Shit."

"Calm down, old chap," I said through gritted teeth. "They're the ones who are dead, not you."

Otto looked back and forth between us, and I was pleased to see he'd put his gun away. "What the hell are you two doing here?"

"Long story," I said. I looked back down the track, wondering if the guys grilling their dinner had heard. I expected to see them appear behind us with cell phones in hand, maybe even weapons, but either they were used to gun shots out here or the steaks and beer had obliterated their hearing. Whatever the reason, I was pleased to see a still-empty track behind us. I looked back at Otto and dosed up my voice with surprise. "What the hell are *you* doing here?"

"Working. Security." He looked at the bodies. "This is fucking nuts. Are they both dead?" Otto had reverted to his sweating and terrified self. He started toward the security guard, reaching for his phone as he remembered his line. "I'll call it in."

"No, you won't."

"What do you mean?"

I gestured with my gun, not exactly pointing it at him but as if reminding him that I held it. "Put that away Otto."

He lowered the phone and looked around as if he was missing something. He looked back at me. "What the fuck's going on?"

His eyes were pleading with me because the script had just changed, rewritten from a fun and lucrative little heist to a thriller that looked like it might end badly. Clearly, he didn't know how to adapt and was assuming that, as the director, I did.

"Here's what you do," I told him. "You go back to the other side of the park. Do you have another gun?"

"Another gun?"

"Yes, Otto. Answer the question, do you have another gun?"

"In my car, yes."

I walked toward him with my left hand out. "Then give me yours."

He looked down at it as the wheels turned in his head. He realized that when the cops arrived, they might check to see if it'd been fired, and if so they'd take it and test it against the bullet from the guard's body. He handed it to me and looked around. "What's happening?"

"It's dark, no one saw you. Now go get your gun and finish your shift."

"But why?"

"Just listen to me. Either we all get rich or we all go to jail." I stepped closer, my voice a hiss of urgency and threat. "Otto, the situation's changed but the rules are the same. Remember who fired first."

"Wait, but—"

"No, listen," I snapped. I didn't want to perform for Tristan, so I kept it short. "You do as I say, and when you get off duty you come to my house and find yourself richer."

Otto glanced at the bodies lying on the ground then back at me, and I knew what he was thinking. He'd not bargained for this, but it was too late to pull out. As a former cop, he knew that if people die during illegal activity, that's felony murder, capital murder. The needle.

I told him my address and made him repeat it three times. He turned and walked away, looking left and right, into the dark.

"Unbelievable," I said, then turned to Tristan. "Let's get the fuck out of here."

"You said no guns," he said. "You said it, loud and clear, no fucking guns."

"Yeah, well, they started it," I said.

"And we fucking finished it, all right," he said. "Now can we go?"

"In a moment, we need to do this right."

"Do what?" Tristan's voice wobbled and I wondered whether I should slap him. "No, we have to go."

"Give me the bolt cutters, we're not leaving without the money." Tristan threw me a scared look but did as he was told, running to the car like someone was chasing him. He handed me the cutters.

"Please hurry," he said.

"I will, but just in case, hold this." I gave him my gun. He hesitated, so I wrapped his hand around it, making sure he had a good grip. "It's just in case. You won't need to use it. I'll be right back."

I pulled surgical gloves on as I ran the twenty steps to the Transit van, looking around and still seeing no one. Gun shots out here wouldn't be all that unusual, but sooner or later someone would come to investigate, if only out of boredom and curiosity. I leaned inside the van and set the blades of the cutters against the padlock. It took less than a minute to bite through it, open up the cage in the back of the van, and pull the two bags out. They were heavier than I'd anticipated, but that meant they were full, a pretty powerful motivator to carry them. I put a bag on each shoulder and started back to the Honda. The most direct line brought me back to Silva's body and, as I stepped over his legs, one of the bags fell.

I froze as the duffel thumped onto his left leg, and instinctively I looked at his face for some reaction. He lay as still as before. I was in a hurry, I knew I was in a hurry, but I wanted to see him up close. I knelt and pretended to check the man's pulse, even though I knew there would be none. My gloved hand lingered on his throat, where the loose flesh was drawn downward by gravity. I closed my eyes and felt taut sinews under my fingertips, like thick guitar strings, and let my hand drift over the firmness of his windpipe, my fingers tracing its edges like they did the neck of my guitar.

"Dom, what are you doing?" Tristan was coming toward me. "He's dead. Give me one of those bags."

I waved him away. "I got it. Just make sure no one's coming." I grabbed the bag and hurried to the back of my Honda. As I dropped them in the trunk, I saw the blood on my fingertips and couldn't resist the temptation. I unzipped one bag, just a little, and wiped the blood on a stack of dollar bills. I smiled to myself, *Tristan's share?* I heard him muttering, so I rezipped the bag and slammed the trunk shut. I snapped the gloves off, turned them inside out, and stuffed them into my trouser pocket.

"Let's go," he said. "And thank God you're an ADA. If the cops pull us over, they'll let us go. You have your badge, right?"

He was remembering what I'd said earlier, which showed that his brain was back in gear. But I didn't agree, not anymore. I looked to my left, across thirty yards of rutted scrubland to the woods.

"I have a better idea," I said. "And we need that camera."

Tristan was already in the car, the door open and his hand still clutching my gun like it was a comfort to him. I took it with gentle fingertips, dropped it into my pocket, and moved to the trunk of the car. He leaned out and looked back at me. "No, dude, let's just go."

"Not without the camera. The cops might find it, and if they do, we're well and truly fucked. And the woods are perfect for stashing the money for a day or so." Before he could argue, I popped the trunk and put a flashlight in my back pocket. I heaved a duffel bag back onto each shoulder. "Wait here."

I trotted away from the car, looking back over my shoulder but still seeing no one. I was starting to think that the kinds of people who lived in the tornado magnets out there had learned to steer clear of trouble, not poke their noses into it. Gun shots might mean cops, and cops were never a good thing for people who lived in their cash society on the edge of the grid.

I hit the woods and stopped, working the flashlight into my right hand and flicking it about until I saw the first of the white strips on the trees ahead of me. I started forward as fast as I dared, my eyes darting between the narrow path at my feet and the strips of white tape that guided me out of view and to the camera. A rustle ahead of me stopped me in my tracks. I knew it wasn't a person—it was too low and gentle to be human—but for me, the alternative was little better. Maybe it was the comparison to sociopaths and psychopaths in books and movies, but I'd come to loathe snakes. Cold-blooded, dead-eyed, calculating, and ruthless, hiding in plain sight. Yeah, an easy comparison to make: me, snake in a suit. Maybe that's why I didn't like them, and as I stood on that earthen path I realized that snakes and I had gained another thing in common—we both killed to survive.

All around me, crickets and cicadas shredded the peace and quiet of the woods, upping my adrenaline as I scanned the brush around my feet for slithery movement. I saw nothing, heard nothing more, and kept going. In less than a minute, the tree loomed familiar, it's gaping *U* shape a welcome sight. I looked around before dropping the bags behind it, kicking them into a narrow ditch that might once have been a stream. There were enough leaves to cover both bags, and I threw a few sticks on top and tried to make it look as natural as possible. But I didn't have much time.

I hauled myself into the bend in the tree and leaned over to get the camera but froze as a dark silhouette moved between the trees no more than fifteen yards away. The figure stopped, but I couldn't tell if he was facing me or the other way. My hand moved slowly toward my trouser pocket. Another movement, and a second figure, a little shorter, joined the first and their heads came together for a moment. I stayed where I was, hardly daring to breathe, not wanting to kill anyone else. After a few seconds, the silhouettes separated just a little and moved away from me, deeper into the woods.

Young love, I thought. *All three of us getting lucky.*

Once I'd pulled the camera down, I went back to the bags and put it inside, then re-covered them a little more carefully. I almost sprinted back to the car and about fell into the driver's seat.

"Jesus, Dom, let's go." Tristan was sweating and, quite literally, sat perched on the edge of the passenger seat. "I don't understand why that was even necessary."

"Look, what I said to you before, about the cops letting me go if they stop me? That's out the window now. That shit works if I'm speeding, and maybe the cop'll give me a ride home if I'm driving drunk. If I know him. But if they've got reports of two people shot and a description of this car leaving the scene, my badge means something very different to a cop who pulls us over."

"Like what?"

"Like he'll be extra careful about how he does his job. We match any kind of description, we'll be out and in handcuffs while they search this car. Thanks to me, they won't find a damn thing."

I fired the engine and spun the wheels in the dust, bouncing from the dirt track of the mobile-home park onto the main road. Once on pavement I slowed, driving carefully all the way home, sticking to the speed limit and signaling each turn and lane change.

Like every good criminal should.

O

As soon as we were safely away, Tristan turned to me. "What the fuck was the deal with Otto?"

"Meaning?"

"Did you know he was going to be there?"

"Working there? Hell no."

"He wasn't part of your little plan all along?"

"No. Of course not. Why would I hide that from you?" I glanced at him, trying to look outraged. "And why are you so pissed anyway? We should be glad he showed up; that dude saved our bacon."

"Maybe." Tristan looked at me a while longer, and I knew he wasn't sure whether to believe me. Eventually he turned and stared out of the window. We didn't talk the rest of way home, although every now and again he muttered *You said no guns, no guns.* But he didn't seem to want an argument, so I kept quiet except to tell him to keep an eye out for cops. He seemed happy for the distraction, and I used the quiet to put myself in his shoes, and Otto's, to think about how they might feel. It was hard, because I knew they were terrified of being caught, but they'd also feel something about the two dead men. That, of course, was the part I had trouble with. The fact that both had weapons and would have merrily used them on us was all the justification I needed, and I didn't need much. They'd escalated the situation, turned a simple theft into a double homicide. I hoped my chums would appreciate, in the midst of feeling sorry for themselves, who was left lying in the dust.

Otto's car was already parked outside our apartment building, and he was pacing the hallway inside, his head down, muttering. When he heard us, he looked up, and his face looked like it had melted, a sweaty mix of wide eyes and slack jaw, relief and terror.

"Gentlemen," I said quietly, "I believe you know each other."

"Yeah," said Otto, "and we're a little past polite introductions."

I unlocked the door to the apartment, and they both rushed in, like the answers to all our problems were laid out on the coffee table. Tristan collapsed on the couch, and Otto went into the kitchen, where he opened and closed cabinet doors for no obvious reason.

"Need something?" I asked.

"A drink. Fuck, you don't drink, do you?"

"No, but Tristan does. Try the cabinet over the microwave. Brandy, I think."

He poured himself a tumbler, more than I wanted to see him drink, but I didn't say anything.

"So what the fuck is going on?" Otto demanded. He looked directly at me and gave a minuscule nod that said, "I'm back to the script."

I played along, too. "It was supposed to be a theft. Just a simple, easy theft," I said. "Take a couple of things from that guy's van and be on our merry way."

"Who were those people?" Otto asked.

"One of them owned a bunch of trailers, in that park and elsewhere. He fleeced immigrants for rent money, let his trailers basically fall apart, but he still made his tenants pay. He was a worthless piece of shit."

"Yeah," Tristan chimed in. "A worthless piece of shit who collected his rents in cash once a month."

Otto shook his head. "I never took you for a thief, Dom."

"It's a good chunk of money, Otto, and you don't need to worry
about my motives." I cocked my head. "What the hell were you
doing there?"

"A new security job."

"So what the fuck do we do now?" Tristan said. He stared at me,
like this was my fault. "We just committed murder. We killed two
people, and that's murder."

"Capital murder, technically," I said.

Otto moved from the kitchen into the living room. He looked
up from his glass. "How can you be so fucking calm? Tristan's right,
we're in deep shit."

"No, wait. You're the ones in deep shit," Tristan said. "I didn't
kill anyone. You two did."

"Sorry to disappoint you, but we're all in this together," I said, irritated. "It's called the law of parties, Tristan. Everyone involved in a crime
is responsible for what happens, even if they didn't pull the trigger. Like
the getaway driver at a bank robbery. Same thing, so if we're in the shit,
we're in it together and we need to stay together. Got it?"

"Sure. But how can you be so fucking calm?"

"A touch more sensible than panicking, I would think."

Otto sat on the couch beside Tristan, his elbows on his knees.
He was back to staring at his drink. "I can't believe that happened."

"Yeah, well, I hate to be the bearer of bad news, Otto. And just
in case you're thinking you can bail out of this, it's a little late."

"You sure about that?" Otto asked. I wasn't sure if he was still
play-acting, so on the off chance he was seriously wondering whether
he could save himself by frying us, I laid it out.

"You shot a man during a robbery. You can tell people you didn't
know what was going on, but we'll both tell it differently. And given
your financial situation, the fact we know each other . . ." I shrugged.

"And the kicker is that you fled the scene and met us back here, after disposing of your weapon."

"But you told me to give it—"

"What happened and what it looks like to the police, Otto, are not the same thing. You're in it now, so I suggest you start looking on the bright side. We got away, and you're a whole lot richer."

"That's true," he muttered.

"In theory," I added.

"What does that mean?"

"I hid the money in the woods before we left. Couldn't risk being caught with it, plus there was blood on some of the notes."

"You *hid* it? What the fuck is this, *Treasure Island*?"

"Calm down, Otto. We'll go back in a couple of days; it'll still be there."

"So what do we do now?" Tristan asked.

"We lay low. Do nothing, say nothing. Act normal, or as normal as possible."

They didn't respond, just sat there in silence, staring at the floor. I felt a sudden rush of annoyance. Not only had we avoided being killed out there, but we'd just gotten away with money and murder, free and clear. I took a deep breath and instead of yelling at them, I tried a pep talk. "Look, we didn't leave any evidence behind. There are no finger prints, there's no DNA, no surveillance cameras. All the cops have is a couple of dead bodies in a shitty mobile-home park. For all we know, they'll assume they shot each other. If that's the way they want this to look, maybe that's the way they'll interpret what little evidence they have."

"No way, man," Otto said. He shook his head slowly. "No way. I mean, the only evidence they have is ballistics. Once they dig the bullets out of those guys, they'll compare them with the guns and see two other people were involved."

"Yeah, we should have taken their guns." I cursed myself for that oversight, then had a thought. "Maybe the scavengers who live at that place will help themselves to the guns, and the cops won't be able to make that comparison."

Otto's brow furrowed and he studied me for a moment. "Why do you hate them so much?"

"Who?"

"Poor people. Or is it Mexicans? Maybe all South Americans?"

"No idea what you mean."

"Bullshit. This isn't the first time you've talked shit about the people who live out there, in places like that. Like they're animals or something."

"Relax, Otto, I don't care about them one way or the other. I'm sure many of them are wonderful people just trying to make a living."

"Don't bullshit me, Dom. You don't think that at all." He sat up straight, and I pictured his spine finally growing in. "So which is it, poor people or Mexicans you don't like?"

I held his eye for a moment. "Like I just said, Otto, I don't dislike anyone. I don't give a fuck who's poor and who's not, and I know you're part Mexican and I don't give a shit about that either. So if you're looking for a fight, you won't get one from me. Not about that, and sure as hell not right now."

He looked at me for a second longer and then took a drink. He sat back and spoke to Tristan. "What do you think we should do?"

"About what?" Tristan asked.

"About not getting caught."

Tristan nodded toward me. "Like he said, I guess we just act normal. And hope for the best, right?"

"Right," I said. "Also a good idea not to be seen together too much. Tristan and I are probably okay as we live together, but Otto you need to steer clear of this place and us for a while."

"Yeah, sure," Otto said.

"Good. Now, as you're a security guard there, the police will want to talk to you, find out if you saw anything. Can you handle that?"

"Yeah. I was supposed to knock off at ten, so I'll tell them I left before it all went down. I can handle that."

Tristan spoke up. "What about your friend Gus. Can you handle him? Do we need to worry about him going to the cops?"

Otto looked at me. "Who the hell is Gus?"

"A friend of mine. This whole thing was his idea in the first place, only he backed out so Tristan stepped up."

Otto's eyes widened. "Someone else knows about this? Oh my God, we're done, we're finished. As soon as he sees the news, he'll call the cops."

"No," I said. "Not at all. I'll keep an eye on him, but there's no way. I promise, he's cool."

"He'll be cool about a double murder, are you kidding me?"

"He's my best friend. Trust me, he won't call the cops."

"You better be right about that. And just make sure you do," Otto said. "Keep an eye on him, that is."

"I said I would. We can go back in a couple of days, once they clear the crime scene. Maybe I should go alone. As a prosecutor, I'd have a reason to be out there."

"We'll go together," Otto said. "Or meet there. Not that I don't trust you, I just need to look out for myself, you know?"

"No, I don't know, Otto." I glared at him. "We need to be smart, not greedy, right now. How're you going to explain being out there if it's not your shift?"

"So we go when I'm working."

"I'm going too," Tristan said. He looked at Otto. "Man, you adjusted to this very quickly. You just killed a guy and all you're thinking about is the money."

"So? What's done is done. And with the money I can get the hell out of here. What do you care?"

"You're scaring me a little, is all. Both of you. I know the money's important, but two people are dead. Fucking dead. Neither of you seem to care about that, which is stone fucking cold and it scares me a little."

And that suited me perfectly.

CHAPTER FIFTEEN

LIPS THAT WOULD KISS

Tristan holed up in his room. I watched the eleven thirty news by myself, and the shooting already was the lead story. The footage consisted of a lot of flashing red-and-blue lights, and nothing of the crime scene. The reporter spoke in that excited calm reporters are taught, that earnest intensity, and gave the same few details three different ways: two bodies, both shot and declared dead at the scene. APD homicide detectives on the scene. No suspects in custody. No indication of motive or gang activity. Rinse and repeat.

When the weather guy appeared at 11:53, I got up to make myself a sandwich, my stomach reminding me I'd not eaten since lunch. I was halfway through it and an episode of *The Simpsons* when someone knocked on the door.

I did a mental inventory of my evening, the one I'd agreed with Tristan; basically, we'd spent the evening at the apartment. The building didn't have security cameras in the parking lot, so if anyone said they'd seen us drive out, it'd be their word against ours. Otto had potentially complicated things a little with his presence, but that was unavoidable. I hoped this wasn't him on a return visit.

Tristan was quiet in his room, so I went to the door and looked through the peephole. I smiled as I opened the door.

"You keep showing up," I said.

"Oh, I think you know why I'm here." She wore black jeans and a white tank top, that luscious hair falling all over her shoulders, and I itched to run my fingers through it. She breezed past me and stood in the middle of the room, checking the place out, a clutch handbag under her arm. "And, if you don't like it, you can kick me out, I guess," she added.

"No, I forgive you." I pointed to the sandwich on the coffee table. "I was just having dinner. Care for anything?"

"Water's fine. Thanks."

"Absolutely. Have a seat."

"Is anyone else here?"

"My roommate. In his room."

She cocked her head and said, "Then let's go to yours."

I was the one to knock people off their game. I did it with charm and wit and by being overly, overtly forward. I didn't trick girls into bed, I basically told them where things were headed and either they went along or I moved along. James Bond–style. Girls didn't lead 007 by the nose, not even into the bedroom, so I hesitated, not so much wary as unaccustomed.

She raised an eyebrow. "Like I said, you can kick me out."

Given the two options, I made up my mind and left my sandwich for later.

My room was a good size, but I'd put a single bed in there intentionally, a simple wooden frame with a headboard of slatted pine. It was something a poor student would have, and a discouragement to anyone wanting to stay overnight with me. For the first time, I regretted not having something larger.

"It's like a little boy's room," she said.

"Glad you like it."

She smiled finally, and looked at me. "I saw the news."

"That so?"

"Yep. Seems like someone went out to the east side of town and did something pretty bad." She clicked open her purse and pulled out a pair of steel handcuffs. "I thought maybe these would be appropriate. Why don't you come over here?"

O

We made a lot of noise but ignored Tristan when he banged on the door, and after a while he gave up. So did the neighbor who slept just the other side of my bedroom wall, a geek who lived his life between headphones anyway.

She hadn't been kidding about me being bad, and she used my own belt on me, attaching me to the bed with her cuffs, teasing me when I winced and laughing when I cried out. When I was ready to break the slats, and her, she stopped and lay her naked body on me, whispering that she was sorry, and then she made me use the belt on her. She laughed and screamed, and the geeky neighbor made his way to our door to yell at us, as Tristan cowered in his room. She kissed me, a lot and all over, but she didn't let me fuck her. I got close to taking her anyway, oh, so close, but I saw in her eyes that even though she wanted me to put a hand on her throat and another in her hair, that was all she wanted. That girl was like quicksand, drawing me in and holding on to me, squeezing me with her grip and making me cry out in frustration. I struggled and gave in, then struggled some more. When she finally let me go, I was soaking wet, exhausted, and utterly disoriented.

I fell asleep around 4 a.m., nestled into her thighs, stomach, and breasts, her arms locked gently around my chest. When I woke four hours later, she was gone.

CHAPTER SIXTEEN

FILLED WITH STRAW

Tristan was gone, too, or extremely quiet, but because I didn't know which, and I didn't like the idea of him popping out of his room again like a sneaky jack-in-the-box, I tapped on his door to make sure. No answer.

I made a cup of tea in my undershorts and drank it while watching the news. The information looked to be the same, but the TV crews were all over the mobile-home park, talking to residents and taking angled shots of the crime scene, which was back to being a dirty patch of ground. Every time the shot was right, my eyes were drawn to the line of trees, and I was pleased to see a distinct lack of activity in that direction.

I dressed in jeans and a T-shirt and was hunting for my flip-flops when the doorbell rang. Almost nine on a Sunday morning, when good people were in church or at Starbucks, and bad people were recovering from a night of sex and murder. Not expecting guests. I checked the peephole and saw a twitchy Gus trying to look in on me.

I opened the door, and he just stood there for a moment. Then he started to cry.

"Gus, for fuck's sake, come in. What are you doing here?"

He looked around as he walked into the apartment. "Is it safe to talk?"

"Yes, Tristan's not here and I don't think he bugged the place."

He wiped his nose with his sleeve, back in control. "Dom, what the hell did you do last night?"

"No idea what you're talking about. Do I look rough or something?"

"I'm serious. I saw the news. That's the mobile-home park where—"

"Gus. Shut your mouth." I said it firmly but put a hand on his shoulder and squeezed to show him I still loved him. "Not just now, but always and forever. When you leave a party, sometimes you miss out on the juicy details. And when those juicy details can get people in trouble, asking questions just isn't polite."

"Polite? What the fuck are you talking about? Look, I'm potentially in a whole—"

"No, you're not," I interrupted. "You left the party. You didn't even know the party was happening. So be quiet for a moment and think about those who might actually be in a whole world of whatever you think might happen to you. You understand?"

"I just want to know—"

"Do you understand?" I looked him in the eye. "Go home. Be normal. And don't ask anyone any questions about anything. OK?"

He sagged, but the message seemed to have gotten through. "Fine." A concerned look fell over his face and he looked at me. "But you're not hurt, you're OK, right?"

I smiled. "Peachy. Never been better."

"Were there others? Helping you?"

"There are no others. Just like there are no questions."

"Right, right. Sorry. I've not done this . . . Anyway, I should go. I gotta get going."

I walked him to the door and shook his hand without another word, then growled in frustration when another figure came down the hall toward us. Otto. They nodded at each other as Gus scurried away. I let Otto in.

"Short memory you've got," I said.

"Huh?" He stood there, breathing hard and looking angry. I didn't care that he was mad, but the whistling coming from his nose irritated me.

"That whole discussion about not seeing each other for a couple of days. Ring any bells?"

"Who was that?"

"My friend Gus, remember that name? He popped by, we had a chat, he'll keep his mouth shut, just like I said."

"You're still sure about that?"

"Actually, I'm double-crossing you, Otto. I've given him the coordinates so he can retrieve the hidden treasure and then we're eloping to the Bahamas together."

"Why is everything a joke to you? Do you have any fucking idea what kind of shit we're in?"

"We're not in any shit, Otto. But if people keep coming to my door and acting mad, and sad, and pitching their hissy fits every fucking minute then, yes, I'm guessing someone will cotton that all isn't as it should be. So how about you go home, shut the fuck up, and I'll see you in two days? How about we do that?" This was my controlled anger, the one that tended to scare people the most. I could turn it on when I wanted to, but this had flared up all by itself. A genuine emotion from me, quite the rarity, but the strongest instinct in my body has always been the one for self-preservation, and I truly didn't like this procession of empaths bringing their insecurities and paranoias to my door.

"Who died and put you in charge?" He sounded hurt more than angry now, so I dialed it back a little.

"Two people, but I'm not in charge. Although, this was my plan and I seem to be the only one thinking straight, and calmly, right now, which means I might be the best placed to figure out what we should do next."

"I don't like leaving the money out there."

"Neither do I. But I didn't feel like it was safe to bring it here, not after everything went sideways. And it sure as hell isn't safe to go back out there for it right now."

"What if someone takes it? Or reports it?"

"If they take it, then we're no poorer than we were this time yesterday. It's not our money, remember."

"It fucking should be after what we did," he said. "Did you wipe everything down? If someone finds those bags and reports them to the cops, they can collect DNA or prints or something."

"Won't happen."

"Why not?"

"Otto, come on. You saw that shit-hole of a place. Fine, tell me I'm racist and classist, but do you really think anyone, anyone at all, from that trailer park who finds tens of thousands of dollars in cash will say to themselves, 'Gee, I should probably turn all this lovely money over to the authorities,' or do you think it's more likely they'll say, 'Hallelujah, now I can get the fuck out of this dump and go rent an actual apartment'?"

He chewed his lower lip and eyed me. "Probably right about that."

"We both know I'm right. Plus, I was wearing gloves and didn't take the time to run my tongue all over those bags. There's no DNA, no prints to be found. On that score, at least, we're in the clear."

Otto nodded, then looked down the hallway toward Tristan's room. "Where's he?"

"No clue."

"You don't think he went back there, do you?"

"He's not stupid, Otto. And there's no need for anyone to get impatient or greedy. We waited weeks to do this—we can sit tight for a couple more days."

He sighed and his whole body seemed to relax. "I'm sorry," he said. "For busting in here all antsy."

"Forget it."

"I'm sorry for shooting the guy, too."

"Don't be, he drew first. No way of knowing what he was about to do."

"No, I don't mean that. I mean . . . I'm sorry he's dead. I've never shot anyone and I don't feel good about it. At all."

"Me too. I feel horrible that those men lost their lives. We didn't go there intending to do that, Otto. You can't beat yourself up like that."

He cocked his head and looked at me. "I don't get you."

"No harm in that."

"No, I mean it. I couldn't sleep last night because I killed a man. Not a very nice man, sure, but I took his life. He's someone's son, maybe a husband and father, and they'll never see him again. And you know what else I thought? Maybe everyone in that trailer park will lose their homes because of this. Maybe, thanks to us shooting Silva and that guard, a whole bunch of families, kids, will be living on the streets."

"I don't see how—"

"And you're not particularly bothered by any of it. Also, the guy I killed, he was one of us. Law enforcement."

"Otto, a polyester suit and a plastic badge don't make you—"

"That's what I mean," he interrupted. "It's all laughs and jokes to you. And you're a fucking suit-wearing lawyer; it's not like you're a combat veteran or some shit like that."

"You're a shrink now?"

"No, man, it just creeps me out, the way nothing seems to bother you."

"It's just how I deal with it all. A different way than you do, that's all."

He unwrapped a stick of gum. "Yeah. Maybe."

"And I should probably thank you for saving my life," I said.

"Now you're working me."

"No, I'm serious. The guy had a perfect right to shoot me, and as far as I'm concerned, he was just about to. In fact, you may not realize this but you actually have a decent defense if . . . you know."

"How do you figure that?" He folded the gum into his mouth and chewed slowly.

"You can argue that you were out there working when you saw

this going down. You recognized me but had no clue why I was there, but you saw some guy with a gun about to shoot me. Your law-enforcement instincts kicked in and you shot him first."

"And how do I explain disappearing from the scene? Not calling the cops or even giving a statement."

I shrugged. "Easy. You realized what we were doing and how it looked. You panicked. Shit, Otto, it's a better defense than I've got, that's for damn sure."

He smiled. "Yeah, I guess it is. Thanks for the idea."

"Hey, like I said, you saved my life. The least I could do."

He left five minutes later, mollified if not happy. I sat in the living room, perched on the arm of the sofa with my guitar. I wrapped my left hand around its neck and pressed my fingertips onto the strings, not seeking any chord in particular but just for the feel of it, that cold, familiar bite of thin metal, soft and serrated, still yet ready to hum like a human vein and give me that wonderful throb beneath my skin. With my right hand I caressed the guitar's body, enjoying its smooth curves and the hollow sound when my thumb tapped the wood. I closed my eyes and saw Ambrosio Silva's face, empty and cooling in the dust, his eyes half closed, just marbles. As I sat there and thought about what we'd done, I didn't feel the panic that had bitten Otto and Gus. And I didn't feel like hiding myself away, if that was what Tristan was doing.

No, all I felt was a sense of calm and a slight tingle of excitement at the thought of what might come next.

CHAPTER SEVENTEEN

THE STUFFED MEN

W e didn't get back there until Friday night. The murders had caused more problems at the trailer park than we could have imagined, mostly stemming from a slow response from police. The same lethargy that helped us escape free and clear was stopping us from going back because the locals were furious. And when the *Austin Statesman* started interviewing people, the paper uncovered a pattern of slow responses. To make amends, APD and the Travis County Sheriff's Office kept a couple of men out there that week, which screwed with our plans because it meant the management company didn't need Otto. We took turns driving out to the park, but every night those police cars were sitting in the dirt near the woods or roaming the trailer park, looking for trouble. Nothing those cops would have loved more than to nab some suspicious characters to show they cared, after all.

I hadn't seen Otto all week, but I imagined him raving with impatience at his place, the same way Tristan was acting bipolar at ours. The cops had interviewed Otto, of course, but he'd played dumb, said he left the property at the end of his shift, like we'd discussed. He told me they believed him, and why wouldn't they?

When we weren't at work or driving past the mobile-home park, Tristan and I mostly kept to our rooms, neither of us wanting to say something we might regret as a result of this pressure. The good thing was, no cops came knocking that week. I kept reminding myself of that.

But by Friday we couldn't stand it. The previous night, only one cop had been at the trailer park and we figured the scale-back was permanent. We piled into Otto's piece-of-shit car and drove east, eyes peeled for a police presence that might undo us. As we pulled to a stop, we didn't see any cops at all. Maybe one was driving through the park, but there was no one right there, which meant we could park and head into the woods. I was glad we'd taken his car, of course, as it fit right in, with an almost zero percent chance of being stolen while we weren't looking. Even out there, where people were dirt poor, Otto's most expensive possession looked pathetic, the envy of no one.

We stood outside the car in that blind spot, three silent watchmen. We heard nothing, saw no one. The day's heat lingered, but a slight breeze ruffled the coarse grass at our feet. Otto was sweating already. On my signal, we crossed the open patch of ground in the pitch black, not wanting to draw attention by using lights. When we got to the tree line, I looked at my watch. Ten o'clock. We looked back toward the homes, rows of low boxes that were little more than black silhouettes. Each one had a little squares of light glowing in the dark, but I couldn't see inside any of them. A man's voice floated over to us and a dog started barking. We pulled out our flashlights, and Tristan led the procession into the woods. Just inside the tree line, he tripped on a fallen branch and cursed.

"You weren't in the military, were you?" Otto whispered from the back of the line.

"What's that supposed to mean?" Tristan replied.

"You're shining your flashlight too far ahead of you. In this terrain you need to point it just in front of your feet, so you can see the ground you're walking on."

"Thanks, General Otto. Any other words of wisdom?"

Otto grunted a response and we moved on again, my flashlight flicking over the trees as I searched for my markers. I'd wondered whether the cops might find the tape, but once I saw the first strip I stopped worrying. In the few days since I'd attached them, they'd been chewed up by the sun and the bugs, and now resembled peeling, off-white strips of bark. They were barely noticeable, and not even slightly suspicious.

Our lights flickered up and down as we walked, as concerned about prying eyes as hazards lying across the path. I tried to listen for outsiders, but our shuffling feet and the cacophony of insects made that impossible. I just hoped it also made it hard for people to hear us. About twenty yards in, we froze at the crack of wood to our right, all three beams of light snapping toward the sound. Two deer stood either side of a sapling, their eyes like reflective pennies in the darkness. Otto stooped and picked up a stick. He took aim and threw it toward the deer, who skittered backward, then disappeared from view.

"What was that about?" Tristan asked, sounding annoyed.

"Stupid deer. About gave me a heart attack."

"More money for us, then," I said, but no one laughed. I turned serious. "U-shaped tree, should be just up ahead."

Tristan kept going and we followed close behind, and it seemed like the excitement in my chest powered up with every step we took. I was staring at Tristan's heels, trying not to step on them, when he stopped.

"That's it," he said. "Right?"

"You sure?" Otto asked.

"Dude, look at it. See any other U-shaped trees out here?"

"No, dickhead, mostly because it's dark."

"Chaps, please, can you keep it down? Better yet, zip it so we can concentrate on finding the bags and get out of here." I moved forward past the tree, my flashlight sweeping the ground. I was looking for the edge of the ditch, and spotted it quickly. I trained the light where I thought I'd hid the bags.

"Fuck," I said.

"What does that mean?" Otto growled.

"Looks like it's been disturbed." I walked to where the ground dipped and stepped down beside the litter of branches and leaves. "Animals, let's hope."

"Shit, I knew we should have come back yesterday," Tristan said.

"Just shine your light over here, will you?" I put the handle of mine in my mouth and used both hands to start pushing aside the branches. Behind me, Otto and Tristan shifted on their feet and tried to ignore the sounds of the woods to keep my little patch of leaves and twigs lit.

"A bag," Otto said, as I pulled one of the camouflage duffels out.

I shook the debris off it and let it dangle from my hand. "It's too light."

"It looks full, though," Tristan said.

"Just fucking open it," Otto snapped.

I put it on the ground and knelt beside it. A leaf had stuck itself in the zipper and I cleared it out. We all held our breath as I drew the zipper down. I opened the bag and looked in, knowing Otto and Tristan couldn't see.

"Empty?" Tristan whispered.

"Full," I said. "Of newspaper."

Otto stepped forward. "Newspaper? What the . . ."

I let them lean in, their lights poking into the bag as they stared. Otto sank to his knees and started scooping, balls of newspaper flying over his left shoulder as he emptied the bag. To our left, Tristan kicked the leaves and broken branches, his flashlight dancing over the forest floor like a manic searchlight.

"Here's the other bag." He sat on the edge of the ditch and put his flashlight in his mouth. With both hands, he pulled the second bag onto his lap, unzipped it, and opened it wide. The flashlight dropped. "Fuck. Fuck. Newspaper."

"Jesus. *Both* of them," Otto said.

"Is the camera in there?" I asked. "Our guns?"

Tristan turned the bag on its side and shook more crumpled

newspaper out. My eyes strained in the dark as they fell to the ground, some wadded up tight, others hardly scrunched at all. Like snowflakes, each one a different shape, all unique. And all utterly worthless.

Tristan let the bag fall to his side and looked at us. "No camera, no guns."

"Oh, Dom, you fucked this up bad," said Tristan. "I mean, two people are dead. We killed two people and not only is the money gone, but the guns are, too."

"Shit," I said. "I'm sorry. I'm really sorry guys, I was thinking on my feet. If someone finds those guns . . . the serial numbers will show who they belong to."

"Can you report them stolen?" Tristan asked.

"Not now," I said. "It'd be too suspicious, especially if we both did it. No reason to draw attention to ourselves."

"Then what the hell do we do?" Otto asked. His flashlight shone into my eyes and I blocked the beam with my arm.

"Get that off me." Anger flashed through me, but I calmed myself as the light fell away. "We stay cool, we stay together, and we think about this. Grab those bags and let's get out of here."

"Wait," Otto said. "Let's just search the area, make sure."

"No. There are cops out there," I said.

They ignored me and started looking, so I joined in. We spent five minutes kicking through the dead leaves and twigs, flashing our lights at anything and everything that looked like money or a gun. Dust started to swirl around our ankles like smoke, each of us muttering with frustration and desperation as we widened the circle. Eventually the sound of a siren froze us in place, brought us back to the reality of our situation.

"Guys, we should go," Otto said.

"That can't be for us," Tristan whispered. "It can't be."

"It's not," I said. "But Otto's right. Everything's gone, and we'd have a hard time explaining why we're standing in the woods holding empty bags. Fifty yards from a double-murder scene."

Tristan and Otto each carried a bag, clutching them close to their bodies as we exited the woods as if self-conscious, embarrassed by the duffels' drooping and useless emptiness. Climbing into the backseat, Tristan threw down his bag and slammed the door a little too hard.

"Take it fuckin' easy," Otto snapped.

"Guys, let's stay calm."

"Which is real easy to do," Tristan said. "We killed two people for nothing and now someone has our money and the fucking guns that put you at the crime scene."

"Us and not you," Otto said, "so zip it."

Tristan did. We all did. The only sound for several miles was Otto grinding through the gears as he took us out of the dark and into East Austin. The sense of unreality remained as the city sprang up around us, the part of town once known for hookers and blow now a hub for those who didn't loosen their ties until six, at the earliest. I looked out of the window at the brightly colored food trailers that sat cheerily on once-scrubby patches of land, at the new bars and restaurants that were too cool, and too busy, to take reservations. Two of them, I noticed, had white-shirted valets running back and forth from nearby lots, where shiny cars took refuge in the dust of the torn-down crack houses that had sat there only months before, firetraps targeted by cops and junkies to justify their existence, both replaced by valet parkers flitting about like moths in search of their flame.

As we got close to Otto's place, where we'd left my car, I spoke. "I do have one idea. It's a long shot, but since we're not overwhelmed with options, I say it's worth trying."

CHAPTER EIGHTEEN

IN OUR DRY CELLAR

We gathered around the computer at Otto's place, a clunky, black laptop that looked like it'd been around since dial-up modems. At first, Tristan was horrified by the device, but then I think he become fascinated by its antiquity. It gave him something else to focus on, a momentary distraction from the horror of losing a lot of money and possibly giving away some dangerous evidence. As we waited for the computer to boot up, I listened to their banter and wondered why I wasn't getting more blame. I was the one who'd hidden the money and the guns together, who'd failed to cover the bags well enough.

And I wondered if they were thinking about what we'd found instead of the guns and money. Tristan, it turned out, was.

"I have a question," he said. "Who the fuck put balled-up newspaper in those bags? I mean, why?"

"Fuck knows," Otto grunted.

"I'm with Otto," I said. "It makes no sense at all to me. I can't . . . I just can't see why they'd bother. Why not just take the stuff and get the hell out?"

"Like I said, fuck knows. . . . And here we go," Otto said. "Internet up and running."

"You really think the stuff might be on Craigslist?" Tristan asked me, doubtful.

"Maybe. The camera only, though, they don't allow gun sales. But if we find the camera, we'll find who took our money."

I gave Otto the brand and model of the camera and two fat index fingers typed the information in, far too slowly for Tristan the computer whiz.

"How can you type like that? Take lessons or something."

Otto ignored him, maybe slowed down a little, it was hard to tell.

"There," Otto said. We leaned over his shoulders and peered at the search results. "Why is it listing cars? Blackberries? I typed *security camera*, you saw me."

"It picks up the words and gives you anything that includes them," Tristan explained. "Just look down the list for anything close, the title description should tell us."

"Just one that I can see," I said.

The ad read:

Weatherproof Camo Security Camera with Night Vision—$150 (S. Austin)

"How much did you pay for it?" Otto asked.

"About two-eighty." We leaned in closer as Otto clicked on the link. "Dude, is that it? Is that our fucking camera?"

"Sure looks like it," I said.

Tristan looked at me and said, "So how do we handle this?"

"We do it nice and simple," Otto said. "We make an offer, meet the guy in a deserted parking lot somewhere, and politely request our guns and money back. If he declines, we become less polite."

"I don't think so," I said.

Otto twisted in his seat. "Why the fuck not?"

"Yeah," Tristan said, "I'm with him. We don't have time to pussy-foot around. We take a day or two to come up with a clever plan, he'll have sold the camera, spent the cash, and ditched the guns. We need to move on this, and now."

"Diving in headfirst didn't turn out so well last time," I said. "You know, guns blazing and all that. Why do you think we're in this mess?"

"Fine, we'll wear masks," said Tristan.

"Masks."

"Yes. Like ski masks." Tristan nodded like it was actually a good idea. "They won't see our faces; we'll be in and out in a minute."

Otto stood. "I'm taking a piss. You two are the smart ones, figure it out and let me know."

We watched Otto walk out of the room, and I turned to Tristan, trying to conceal my disdain. "So, then. Masks."

"Yes. Fucking masks."

"How does that work exactly? We roll up and find some dude with a camera for sale. 'Hang on,' we say, 'just need to put on some masks, please don't look until we're ready.'"

"Very funny. We put them on before."

"Right, because three idiots driving along in Austin wearing ski masks, that won't attract attention. Or maybe we wait until we pull into the parking lot where we're going to meet this guy. Who, by the way, we're hoping is a criminal, which means he'll be keeping a beady eye out. So we're driving toward him, pulling on ski masks. That sounds like a successful approach method to you?"

"I suppose you have a better idea."

"I do, as it happens."

Otto appeared in the doorway. "You do what?"

"He has a scheme to get the camera back," Tristan said.

"Oh?" Otto looked at me. "What about the money? And guns."

"Maybe," I said. "But we'll have to be patient, and we may have to put a bit of a scare into the dude. Think you chaps can manage both of those things?"

"I think we've shown that we can. The scare, anyway," Otto said grimly.

"Just a scare Otto, nothing more than that. And even that may not be necessary."

"Yeah, no worries."

Tristan nodded.

"Good," I said. "Then one of you guys call him and arrange the meeting. And the sooner the better."

"Why does one of us have to call him?" Tristan asked.

"We're trying to remain anonymous," I explained. "Having the English guy make the phone call would undermine that plan a little, don't you think?"

"Fine," Tristan said, pulling out his phone. "I'll do it, I was just asking."

"Where's your burner phone?" I asked.

"At our place. Otto?"

Otto went into his bedroom and handed Tristan his prepaid phone, and we watched as Tristan dialed. "Yeah, hello? I'm calling about the security camera. . . . You still have it?" He looked at me and smiled. "Awesome, I'd like to buy it. As soon as possible."

CHAPTER NINETEEN

SHADE WITHOUT COLOR

The next morning, Otto drove over to our apartment, arriving just after seven. We went over the plan one more time, and when we were all agreed, we headed for the door. On the way out, I grabbed the original box the camera had come in, for the serial number stenciled on the back.

"Three fuckin' amigos, here we go again," Otto muttered as we started down the hallway.

"Let's not hurt anyone this time, okay?" Tristan said. He seemed genuinely worried.

"Every time we hurt someone, we're committing a new crime and creating witnesses and evidence," I told him. "It's not in our interests to do that. Right, Otto?"

"Hey, I'm with you. We'll do it the way you said, nice and safe."

The plan called for me to follow in my car, so I tucked in behind Otto's piece of crap, glad for the peace and quiet. Just like before the theft (fine, let's call it the double murder, but that's not what it was when we set out), I could feel them getting tense in the apartment. Empaths fidget and get snippy with each other, I'd learned—and whoever said, "Just stay calm" the most, was the least calm.

Even though I was fine, I understood why they weren't: we were pretty sure this was our camera. The guy on the phone had told Tristan it wasn't in its original packaging, that someone had given it to him as a barter, and he seemed as eager to sell it at the crack of dawn as we did to buy it at that hour. Plus, he didn't know a damn thing about its specifications.

Tristan had drawn the short straw. Literally. He was the most innocuous looking, didn't have a foreign accent, and didn't have a hot temper. And while I was unarmed this time, I wasn't so sure about Otto. I didn't ask because I didn't expect him to admit it if he was. So it made sense all around for Tristan to make the buy. And as the guy holding the two straws, I made sure that's what happened.

I drove with the windows down, the hot morning air a reminder of something real and a cure for the sense of detachment that had settled over me. Ten seconds of crazy had gotten us here, a simple plan for theft cascading into murder and desperate, amateur trickery. The weekend traffic on Loop 360 was going the other way, heading toward the parks and breakfast joints in Austin, two lines of cars shuffling up to the traffic lights to await permission to proceed to the next set of lights. I saw a few cars twitch their noses and nip into the other lane, maybe a couple of seconds gained, but probably not. Half the people I passed were looking at their phones, a few of the women were applying makeup. All of them were anonymous nobodies to me, a procession of ants on their way to the nest, ready to fuck, feed, or die for their queen. All of them living the bland and repetitive life I'd struggled to hold on to and was now fighting to regain.

We pulled over just before entering the parking lot of Barton Creek Mall, our eyes searching the acres of asphalt that in a few hours would bake in the summer sun. The place was empty, just a sprinkle of cars near the main entrance to the south side of the mall. Cleaners, security guards, and a few early-rising store keepers, I assumed. The meet was on the north side, so I called Otto's burner to let them know I was staying put per the plan and was ready for them to go.

Tristan answered. "Okay dude, we'll see you in a couple minutes."

"Right. And remember," I told him, "just do the deal, don't talk or answer any questions. If it's our camera, he won't be asking any."

"Suddenly you're such an expert," he said.

"I've read a thousand offense reports and victim statements. So I've been an expert at this for a while."

"Yeah," he said, "in theory."

As long as you're the one risking your neck, it'll stay theory. I decided to keep that less-than-motivational thought to myself. Sometimes my charm and humor didn't go over the way I intended. Especially in stressful situations, I'd noticed.

I watched Otto's car disappear around the side of the mall, heading for the north parking lot where the buy would take place. Otto was with Tristan and not with me because, as I'd pointed out, it'd be good for our seller to see that Tristan had company, just in case he tried some funny stuff.

My job, of course, was the funny stuff.

I waited calmly, my left elbow out the window, my eyes scanning for unusual movement. My burner phone rang after four minutes.

"White truck, one guy only," Otto said. "Mexican dude with a mustache."

"As opposed to all the other white trucks leaving the mall at seven in the morning."

"Fuck off."

"I'm just about to. The serial numbers?"

Otto read them off. Just as he finished, the white truck appeared on the road that ringed the mall, heading toward me and the exit. "That's a match. I've got it from here."

"You sure?" Otto was uncertain. He had been from the start of the plan. I was to follow the guy and talk to him whenever I felt it safe to do so. I'd wear my DA jacket, let my ID swing loosely around my neck, and terrorize him with my badge. I was to tell him he wasn't under investigation, but the guys he'd sold the camera to were suspects in a theft ring. If he had anything stolen, more cameras, money, or guns, he was to hand them over or find the FBI crawling over his ass, and then find a few meaty inmates crawling up his ass.

As for any cash, which he'd be the slowest to give up, I planned to tell him he'd actually get it back unless we could source the owner, assuring him that would be unlikely if it was small denominations. Which, of course, it was.

Not a great plan. A million miles from foolproof. But if I thought he was lying, we had a backup plan ready to go: a night-time visit with guns and masks and instruments that would make a grown man beg to tell the truth. Tristan had suggested there was no way in hell that we, decent people, could carry out plan B. Otto had grunted, which I took to be a sign that he was in agreement with Tristan. I remained confident we wouldn't have to.

I tucked in behind the truck, turned left onto 360 toward Austin, and followed him all the way to a taco stand on the east side. I put two cars between us at all times and parked four spaces away. We opened our car doors at the same time. He was Hispanic and looked like a gaucho cowboy with his big, brown eyes and a drooping mustache. He wore battered boots, a checked shirt, and jeans so faded they were almost white. He walked with a kind of tired swagger, and I caught up with him ten yards from the taco stand, where three young men in business casual were putting in their order and nervously eying the BMW they'd arrived in, ready to dash back to their Saturday workaholic office and brag about the hole-in-the-wall they'd discovered.

"Good morning," I said to him. "Never got tacos from here. They good?"

CHAPTER TWENTY

GESTURE WITHOUT MOTION

I called Tristan on his burner phone from the taco stand. "He doesn't know anything. He's not the guy."

"How do you know?"

"He said he found it in the parking lot of his apartment complex, lying on the ground next to his truck."

"And you believed him?"

"I did. Honestly. He was terrified by the badge and all that stuff. He'd have given up his own mother to get me to go away, and when I mentioned the feds, he about dropped his taco. By the way, I went with INS instead of the FBI."

"And you really believed him?"

"It was written all over his face, the idea that he was going to get deported for finding a camera on the ground. He started telling me about his wife and three daughters, just trying to make a living."

"So you felt bad for him."

"Of course." *With all that empathy I have.*

"I dunno, man."

"He showed me paperwork for his apartment. He's nowhere near that mobile-home park."

"Maybe he has friends there."

"Maybe he does. If so, he'd be grilling out and drinking beer with them, not strolling around the woods. Also, his place is halfway between there and Austin, right off 290."

"So?"

"So, it's a perfect place to dump stolen goods. Pull off the road, drop it out the window as you pass some dolt's truck . . ."

"But why take it if you're just going to dump it?"

"I don't know, Tristan. Maybe he didn't know what it was or changed his mind about keeping or trying to sell it. I'm telling you, raiding this guy's apartment and scaring his family won't do anything for us. It's a dead end. And maybe that's a good thing."

"How so?"

"If the police somehow track him down, he's not spilling his guts because he's got no guts to spill."

"So we just let it go?" Tristan asked.

"Yeah, I think it's the only thing we can do. Loose end tied off."

"I've been thinking about that other thing that's weird."

"Which one?"

"The scrunched-up newspaper in the bags. I just don't get it."

"Me neither, matey. It's weird, for sure."

"Yeah. So what now?" Tristan asked.

"I'll dump the camera, for good this time."

"Okay. Oh shit."

"What?"

"There's someone at the door, hang on." I heard movement in the background, Tristan's breathing as he went to the door. His voice was quiet when he next spoke, like he'd looked through the peephole and didn't want the visitor to hear him. "Dom?"

"Yeah, I'm still here. Who is it?"

"Should I let her in? It's your new girlfriend."

○

I lied. I wasn't at the taco stand when I called Tristan. I was at her house. More accurately, in my car half a block away from her house, watching it, waiting for her to appear. Not that she was expecting me; I wanted *her* to be surprised for a change. So much for that.

She'd been easy to find. I knew she lived with her brother, and his information, including his address, was in the juvenile system. Easy peasy.

Her house was like so many in this part of town, small and ramshackle, circled by a broken fence. Since she wasn't home, when I hung up with Tristan I got out and walked along the cracked sidewalk. Her front yard was only slightly bigger than a large dining table, just not as neat. Hip-high clumps of grass and weeds grew up around, and swallowed, an old hand-cart and a rusted bicycle that had no wheels. At some point, the homeowners on the street had painted their houses red, blue, yellow, and green, as if color could make up for poverty. But those colors had long since faded and the whole street looked old and tired, like it had given up hope of being cared for or was waiting for the clean cut of the bulldozer to end things. Her house was a sun-bleached yellow, with the gutters poking away from the roof like strands of wild hair.

I paused when I saw movement in a window. A moment later, the door opened and her little brother came out, baggy jeans, a hoodie, and wary eyes. He had pale skin, like he was sick, but his eyes were dark brown and clear.

"You fucking my sister?" he asked. I couldn't tell if he was annoyed, interested, or trying to get a reaction.

"Not right now."

"Where you from?" His head was cocked to one side, and while he may have been studying me, he didn't seem scared of me. A good thing, if I was going to be fucking his sister.

"England. Near London. Know where that is?"

"You think I'm an idiot because I live here? Because I picked up a case?"

"Most Americans couldn't find New York on a map," I said. "Let alone London. I was just asking."

"What are you going to do with my case?"

"I'm not allowed to talk to you about that."

"Are you the prosecutor on it?"

"No, I'm not."

"Then why can't you talk to me about it?"

Jesus, twenty fucking questions. I like this kid.

"Where's your sister?" I asked.

"Where's yours?"

"Dead."

"Oh."

"Not really. You want to tell me where she is?"

"Nah. That's her business."

"And what's yours?"

"School. Good grades. Not getting caught." He shrugged. "I'm on paper." *On paper.* Otherwise known as probation. For people like me, white people with a job, probation was the death knell to a career because it meant you had a criminal conviction. Out here, for kids who idolized rap stars and for whom a job promotion meant slinging crack and meth instead of weed, being on paper was like a Cub Scout merit badge.

"Instead of not getting caught, how about not committing crimes?"

"Sure. I was planning to do that this afternoon."

"Just the two of you live here?"

"Why, you gonna break in when I leave?"

"No. I'm a prosecutor."

"Don't break the law, huh?"

"Try not to. Well?"

"Yeah. Just us."

I reached into my pocket and took out my wallet. When I opened it up, his eyes fixated on the gold shield. I took out a ten and held it out.

"What's that for?" he asked.

"Help you stay out of trouble. Go to the movies or something."

He took it with a sly smile and eyed the bill. "By myself, huh?"

I laughed and gave him another one. "Take a girlfriend. Boy-friend. Whatever."

He tucked the money into a pocket. "Right. Gotta split," he said, then turned and strolled away down the sidewalk. He looked once over his shoulder, and half raised a hand to wave good-bye. I just nodded.

I thought about waiting there for her, but I wondered if we were in the middle of some sort of power play, and waiting around in the hope someone shows up never looks good. Plus, it was bloody hot outside.

On my way out of the neighborhood, I drove past little Bobby. He was sitting on a low brick wall with a friend, a black kid wearing the same uniform of baggy pants and a hoodie, plus a baseball cap, its oversized beak as big as his face. They both stared at me as I cruised by, and I wondered if Bobby had told him anything. I hoped not.

CHAPTER TWENTY-ONE

IN THE WIND'S SINGING

When I got to the apartment, she wasn't there, but Tristan was acting like he had hot rocks in his shoes. He kept coming and going from his room, checking what was on TV or getting ice from the fridge.

"She stay long?" I asked. "Not still in your room, is she?"

His mouth dropped open, then he realized I was joking. "Yeah, right. She sure is."

"Is everything all right? You're being weird."

"I'm fine, just … you know. Nervous about everything. Seen the news?"

"Not today."

"I can't decide whether to watch or not."

"Don't bother. If there's a major break in the case, one that's bad for us, we'll find out before they put it on TV."

"Very reassuring, Dom."

We both looked at the door as someone knocked. "You expecting company?" I asked.

He shook his head and went to the door. He looked through the peephole and seemed to hesitate before opening it. "Your girl-friend's back," he muttered.

"Then let her in."

He did so and she floated in, giving Tristan the kind of smile that makes a man jealous. He wouldn't look at her.

Mother fucker.

"Hey guys. I left my keys here, I think." Her voice was soft, matter-of-fact. "Mind if I look?"

"Err, well . . ." Tristan said, but she didn't wait for a complete answer. She went straight to his room, opened the door, and disappeared inside. I stared at Tristan.

"She used my shower," he said, eyes on the floor and his voice low.

"That's weird, because I have a shower in my room, too."

She reappeared, jangling her keys. "Thanks, guys. I wouldn't mind so much if I had a car. Backtracking on the bus is a pain." She looked me in the eye. "But I do have a phone. I'll call you."

"Yeah," I said. "Do that."

Tristan and I stood in the living room like statues, watching her and each other as she moved to the door and let herself out.

"So," I said to Tristan, once she'd gone. "You were saying?"

He collapsed onto the sofa. "Dude. This week, it's been all fucked up. I don't know what's happening anymore. Who I am or what I'm doing, I mean it's crazy, it's all so crazy."

He was starting to sound like me, changing the subject and going for sympathy with one, well-executed ramble. Except, not so well-executed. "Did you have sex with her?" I asked.

He looked up, his eyes wide. "No, dude, I didn't. I swear."

I couldn't tell if he was lying or not, so I just stared at him. "Then explain."

He held his breath for a few seconds, then let it out with a sigh. "Fine. And you can yell and scream and punch me in the face, I don't care. I don't fucking care."

"Tristan, what did you do?"

"She showed up, looking for you. We talked for a while, she asked me a lot of questions about myself. She's kind of . . . hard to talk to. Like, she wouldn't talk about herself. Anyway, after a while, she said the water in her house wasn't working and could she take a shower. I thought it was a little weird, but fine, and I thought she was asking for permission to use your room, your shower. I was in the kitchen, making toast, so I just waved her on, but she went into my bathroom. I didn't know what to do, I just stood there. You know I don't like people in my bedroom or bathroom. I figured she'd realize it was mine and come right back out but . . . I heard the water running."

"And then?"

"She called out to me. My name." He swallowed heavily. "She said she needed a towel, she was kind of laughing like she'd been silly not to think of it earlier. I got a towel from the dryer and stopped in the hallway, but it was wide open, the bathroom door. She asked me to bring it in there."

"So you did."

"Yeah. I shut my eyes, man, I did. But then I had to open them to see where to put the towel, like on the sink." He sighed again. "Then she opened the curtain, like, actually put her head out. And her hand, with a bar of soap. She told me to wash her back."

I could have laughed. "She told you to."

"Yes."

"So you did."

"She made me close the bathroom door to keep the heat in, then she opened the curtain and turned around, turned her back to me. Dude, I'm telling you, it was like . . . I was just standing there with the soap in my hand. What was I supposed to do?"

"Wash her back, apparently."

"Yeah." He nodded like he was remembering a dream. "So I did."

"How was it?" My voice was quiet and he looked up, surprised, like he expected me to be yelling.

"It was weird. I didn't touch her anywhere, man, I promise. I just washed her back with the soap, and the wash cloth, and that was it. She said thanks and closed the curtain. I left, and closed the door behind me. I promise, Dom, I didn't touch her, like *that*. She just wanted me to . . . you know."

"Yeah, wash her back. Why, do you think?" I asked.

"I don't know man." He sat quietly for a moment, then shook his head. "I don't think I get it. Get her, I mean . . . I just can't decide if she's fucking with me or," he stopped talking and shrugged. "Or maybe it's you that she's fucking with."

"Yes," I said. "I was rather wondering the same thing."

O

Tristan left me alone pretty quickly. He wasn't sure how badly he'd screwed up, but I could tell that a part of him wanted to brag a little—given his job and personality, I was pretty sure this was the closest he'd been to a naked girl for a while.

I sat on my bed with my guitar but didn't feel like playing. Something was bugging me and I couldn't figure out what. As it turned out, I wasn't the only one with concerns, because at two o'clock Otto called.

"Can we meet?" he said.

"Why?"

"We need to talk about something."

"So talk."

"No. Just the two of us."

"Has something happened?"

"That's what I want to talk about," he said.

"We're not supposed to be seen together, remember?"

"I don't care. This afternoon."

"Fine, meet me at Gillis Park." I checked my watch. "An hour from now."

I lay back on the bed and stared at the ceiling. *What the hell did he want?* It had something to do with Tristan, obviously, but what? I didn't get anywhere thinking about it, so I logged on to my computer and did some work. I'd gone from trying cases to processing forms, and while I minded the downgrade, I found the repetitive nature of the work soothing. Fifteen minutes before the rendezvous, I logged off and went into the living room. Tristan was sprawled on the couch, watching a home-repair show.

"Can I ask you something?" he said.

"I'm on my way out."

"Where?"

"Get some fresh air."

"Want company?"

"No, not really."

"I can't stop thinking about the money. Specifically, the scrunched-up paper. Have you thought about that?"

"A lot," I said. "You have a theory?"

"Sort of. I mean, think about it, the only reason to do that is to make the bags look full, right?"

"Sure, I guess so."

"Must be. So all I can think is, whoever took the money and put the paper in there must have wanted us to retrieve the bags and leave the area before realizing they were empty. Plus, no one drives around with newspaper in their car."

"So you think the person who took our money lives at the mobile-home park?"

"They must. And since most people there are . . . well, probably don't have bank accounts, I'm guessing the money is still there. Sitting in someone's trailer under a blanket or stuffed into an ice chest."

"Maybe, but there are a hundred trailers in that place. You have a way to figure out which one has our money?"

"Nope." Tristan smiled. "That's about as far as I got."

"Makes sense to me." I started toward the door. "I'll think about it. Maybe surveillance cameras again, but I don't really know what we'd be looking for."

"Maybe someone showing up in a nice new car?"

"Could be. Keep thinking." I left him on the couch and walked out.

Otto was already in the parking lot, pacing in front of his car, which surprised me because it was ninety-five degrees out there. I could see dark circles of sweat under his armpits. I'd chosen Gillis Park because it was the kind of park where people minded their own business. Illegal business, usually. Kids bought and sold weed, scraggly crack heads shuffled about, hoping their dealer would show and be generous, and the public restrooms were no-go zones for kids. As long as you kept your head down and didn't get in anyone's business, you'd be unnoticed and unremembered. I'd handled an aggravated-robbery case that happened there. Three men with guns robbed two other men in broad daylight. Police had arrived on scene within minutes and detained nineteen people for questioning. No one had seen anything. Nothing.

We walked slowly toward a stand of trees beside the basketball court, where three black guys were teaching a Hispanic girl how to shoot hoops. The men were shirtless, their muscles like knotted rope, glistening with sweat. It looked more like a mating dance to me, the men competing for the pretty lady's attention with their bodies, their words, their moves.

"So what's up?" I said.

He stopped and looked at me. "Take your sunglasses off."

"What?"

"Take them off, I want to ask you something. And I want to look in your eyes when I do."

"My eyes?" I smiled. "They won't tell you anything."

"Dom, I'm not kidding."

"Fine." I removed my sunglasses and looked him in the eye.

"Do you have the money?"

"What?" I was genuinely surprised. Of course, if I'd had the money, he was hoping to see panic. He wouldn't have seen it, because that's not something I do. Lying is what I do, and there's no way in hell he'd have been able to tell. But I couldn't believe he was asking me that, so the surprise he saw, that was real.

"Answer the question."

"No, Otto, I don't have the money."

He shook his head and smiled. "I know that. I know you don't. Just wanted to ask."

"What the hell are you talking about?"

He chewed his lip for a moment, then said, "I've been thinking. I don't know, man, I want to be wrong about this, but . . ."

"But what?"

"Dude, I think Tristan has our money."

CHAPTER TWENTY-TWO

ON A BROKEN COLUMN

We sat on a graffiti-covered bench, a slight breeze coming through the trees and in the shade the temperature was almost bearable. But I could smell Otto beside me, dank and strong. I inched away.

"I know it sounds crazy," Otto said. "But I really think he went back for it."

"That makes no sense."

"To you, maybe, but to me it does."

"Explain."

"It's not one thing he's done or said—it's a bunch of little things."

"You being an idiot is one of them."

"No, man, I'm serious. I'll run through them, and you can tell me if I'm still an idiot. First, he's way more worried about the dead guys than the money."

"We shot two people. That's a big deal, Otto, how would he *not* be concerned about that?"

"Because he didn't do the shooting. And I know that doesn't make a difference legally, but as far as how he feels, that should matter. Plus, those guys weren't angels, and that's a shitload of money he doesn't seem to care about."

"Weak. What else?"

"He's acting weird. He won't look me in the eye, and have you noticed how he's taken a backseat to all the planning and figuring out of stuff?"

"I didn't notice that, no. And he won't look you in the eye because he's a computer nerd and basically has Asperger's."

"Yeah, well, I saved the best for last. We each rode out there to check on the police situation, right?"

"Right."

"Get mad at me if you want, but I kept an eye on you both."

"Otto, seriously?"

"Be glad I did. You drove out there, did a quick turnaround when you saw the patrol cars, and came home. Same thing I did. Tristan did something while he was out there, though."

"Like what?"

"There's a patch of dirt on the other side of the road from the entrance to the mobile-home park. That's where I watched you both from, backed in between some trees. I think there's a bus stop there, but it's pitch black at night, no light there at all, so a good place to watch from. Anyway, like I said, you went in and out. Tristan went in, drove to the left side, where it all happened, where the woods are. He parked his car, and got out, walked in that direction."

"What direction?"

"Toward the trees."

"Did he have a bag with him?"

"I couldn't see. He went between a couple of double-wides; they had outside lights but it was like he was half in and half out of light, so I couldn't tell. Plus, he was about fifty yards away so it was difficult to see."

"How long was he gone?"

"He was out of my sight for nine minutes and twenty seconds. Used the stopwatch on my phone."

"Maybe he was just checking the place out."

"Maybe. And maybe he was taking our money. You know, he's a lot smarter and sneakier than he acts."

"Possibly, but then again he's not the one spying on his colleagues."

"You should be glad I did, because I haven't told you the best bit. He went from the mobile-home park straight to a self-storage facility."

"Oh? Now I'm mildly interested."

"Yeah, figured."

"What did he do in there?"

"No clue. They had a security gate so I couldn't get in."

Two young black men walked toward us with that cocky swagger kids adopted when trying to look tough. One wore a red ball cap, Chicago Bulls shirt, and red shorts; the other was dressed in all blue. The first time I'd seen this, a Crip and a Blood hanging out together, I'd been on a police ride-along. "It's not like LA here," the young cop had told me. "They don't take the gang stuff so seriously in Austin, except for the Mexican gangs. Here, it's about selling dope, not owning turf. There's even a saying: red and blue makes green. It's all about the money."

We watched as the two men angled off to our right, heading for the outdoor swimming pool where half a dozen families were splashing about. They edged around the pool to the lifeguard. He hopped down from his high chair, and they exchanged fist bumps and half hugs. They were a hundred yards away, so I couldn't be sure, but it looked to me like the kid in blue handed off something to the lifeguard.

"So," I said. "Nice as it is out here, I feel the need for some air-conditioning. Maybe lunch."

"That an invitation?"

"No. Are we done here?"

"What about the storage facility? What are you going to do about Tristan?"

"Nothing. There's nothing to be done. Which means that you're going to stop being paranoid and leave him alone as well."

"Seriously?"

"Look. I didn't know he had a storage locker. I also don't know what kind of underwear he has on. I don't believe he has the balls to go back into those woods, while the police are standing right there, and haul out all our money."

"You think that's more unlikely than someone wandering aimlessly around in the trees and stumbling on two bags that you buried?"

"I didn't bury them, I covered them up. And not very well, apparently." I stood and looked down at Otto. "Look, it fucking sucks we lost the money. But we committed capital murder and so far we're free and clear. It's been a week and the police aren't anywhere near us. We need to hold it together, individually and as a group. We start pointing fingers at each other, Otto, things will go downhill very fast indeed."

He nodded. "I guess. But keep an eye on him. If he starts buying himself expensive new shit, I want to know about it. And do me a favor. Call your buddy Gus. You seem to think we can trust him, but . . . just call him, will you?"

"Yeah, sure." I smiled. "So how do you know I'm not in on some scheme to defraud you? With Tristan or Gus?"

Otto shrugged. "We go back, me and you. And I'm a good judge of character. I just don't think you have it in you to double-cross me like that."

○

When I got back to the apartment, I called Gus's phone like I said I would, and left a message. Ten minutes later, my phone rang, and his name showed up.

"Howdy, Gus."

"Dominic, it's me." Gus's wife, Michelle.

"Oh, hey, how're you?"

"Not good. Have you seen Gus?"

"Not for a few days, actually. Everything okay?"

"I don't . . . I don't know. He went to work yesterday, had meetings all day so I didn't talk to him. He didn't come home, so I tried calling his phone and it rang by the bed, he'd left it at home."

"Did he play a gig maybe? Get stuck out at a bar?"

"No, he'd have told me and there's nothing on the calendar on his phone. Plus, why would he stay out all night?"

"I don't know. Has he done this before?"

She hesitated. "A couple of times." *So much for the perfect, doting husband.* "He's not . . . he loves me, he just sometimes gets . . . side-tracked. He gets so into his music when he's playing, and so do other people, girls. You know how it is. Then, if he stays at the bar and drinks, well . . ."

Only I'd never seen him like that. And no reason he'd hide it from me because I didn't care who he slept with, and I'd told him that. In fact, he'd screwed up a couple of great opportunities for me by bailing out of a foursome and going home. The idea that he'd go to work without his phone, stay out all night without letting Michelle know, not go home the next day, *and not include me*, just didn't compute.

"Honestly, Michelle, I've never seen him with anyone else. Even show interest in anyone else. I really mean that."

"That's nice of you to say. But it's okay, I don't expect others to understand our relationship."

"Hey, if you ask me, you never know anyone else, Michelle, unless maybe you're married to them. Whatever you guys have going on, I'm not doing any judging."

"Thanks. Right now I just want to find him, make sure he's okay. It's not like Gus to not call."

"I agree. I spoke to him a few days ago but haven't seen him or heard from him since . . ." I thought back, "I guess since Monday or Tuesday."

That hesitation again. "Can I ask you something?"

"Sure."

"A few weeks ago, he was being weird. Not very weird, and with him it's hard to tell sometimes. But he was all excited about something, nervous but giddy as well, like that time he put his album together. This time, though, he wouldn't tell me what it was about, and I'm pretty sure it wasn't about his music."

"I don't think I noticed . . ."

"That's the thing. It had something to do with you. He kept disappearing off to meet with you, and you came over here one time. I thought maybe you were working on something together."

"No," I said. "I mean, we play together sometimes, critique each other's songs, but I don't really know what to tell you. I don't recall him acting weird, and we weren't working on any project together."

"What about that girl, the one who called here?"

"She's my girlfriend—he didn't tell you that?"

"He did. I just . . . wanted to be sure."

"She is. Her idea of a practical joke, sorry."

"Huh. Okay. Well, if you have any ideas, please call me. I'll have his phone with me. This just isn't like him." Her voice caught, like she was going to cry. "If he's not back tomorrow, I'll have to file a missing-person's report."

○

This didn't sound like Gus. Turns out he could be an asshole, like most men, but not getting in contact with Michelle for so long? Obviously I didn't know him like I thought I did; I'd swallowed the perfect house/husband line, but that wasn't even what Michelle was worried about. If he could get away with the occasional dalliance, why wouldn't he call home if he'd done it again? The closest you can get to knowing someone, as I'd said to Michelle, was being married to them. Apparently that didn't always pan out. Despite the prevailing wisdom about people like me, I'd never tried marriage.

I scored a rare zero on the Hare checklist question that asked about "Many Short-Term Marital Relationships," not because I didn't have the urge, the raging impulse to impress the hell out of some girl by professing my love and proposing marriage, but because the smarter side of me knew that it wouldn't work. She'd get to know me and my cover would be blown. And the marriage blown too, of course, but that'd be a big deal to her, not me. Maintaining cover was my main goal, not marital bliss. Or disaster, as the reality would be. But Gus . . . it sounded like he had some kind of accord with Michelle, if not acceptance then tolerance, and if not tolerance then studied ignorance. But that didn't include abandoning her, clearly, because that was her concern. That Gus had fallen in love and skipped off with a bar-room floozy.

I didn't think that for a minute.

Gus knew about our plan, and I was pretty sure I knew what Otto and Tristan were worried about. That he had some kind of revelation, some change of heart. They were wondering whether he followed us and saw where we put the money, then went back and helped himself. Maybe he filled his pockets with our loot and left his wife, because maybe that shack on a Costa Rican beach looked like a possibility to him. At Michelle's expense. And ours.

But me, I didn't think that for a minute.

CHAPTER TWENTY-THREE

WITH DIRECT EYES

On Sunday, Tristan went to church. I didn't know he even owned a Bible, and once he'd gone, I tried the handle to his bedroom in the vague hope he'd forgotten to lock it. No such luck.

It wasn't that I believed Otto, or thought he was right about Tristan. No, that Poindexter barely had the balls to drive past the mobile-home park at night, let alone sneak in there and go digging up the forest floor with cops lingering nearby. I figured Otto had exaggerated, letting his paranoia see more than there was to be seen. At some point, I'd come out and ask Tristan about his trip to the trailer park and his storage locker. But, as any good trial lawyer will tell you: when the stakes are high, don't ask a question you don't already know the answer to.

One thing, though, I didn't like Tristan's change in routine. This disappearance to church, it made me nervous. I sure as hell didn't want him getting all religious and confessing his sins to some guy in a dress with an overly tuned sense of right and wrong.

The other problem with straight out asking him was that I'd have had to wait, and waiting was hard for me at the best of times. My music usually provided enough stimulation to keep me out of trouble, but Otto's accusations, and events generally, had put pressure on my natural self and forced cracks in the shell I'd constructed, and dangerous little pieces of me were looking to squeeze out. When self-preservation, my own life and freedom, were at stake, my incapacity for inaction always became unbearable.

So, assuming he'd be out for another hour at least, I rattled the door to his bedroom one more time, then picked the lock.

Both of our doors had pin-and-tumbler locks, more secure than those you usually find in apartments where a button on the door handle pretends to be security. I had no idea whether they came with the place or if Tristan had them installed. Either way, I had the tension wrench and pick that I'd bought online, tools I'd practiced with on my own door when Tristan was out.

I knelt on the carpet outside his room and got to work. The tension wrench went into the bottom of the keyhole. I twisted it slightly in the direction the door should unlock, and put the pick into the upper portion of the key hole. I ran it back and forth, picturing the five pins that dropped down into the tumbler, keeping the door locked. I started with the most stubborn of the pins, pressing it up out of the cylinder until I heard a faint click. I upped the torque on the wrench, just a hair's breadth, to make sure the pin stayed up and out of the way, then found the next pin. And the next after that until, with a final, gentle click, Tristan's door swung open.

I went in and looked around.

A queen-size bed lay to the left, taking up most of that wall. A flat-screen TV hung to my right. Opposite me, his windows looked out over the parking lot, and under the windows he'd put two desks, end to end. A desktop computer sat on the left, a laptop on the right, and various electronic debris was scattered in the spaces between, cables, chargers, and mini speakers. Matching bedside tables sat either side of his bed, the one nearest me bearing an alarm clock, the one the other side of the bed carrying a stack of books.

I started in his closet, a small walk-in just past his TV. It was emptier than most closets, but then I wouldn't have expected him to have too many clothes. He was a geek, and not in a metrosexual way. One corner held his laundry basket, another was filled by a tumble of sneakers and work shoes, and the one behind me to my right was a stacking place for three wheeled suitcases, each a different size.

I flipped the light on, unzipped the top case, and peered inside. Empty. I put my hands in all the pockets but came up with nothing. I dumped the case and tried the second, then the third. No money, and no guns.

I restacked the bags and looked in his laundry basket, holding my breath. He didn't empty it as often as he should have, and it took an unpleasant thirty seconds to be sure there was nothing stashed at the bottom.

I went to his double desk next, resisting the urge to go wash my hands first, and checked each drawer methodically. I knew what I was looking for, guns or money, so I went through them quickly, and I couldn't decide whether to be relieved or frustrated when all I found was batteries, instructions manuals, and three flashlights. Not even any porn, though he had the Internet for that. I got to the last drawer, the bottom one in the left-hand desk. I tugged the little handle, but it didn't open. I pulled harder, but it stayed shut. A tiny keyhole told me I'd found the one interesting place in his room.

I perched on the edge of his bed and began the lock-pick routine. The keyhole was small, almost too small, but I managed to get the tension wrench into the bottom of the slot. I slipped up several times, letting the pins pop back into place accidentally and having to start again. Five long minutes later, I was intently focused on the last of the six pins when I heard the front door. I slid the drawer open and quickly looked inside. Its contents had nothing to do with our heist, but I saw why he kept it locked, and I smiled. I closed the drawer, locked it, and twisted toward the door.

"Hey!" Tristan stared at me, bug-eyed, his face reddening. "What the fuck are you doing in my room?"

His eyes left me and went to the little drawer, so I palmed my tools and stared at him, choosing my lie. My options were outrage (*You're damn right I broke in here, you've been acting so weird and Otto thinks you have our money, so what the fuck is going on? Locking your doors, pawing my girlfriend, pretending you're going to church?*

Are you fucking kidding me?) or apology. The former created conflict and gave me a modicum of power over him, the latter defused conflict and gave him power over me. A wonderful weapon, the apology.

"Shit, Tristan." I stood and slipped my tools into my pocket. "I'm so sorry. I know this is wrong and I know you have nothing to hide—"

"Yeah, now you've been through my fucking stuff." He was furious, planting his righteous anger in the middle of my apology, just like I wanted him to.

"I know, you're right, totally right. I just ... everything's been so fucked up this past week or so, like you said yourself ... man you've been weird. I suppose we all have, but you've not been yourself. I mean, I know she asked for it, but walking in on my girlfriend like that. And pretending you're going to church, I mean what's that about?" I held up my hands in apology, not giving him a chance to respond. "But that doesn't make this okay, I know that. I know that, and I'm truly sorry. It won't happen again, I promise."

Tristan stood aside to let me out, then looked down at his door knob. "How did you get in?"

"It was unlocked."

"No, dude, it wasn't. I always lock it."

"I don't ..." I put on my confused face. "I don't know, then. I just tried the handle and I swear it just ... well, you know, I did rattle it pretty hard. Maybe that's what did it? Maybe you locked it and it came loose somehow, when I shook it. That's all I can think, I don't really know."

I went into the living room and sank onto the couch. Tristan hovered near his bedroom door, eyeing it and me. I knew he was unsettled, not just by my intrusion but also by my attitude because he'd never seen me apologize to anyone before, for anything. It was his first encounter with a contrite Dominic, and he didn't know how to handle it.

"Seriously, I'm so sorry. But there's one thing I should tell you, even though now's not the best time."

His eyes narrowed. "Tell me what?"

"The reason I went into your room."

"To snoop. Because you don't trust me."

"Not me. Look, I wanted to be able to tell Otto he was wrong. And I can, I can do that now because there's nothing in your room—"

"Wait, Otto? What do you mean, tell him he's wrong?"

"He called me yesterday. He wanted me to meet with him because he had this stupid fucking idea that maybe you . . . knew where the money was?"

"What?" His eyes widened into saucers, and I knew for sure that he was truly shocked by the allegation.

"I know." I held up placating hands. "I met with him, and told him he was full of crap. I told him we've all been acting weirdly, not just you, and that there's no way in hell you'd try to double-cross us, just like I wouldn't and he wouldn't."

"I don't believe I'm hearing this."

"Good, because I was horrified, too. And now, as wrong as that was, I can tell Otto I went into your room and all I found were some smelly socks and a stack of porn magazines. Actually, no porn magazines."

The joke went by him. "Why would Otto think that?"

"He said he watched both of us when we went out there, when we were checking on the police. He said that you parked and walked around the trailer park for about ten minutes. Did you do that?"

"Yeah, of course. I didn't see the cops so I parked in the area near that shitty office. I didn't want to be driving around so I just walked. The place creeped me out, so as soon as I saw the cop car I left."

"Yeah, I told Otto it was something like that."

"I didn't go into the fucking woods, I'm not stupid."

I watched him carefully for his reaction to my next question. "And the storage facility you went to right after that?"

He was quiet for a second, as his brain traced back to that night, a look of slight confusion on his face. "The storage . . . I went to get some speakers. For my new iPod. When you moved in, I had to pack a lot of my crap and . . . Wait, how did you know I went there?"

"Otto. He followed you. He couldn't see what you were doing, so he got suspicious." I held up both hands as if in surrender. "That's him, not me."

I thought he'd explode with anger, I know I would have, but instead he leaned against the wall and shook his head. "What have we done, man? What are we becoming?"

"Nothing, Tristan. Nothing at all. Just stay cool and everything will be fine. Otto will shut the hell up, we'll all keep a low profile, and everything will work out."

"We can't do that, man, we can't be accusing each other of shit."

"I know, and I agree. Maybe we can have a sit-down with Otto and clear the air."

"Yeah," he said. "I've a few things to say to him."

"No, like you just said, we can't be turning on each other. So when everyone's calmed down, you, me, and him, we'll get together."

Something in my voice made him look at me. "What?"

"No, nothing. Don't worry."

"Dude, tell me."

I paused, as if to think about it. "While we're on the subject, it's my friend Gus."

"What about him? Don't tell me he wants a cut."

"No, no. Quite the opposite, I suppose you could say."

"Meaning?"

"He's disappeared. His wife called me yesterday, he went out a couple of days ago and hasn't come home or even phoned her since."

Tristan looked wary. "That common for him?"

"No. Not at all."

"So you think it might have something to do with . . . our money?"

"Seems like odd timing, don't you think?"

"Yeah, very. What should we do?"

"I think I'm going to head over to his place, talk to Michelle again. I might have a little look around while I'm over there. Anyway, if she's not heard from him, there's only one thing I can do. I hate to, but I don't think I have a choice."

"What do you mean?"

"I think I'll have to call the police."

CHAPTER TWENTY-FOUR

DISTANT AND MORE SOLEMN

Tristan stared at me, like he wasn't sure if I was kidding. I assured him I wasn't.

"There's no way," he said. "You're the last person to be calling the cops. What will you tell them?"

"It's the only way. The trick is to control the situation. If you let others take control or leave it to fate, then you're screwed. If I'm with Michelle and we call, then I'll know what she tells them and I'll be able to tell them I know nothing. Much better than having them snoop around and catch us by surprise with questions when we're not expecting them."

"They won't talk to me. I don't know the guy."

"Which is why I'll be the one going to see Michelle. Look, I know how it works. Some patrol guy will roll up an hour after the call, eyeball this pretty housewife, see me there being all supportive, and figure it's a love triangle, which he wants nothing to do with. He'll take a report, enter it into the system, and that's that. If I'm not there, the hot housewife is a little more alluring, and in the interest of staying longer the cop asks more questions. We don't want that."

"That's for damn sure."

"So sit tight and I'll check in later."

"Do you really think he might have taken off with our money? I mean, you know him best."

"I sincerely doubt it. More likely he got rolled in an alley and has a headache and bad memory in a hospital bed somewhere. Or he's banging some groupie chick who likes the way he sings."

"I hope so."

I feigned awkwardness, shifting from foot to foot. "Hey, I don't mean to be a jerk or anything, but I'd like to put the storage-facility thing to rest."

"What do you mean?"

"I thought maybe I could drive by there on my way to see Michelle."

"My unit?" He chewed his lip. "And what, look inside?"

"Just so I can tell Otto I did. Make him realize he's being an idiot."

"Why not just tell him you did?"

"I don't know, I don't want to lie. He's a cop, they're good at spotting that."

"You know why this pisses me off so much?"

"Tell me," I said.

"Because I've gone out of my way to look out for him, and you. I told you before, you left some stuff on your computer, and I went on and cleared it. Didn't tell you, didn't make a big deal, I was just looking out for you. For us. And this is my thanks."

"Wow, I didn't know that. Thank you, Tristan, really. And look, I'm trying to do the same as you, keep us together and safe. It's just that reassuring Otto has become a part of me looking out for us. Even though you're right, I shouldn't have to, not by nosing through your stuff."

I could see him thinking, and finally he nodded. "Okay, that's fine."

"Great. Thanks. That'll make him feel better, stop being so paranoid." I started for the door. "Oh wait."

"What?"

"With everything that's going on . . . mind if I use your car?"

"Why?"

"Now it's me being paranoid but if someone working there knows your car, associates with that unit and then sees my car pull up. . . . Am I overthinking this?"

"Yeah, a little." He smiled. "But seeing what's happened, I'm fine with you overthinking our safety. I wasn't planning on going anywhere for a while. What time will you be back?"

"Couple of hours, no more."

"Go for it. The code at the gate is all sevens, four of them. I'll get you my keys."

Fifteen minutes later, the gate rattled and shook as it slid out of the way. I pulled though and headed to Tristan's lock-up, which lay at one end of a long row of orange-doored units.

I used the key he'd given me to undo the padlock and yanked the sliding door up. A switch to my left turned on a light bulb that sat protected by its own wire cage. The unit was about ten feet wide and ten deep, and mostly empty. It smelled of dust and some sort of chemical. A battered, brown sofa sat against the right-hand wall, its matching armchair against the left. Various electronic gadgets were piled on the furniture and floor, old computer monitors and processing units, some ancient music speakers, and what looked like miles of cables, white, black, and gray lying on the floor and spilling out of cardboard boxes.

Two old file cabinets, faded green metal, sat side by side at the back of the unit. I moved inside, pulling the door down behind me. I looked quickly under the sofa and chair cushions, then moved the speakers and cables around with my foot. I didn't expect to find anything. I never believed Tristan had double-crossed us, but this way I could honestly tell Otto I'd looked. The filing cabinet was next. I looked through each of the six drawers. Four were empty. One held stacks of papers, old bills and tax forms, musty with age. The other had a small gun safe in it, about the size of a shoe box. It had a combination lock, which Tristan hadn't mentioned, but there was no way it could have held all our money, so I didn't worry about it.

I took one more look around the space, slid open the door, and locked up carefully behind me.

○

I pulled into Gus's driveway twenty minutes later. Michelle met me at the front door, wringing her hands and upset, but it looked like she was glad to see a friendly face.

"No word?" I asked.

"Nothing."

I sat in the living room, and she brought me iced tea, a vile substance that all true Englishmen despise. I put it down on the coffee table. She sat opposite me and wouldn't meet my eye.

"Can I ask you something?" she said.

"Anything."

"And please. Please, be honest, I can handle anything, I just want the truth."

"Sure."

She looked at me intently, her head slightly cocked to one side like a dog waiting to sniff out a lie. "Is he seeing someone else?"

"No." I shook my head, pleased I didn't have to lie. "At least, not that I know of. I promise, I've always seen him as faithful and loving. That sounds trite, but it's true. Even when we were out . . . I know what you said on the phone the other day, but I've never seen that. I certainly don't know anything about him seeing someone."

"Okay." She stayed in that position, staring at me. "One other thing. I mentioned it the other day, but I've been thinking more about it. Can't get it out of my head. That thing a few weeks ago, when you and he met a couple of times. He said something at the time . . ." My face was a mask. *That stupid fucking idiot.* "I can't remember what, and I know he was vague, but I felt like you two were planning something."

"I've been thinking, too, and it had to be music stuff, I'm sure. Otherwise, I don't really—"

"No, it wasn't. You guys always do that here, or at your place. Usually the den here. So I don't think it was that."

"I don't remember, honestly. Although ..." My voice trailed off.

"What?"

"No, I doubt it but ... we've talked about him maybe doing some consulting work with the DA's office, but that was early stages. Not much more than me offering to talk to the hierarchy about it."

"What do you mean consulting work?"

"We're getting a lot of cases with foreign nationals. Mexicans mostly, but other Central and Southern Americans. Every time they pick up a felony charge, their defense attorney comes into court and tries to get us to drop or reduce charges by saying that if we don't, they'll get deported. You know, play the sympathy card about the three kids and pregnant wife who will starve if their client gets booted out of the country. The rules about deportation are complicated, so it'd be nice to have a reliable immigration attorney to consult with, to find out if they're blowing smoke or actually telling us the truth in each case."

"Huh. Why wouldn't he just come out and tell me about that?"

"I don't know." *Probably because it's a steaming pile of horseshit that I just made up.* "Like I say, it wasn't much more than a suggestion. But we did talk about it, to see if he was interested and to see how it'd work. Maybe he wanted to wait until it was a real possibility before saying anything."

"Maybe. Was he acting weird in the last week or two?"

I gave her a kind smile. "I was going to ask you the same thing."

"No. Worried about work, but nothing new there."

Her eyes settled on her phone. "Will you ... will you help me call the hospitals?"

"No need, I already did." *True.* "Nothing."

"Really? I figured they only answer family about health stuff."

"Normally," I said. "Family and prosecutors."

"Ah, of course. Thank you for doing that."

"Of course, Michelle, he's my friend."

"And now?"

"Now I think we should call the police."

○

In my little village back home, there was a constable assigned to keep the peace. His name was Clive Potter, a forty-something single man who lived with his parents and could only ever play good cop, because bad cops didn't have pot bellies and ruddy cheeks. He had a tried-and-true routine for ensuring a peaceful village that began with a morning bicycle ride. If someone had suffered a puncture on the four streets that wound through Weston, he'd keep them company as they changed their own wheel or hold the gate for the farmer chasing his escaped cows back into the field.

Around lunchtime, Constable Potter propped his cycle against the wall of one of the three pubs and made sure there was no trouble inside, accepting a ham sandwich and pint of ale for his trouble. In the early afternoon, he'd work off the sandwich and beer on a park bench on the village green, with ducks for company. He usually read a mystery novel, his version of studying police procedure, an Agatha Christie his criminal-investigation manual. We were pretty sure he nodded off every day, his belly holding him upright, but his bench sat beneath a weeping willow tree, so it was hard to be sure. At around three, he'd stretch himself awake and walk his bicycle to the elementary school half a mile away to make sure no kids got run over at day's end. And, when the summer began, to buy himself an ice cream from old Mr. Miller, who cranked up his ice cream van for a few months and toured the nearby villages in the late afternoons and on weekends.

I'd somehow expected the cop who took Michelle's call to be like Clive Potter. To be the cop who preferred the easy missing-person's call to the higher-priority calls that might require confrontation and running. Jared Carruth was no Clive Potter. In his midtwenties, he addressed us with the politeness and interest of a highly trained customer-service rep, all *Sir* and *Ma'am* in his soft, Texas twang. His pen jotted down everything we said, a modern cop full of efficient concern. And no hint that he thought we were having an affair, no suggestion that this wasn't his most important call of the day.

After he'd gathered the details of name, age, height, weight, and Michelle's contact number, Carruth asked, "What was he wearing when you last saw him?"

"Khaki pants, light-blue shirt, and dark-blue tie," Michelle said. "You gave me his car details. It hasn't turned up?"

"No. I wouldn't expect it to, not without him."

"And you last saw him leaving for work."

"Yes. I didn't talk to him all day, which isn't unusual. Normally we'll text to figure out dinner plans midafternoon, and he'd call from his office to let me know if he had some late meetings. But I didn't notice that he'd left his phone at home."

"Was that unusual, for him to forget his phone?"

"I don't . . . I guess it's happened once before. He can be kind of scatterbrained, which I know is odd for a lawyer but . . ." She shrugged. "Nothing seemed out of the ordinary at all. Nothing."

Carruth hesitated. "Ma'am, excuse me for asking, but I have to. Is there any reason he might take off for a while. Y'all didn't argue or anything like that?"

"No," she said. "Not at all, everything was fine between us. Like I said, everything seemed totally normal."

"Yes, ma'am. And have you called hospitals or the jail to see if somehow he's at one of those places?"

"I did," I said. "I'm a friend of theirs. I work at the DA's office, as a prosecutor. I checked the hospitals and the county jail, nothing."

"Good. Can either of you think of anywhere he might be, anywhere he might have gone?"

We shook our heads in unison.

"No problem," Carruth said. He tore off a page from his small notebook and handed it to Michelle. "That's the case number. If you think of anything else, just call 311 and ask for the detective in charge of the case. You can give the information to him, and if he's not available, the 311 operator will add it to the report."

"So what happens now?" Michelle asked. "I mean, what will you do?"

"I'll write a report, put all this information in there. The report will be forwarded to a detective, I don't know who yet. He'll put out a notice on something called TCIC/NCIC, which will act as a notification system. So, if a cop pulls your husband over and runs his name, he'll show up as a missing person."

"And then what, you'll bring him home?"

"Maybe." Carruth shifted from foot to foot. "See, thing is, he's an adult. The officer will let him know there's a missing-person's report on him. And then, well, it's his choice what to do."

"I don't understand."

"If he tells the officer he's not missing, in other words he doesn't want to return home, then the officer will update the report and the detective will notify you."

"That he was found but doesn't want to come home?"

"If that's his reaction, yes."

Michelle's eyes widened. "So either he's dead in a ditch somewhere, or he's disappeared of his own accord. Either way, there's not much you can do to bring him home to me."

"I'm sorry, ma'am." From the distress on his face, I could see that Carruth hadn't given enough of these speeches to become indifferent. "I promise, we'll do what we can. I promise."

CHAPTER TWENTY-FIVE

BEHAVING AS THE WIND

After Officer Carruth had left, I told Michelle that I was surprised he'd not poked around the house a bit. "Probably a rookie and didn't want to upset you," I said. "But if a man is missing, I don't know, I'd probably want to see if there are signs or indications why."

"You think? How would he know what to look for?"

I shrugged. "Sometimes a pair of eyes from the outside can see things that might be missed by someone close to the situation."

"Well," she said, "you're kind of on the outside. And work in law enforcement. Would you look around, see if you see anything?"

"Sure, if you want," I said reluctantly. "I don't want to be nosing in your stuff; you guys are my friends."

"Gus is missing, Dom, and I've nothing to hide. Look where you want."

"Sure, okay."

I walked slowly up the stairs, keeping my eyes peeled. I was looking, of course, because the things that would explain missing Gus to her would explain them to me. And I knew there was a good chance I'd want to see them before she, or a cop, did. The fact that he'd not left a note, or sent one, was good. I tried to quell the frustration growing inside me. It had been a long time since my recklessness had pushed events out of my control, potentially beyond the point of redemption. A very long time because I'd learned that even recklessness can be channeled, and redemption wasn't necessary if it was channeled into doing something good, or if someone else was there to take the fall.

My parents sent me to boarding school when I was ten, not because I was a bad kid but because it was the done thing, the expected thing in my family. My father and his brothers had gone when they were six, my grandfather, too. But, even though it was a family tradition, the looks of relief they wore as they hugged me and drove away from Maidstone Hall Preparatory School were unmistakable. I actually didn't mind. Growing up on a farm is hard for a kid who experiments with animals. And for a kid who has no one to blame his little fires on. So to be surrounded by wide-eyed little boys and teachers all too eager to bring out their canes was something to appreciate. The school itself was in the Scottish highlands, a rugged and often desolate place, but since I was familiar with the countryside and pretty much immune to atmosphere, I felt at home much quicker than most.

One time, in the dormitory just before lights-out, one of the kids was still in the bathroom brushing his teeth. I had the idea to give him an apple-pie bed, to short-sheet him. Two other boys thought it a splendid idea and leaped into action, stripping away his top sheet and folding up the lower one, then remaking the bed with military perfection. They landed on their own beds just as he came through the door. I'd suggested this particular victim not because I didn't like him but because I knew how he'd react. His name was Faisal, and he was the nephew of a Saudi prince. He and his little brother, Hakim, shared the same sense of entitlement—and the same hair-trigger temper. When they didn't get their way, or if someone didn't accord them the respect they felt they deserved, they would explode, fists flailing, screaming bloody murder. Hilarious if you weren't the subject of their anger.

We heard the headmaster in the dorm next door, so Faisal hopped straight into bed, jamming his feet down under the sheets. It took him a split second to realize what had happened, but when he did, and when he looked up and saw us all snorting with laughter, his face darkened and the lid blew off.

"Who did this? Who did this?" he repeated over and over. When no one answered, he leaped out of bed and to the enormous chest of drawers that held our clean underwear and socks. On top were each boy's hairbrush and nail-scissors. He grabbed a pair of scissors and went straight for the kid laughing the hardest, Michael Moxon. Before Moxy knew it, a pair of scissors was sticking out of his shoulder. Our rugby captain and the toughest kid in the school, this merely served to annoy him, and he went for Faisal with a howl as we sat on our beds, gawking.

In seconds, the headmaster burst through the door.

"What the bloody hell is going on?" he demanded, his face as red as I'd ever seen it.

Faisal and Moxy got up off the floor, the former with a sulky, don't-you-dare-berate-me look, the latter with a pair of nail scissors still protruding from his shoulder. And what happened next was probably the first sign I'd become a lawyer, because when Faisal had explained about his apple-pie bed, as if that was the worst thing that could happen to a boy, the headmaster swiveled on his heels, glaring around the room.

"Who did that to his bed?" he growled.

Understand that there was a code of honor at Maidstone. You could misbehave, you could be naughty, but if your mischief was uncovered, you were expected to own up. No one would ever squeal on you, but you absolutely had to own up—not doing so wasn't an option. Not even for me.

So I parsed his words. "Who *did* that to his bed?" was the question. Not *Whose idea was that?* Not *Who suggested that?* And so I didn't put up my hand. It wasn't just about avoiding the cane. It was about not getting caught, about avoiding the opprobrium that comes with sinning. It was an aversion far more powerful than any fear of pain.

Jeremy Gorst and Anthony de Kruyff put up their hands, spindly arms poking up out of flannel pajamas, and were sent downstairs to wait outside the headmaster's study, which was directly below us. Faisal was ordered to escort his victim to the matron, a burly Scottish woman who lingered a little too long and offered a little too much help on our bath nights.

When the headmaster stalked out, we lay in anxious anticipation. There was only one penalty facing those two boys, and our dormitory lay directly above the HM's study. We whispered among ourselves, wondering how many they'd get. And as we listened to the cane swish through the air, as we heard the crack of it down below us, I looked around at the awe and terror on the faces of the other boys, like unwilling witnesses to an execution. And I looked long and hard into their eyes to see whether they blamed me for this or whether I'd gotten away with it.

The real test was when Gorst and de Kruyff returned. Both sported red-rimmed eyes, but only de Kruyff was still sniveling. Matron, of course, was on hand to inspect the damage, to oversee the ritual showing-off of the marks. She always managed to be there for that. And as she supervised the lowering of the pajama bottoms, I waited for recriminations from either boy, for dirty looks or a *Why didn't you own up?* I got none. No, they were too busy recounting what it was like and how they managed to hold position to their admiring colleagues, and, for a few fleeting seconds, I experienced envy at the attention they were getting. When their tale was over and they'd slid into bed, my role in the caper seemed to have been forgotten. So, as Matron flicked off the light on her way out, all I felt was the thrill of having instigated the crime, and gotten away with it, free and clear.

As I walked into Michelle and Gus's large bedroom, though, I remembered how Gorst and de Kruyff had taken the fall for me. Sure, they'd been guilty, but morally and legally I was in it with them. This time, though, I wasn't interested in seeing someone else take the fall, especially my friend Gus. For one thing, he wasn't guilty. For another, I had no doubt at all that if he wound up on a hard chair in a small room, an experienced detective would have a field day with him. Maybe Gus would exercise his right to silence, but he'd realize pretty damn quick that the cops would be far more interested in his testimony than in pinning a crime on him that he didn't commit. Sooner or later, he'd tell all.

Easier for Gus, though, to avoid the whole situation. To pack a bag and head to his home country and disappear among the brown-skinned locals and the sun-seeking gringos. So that's where I checked first, his closet.

I looked for a row of empty hangers, for a stack of matching suitcases with one missing. Instead, I saw the three Hawaiian shirts he'd rotated, day after day, on the cruise I'd shared with him and Michelle. I saw a pair of flip-flops and only two empty hangers. I saw no sign he'd packed and left of his own accord.

I checked the bathroom next, opening the cabinet above his sink. I turned when I heard Michelle's voice.

"I did that already," she said.

"You looked in here?"

"Toothbrush is there. So's his razor, shaving cream, and deodorant." He could buy all that stuff new, and she realized that. "He loves that razor, I'm sure he'd have . . ."

"All his stuff looks like it's here," I said. "Honestly, Michelle, I have a really strong feeling that he's fine. He loves you so much, and . . ." I cut myself off. "Of course, his guitar. Is that here? He's like me, he'd never go anywhere without his guitar."

"I know." Her eyes filled with tears. "It's the only thing that's missing."

CHAPTER TWENTY-SIX

THIS IS THE WAY
THE WORLD ENDS

On Monday morning, I went to work as normal. It wasn't supposed to be my day in court, but Brian McNulty had called in sick, and Maureen Barcinski asked me to cover his docket.

"It's a short one, about four cases. Most are just reviews requested by probation. I think there's one case set for a plea, but Brian put notes in the system, so just follow his instructions."

I carried my computer into court, barely paying attention to the proceedings. The best thing about being a juvenile prosecutor was that most of the action went on around you, judges and probation officers deciding the fate of the miscreant while we sat to one side and took notes. We only got really busy when a kid killed someone or committed some other kind of crime that caught the public's eye. That was pretty rare, and in my few weeks at juvie, the place had been unutterably dull. Note taking and a pretense at caring, those seemed to be the job requirements. Two things I could manage quite well.

My head snapped up when the judge called the case that was set for a plea. I'd not noticed the lawyer, a public defender, and his client set up at the defense table. I looked across to see Bobby staring straight ahead, smartly dressed and his back ramrod straight, as if he was trying not to look terrified.

"Is the State ready?" the judge said. She was looking at me like she'd said it a few times already, and maybe she had.

"Yes, Your Honor," I said, standing. I glanced over my shoulder, a rush of excitement that I might see little Bobby's sister. She was at the back of the courtroom, studiously ignoring me, but I had trouble dragging my eyes from that pure-white skin, the hair I could almost smell from where I stood.

"Sorry to wake you, Mr. Prosecutor," the judge said, a half smile on her face. Judge Barbara Portnoy had been a prosecutor once, and I think sympathized with the marginalized essence of prosecuting juveniles, the lack of any meaningful involvement. She bought into the idea that kids needed to be rehabilitated and not punished, no doubt about that, but she understood the frustration for us, seeing the same kids spinning through the system time and time again. And it irked her that so often the victims of these little hoodlums were left with no justice and, to them even worse, the financial burden of these potential angels stealing their stuff and crashing their cars. So she cut me and the other ADAs a lot of slack and threw us frequent pitying smiles as she sentenced the next serial burglar to serve six months of probation, at home. With counseling.

"My apologies, judge," I said. "I was looking over the notes for this case—it's Mr. McNulty's."

"We have a plea agreement?" the judge asked, looking at defense counsel.

"We do," Derek James replied wearily. "We'd love to avoid the felony, but, given my client's history, I understand why Mr. McNulty declined to waive the burglary paragraph."

"Your client's mother, or father, not coming?" Judge Portnoy asked.

"No, Judge," James said. "That's Bobby's sister at the back of the room. She basically raises him."

I glanced over my shoulder again and saw her give the judge a sad smile, which she held on to for my sake.

"Your Honor," I said, back on my feet. "I've looked on our system at Bobby's history. It doesn't look all that bad to me. Nothing violent, and he completed a period of deferred prosecution for his previous offense without any issues. As far as I can tell, anyway."

"Meaning?" The judge cocked her head and stared at me.

"I know a felony's harder to get off your record, and he's only twelve. Seems like a fair resolution would be a plea to a lesser-included. Maybe criminal trespass of a habitation."

James about swallowed his tongue. "Your Honor, I'd have to consult with my client, but I'd certainly advise him to take such a generous offer."

"This isn't your case, counselor," the judge said to me. "Are you sure you can make that offer?"

"Yes, judge, absolutely."

I wasn't sure that was true at all. When there was a victim, we were supposed to consult with them before any reduction of the charge. When it was someone else's case, we were supposed to check with the ADA who it belonged to, or Maureen, before reducing it from a felony to a misdemeanor. I hadn't done either, of course, but with a vulnerable and potentially grateful young lady sitting three rows behind me, the benefits seemed to considerably outweigh any likely fallout. And if one impetuous act gave me a sliver of power over Bobby's glorious sister and also pissed off Brian McNulty, so much the better. I didn't stop to think that people might figure out who his sister was, that I might be committing a crime by handling the case of a kid whose sister I was in lust with. Never mind the capital murder, I'd just placed my career on the sharp end of a small act of self-interest. I was manipulating the resolution of a case purely to further my own ends.

Morally dubious, of course, and something the American Bar Association forbade, through Standard 3-1.3, Conflicts of Interest, subsection (f): "A prosecutor should not permit his or her professional judgment or obligations to be affected by his or her own political, financial, business, property, or personal interests."

"Good, then that's what we'll do," said Judge Portnoy, giving me a grateful nod before putting on her formal voice. "Calling case number JV-45-969, In the Matter of Bobby . . ."

O

"Thank you," she said, with a slight smile and a single bat of the eyelashes. She turned to her brother. "Bobby . . ."

"Thanks, Mr. Dominic," he said, his voice small and his eyes downcast. "I really appreciate it."

We were in the main reception area, packed with probation officers and parents, juvenile delinquents and witnesses, all milling around. It wasn't unheard of for a kid's relative to thank a prosecutor, if they'd been given a break. But if we hung around and chatted, curious eyes would lead to awkward questions.

"You're welcome," I said. "Your new PO is probably waiting for you; maybe best not to say anything about knowing me."

Bobby looked up. "I'm not dumb."

"I know. Just . . . We probably shouldn't be chatting. I better get back to my office."

She put a hand on my arm and spoke quietly. "Call me."

I nodded and wandered away toward safety, the security door leading into the DA's office. Standing by it, looking directly at me, was Maureen. "What was that about?" she asked.

"She was saying thanks. I felt bad for them. That was the kid's sister, and from what the PO said, she's basically raising him by herself. They live in a shitty part of town and no parents in sight. PO said he's basically a good kid with some questionable friends, so I gave him a break on his burglary case."

"A break?"

"Yeah, pled him to a criminal trespass."

"You run that by Brian?"

"Brian, as you well know, is an idiot."

She smiled, but like she was trying not to. "Fine. Just wanted to make sure everything was okay."

"Yep, fine."

"Good. I'm headed downtown for a meeting. If anyone needs me, tell them I'll be back tomorrow. And I'll check e-mail tonight."

"Sure. Doing something fun?"

"A meeting. There's an investigation, they think it might be kids so they want to make sure they have their juvenile ducks in a row, in case they arrest someone. Detectives, and patrol, often fuck up when they arrest juveniles, so we're making sure they know to not question them until they're magistrated. More of a training than a meeting, maybe." She sighed. "Anyway, this is one case they don't want fucked up."

"Oh? One I've heard of?"

"I expect so. The capital murder at the mobile-home park, a couple weeks back."

I didn't miss a beat. "Yeah, I read about it."

"Nasty business. They think maybe kids are responsible, but they're not sure."

"They don't have any suspects?"

"No. It happened pretty quickly, and in the dark. Plus, out there people don't much like talking to the cops."

"East Austin, right?"

"Yep," she said. "But far east, kind of in the sticks almost."

"Good place to commit a crime, then."

"Maybe. But they'll catch them, is my bet. There aren't too many unsolved murders these days, especially double homicides."

"You might be right about that."

"I am. Plus, they have some evidence."

"They do?"

"Yeah. The gun that was used, that killed those guys. They think they've found it."

CHAPTER TWENTY-SEVEN

DELIBERATE DISGUISES

I went to my car and took the burner phone from my glove compartment. I dialed Otto's phone and I sat there, impatient, as it rang and rang. Then I tried Tristan, praying he had his phone with him.

"What?" he said.

"Where are you?"

"Going out to lunch. What's up?"

"I'm going out to lunch, too. Meet me at Kerbey Lane Café on South Lamar."

"Wait, I was just aiming for a sandwich at—"

"Something's up. See you in ten."

We were early for lunch so had no trouble getting a booth without anyone around us. I ordered coffee and water, Tristan a Diet Coke.

"What's going on?" he asked.

"There's no easy way to say this, and I need you to stay calm. Remember, we're in public."

His eyes bored holes in me. "I'm calm. What happened?"

"The police think they found one of the guns."

Blood drained from his face. "What?" he croaked.

"I'm not sure which one. And I sure as hell don't know how."

"Oh my God. What . . . what do we do?"

"Depends, I don't know how far along they are with the testing. Maureen told me they'd had a tip, found the gun, but she didn't say whether they'd even started the ballistics yet."

"Oh, God." His eyes filled with tears, and he looked down at the table. "Oh my God, it's over."

"Do you know where Otto is?"

He shook his head. "If it's his, he'll tell them, won't he? He'll tell them everything."

"Stay here and eat." I stood and dropped a five-dollar bill on the table. "I have to go find him. Don't do anything until you hear from me. Eat, go back to work, and for fuck's sake stay calm."

"How can I stay calm?" he hissed. "We're going to prison, and when—"

I leaned on the table and put my face close to his. "No. We are not going to prison. Otto is a smart man, he'll lay low, disappear."

"What if it's yours?"

"Then I'll go back to England. Or Canada. Whoever it is will disappear and lay low."

"Bullshit. The cops can find anyone these days."

"Actually, they can't. Why do you think there's a top-ten most wanted? The FBI has one, every state has one. Shit, every local police department has one. That's a whole lot of wanted criminals on the run, unable to be found. Otto will be just one more, and we'll help him if we have to." I saw Tristan's eyes flick past me and assumed it was the waiter coming back with our drinks. I put my hand out to shake Tristan's. "I'm sorry, family emergency, I'll call you later, yeah?"

Tristan nodded and I gave the hovering waiter a smile and said, "Sorry, gotta go." I breezed past him and out of the door.

I'd handled a murder case where we thought the evidence was all in, and the trial was set. Four days before we picked the jury, the detective located the gun. Just like this time, it was an anonymous phone tip. They seized the gun from the cistern of a public toilet in a park in North Austin, and while the ballistics guy did his tests the detective ran the serial numbers. Finding the gun to identifying its owner took less than twelve hours.

Otto, as far as I knew, wasn't working. His erratic job schedule meant that even if he was, I wouldn't know where to find him. I drove to his little house on Porter Street and saw that his car was in the driveway. I knocked on his door but got no answer. I peered in the front windows, but the curtains were closed and I couldn't see inside.

I started for my car when my cell phone rang, my boss Maureen's name popping up on the screen.

"This is Dominic."

"Hey, Maureen here. Dom, can I ask a favor?"

"What's up?"

"On that double homicide we talked about. They just got some info and want to execute a search warrant. I don't want to talk about it on the phone, the guy we're after is . . . well, I helped them with the warrant affidavit, the judge signed it, but they need someone there when they execute it."

"A prosecutor? That's unusual isn't it?"

"Not for a capital-murder case. If you can cover this one, I'll take back over with whatever else they need. I got a call from my son's school; he's sick and I have to pick him up."

"When are they doing it?"

"Now. They're getting a SWAT team together, just in case. I'll text you the address. Wait, better still, I'll text you the staging point."

"Sure, no worries."

"Where are you right now?" she asked.

"At lunch. I'm done, though. Just text me the location; I'll be on my way. I don't mind waiting."

"Thanks, Dom, I owe you one."

I sat in my car and cursed myself. She'd asked me where I was, and if someone checked my phone log, it'd show I was right here. At the home of a suspect in a double murder. And it crossed my mind, a sharp, painful thought, that this was a trap. That they knew I was involved and they were luring me to my place of arrest. But I couldn't do much except play along, because if they had no idea, the last thing I needed to do was act cagey. Plus, if I was being suckered into custody, wouldn't they have me show up for a "briefing" at the downtown police station? My phone dinged and the message from Maureen came up.

Large parking lot behind Conoco on E Riverside / Montopolis. Asap.

It took three full seconds to realize that she was directing me to the gas station two blocks away. They had Otto's gun.

O

I was the first one there, and I parked my car in the middle of the enormous and empty lot. I couldn't tell whether it was parking for people at the warehouse behind me, or whether the gas-station convenience store was overly optimistic. I leaned against the outside of my car and kept my eyes peeled for the cavalry, but after three minutes, the back door to the gas station opened and a middle-aged man started toward me. He was dark-skinned and wore that expression so many gas-station owners and clerks wear: tiredness, boredom, anticipatory hostility, and an edge of fear.

Behind him, about half a mile away on Montopolis, I saw the procession I'd been waiting for, hoping for, the procession that told me I was still in the clear: an armored vehicle and the bland sedans driven by cops on duty. No lights, no sirens, in stealth mode, for now.

Twenty yards away from me, the man waved a hand and yelled. "You can't park there."

"Who says?"

"I do. This is my lot."

"We're going to be borrowing it for a few minutes."

He was in front of me. "What?" Indian, maybe Pakistani. "It's not for rent."

"I didn't say *rent*. I said, we're going to be borrowing it for a few minutes."

"Who are you? Who is borrowing?"

I smiled genially and pointed behind him as the armored car growled its way through the parking lot toward us, four beige cars fanning out behind it like a wedding train.

"What is this?" The man was indignant, not intimidated, and for a moment I was impressed.

"We're meeting here for a chat, then going somewhere else. Nearby, but somewhere else. Now do me a favor and go back to your business."

He didn't budge, but his eyes got wider as the armored car pulled up near us and eight officers in full SWAT gear piled out. The police cars lined up behind the truck, and doors slammed as more cops joined the circle. I recognized one detective, Megan Ledsome. I'd gotten pretty close to her during a week-long trial when she'd been in Robbery. I didn't know she'd moved over to Homicide. She was blond, petite, and probably the prettiest cop I'd ever seen, and she carried an air of confidence (and a gun) that made her even sexier. Our lunches that week had lingered a little too long, become a little too informal, and when she realized what was happening, she made up for it by talking about her husband, Greg, how hard they were trying to have a baby. That was eight months ago, so it looked like the baby thing hadn't happened yet.

She seemed pleased to see me but keen to hide that fact. We shook hands.

"Who's this?" she asked, nodding to the Indian.

"It's his parking lot," I said. "Apparently, you forgot to make a reservation."

She turned to the man and introduced herself. "Sir, I apologize for taking up your time, and your parking lot. We're about to execute a very important operation nearby. We needed to stage somewhere out of sight of the target location, and this was the most convenient place. If you'll give us fifteen minutes or so, we'll finalize our plan and be out of your way."

"Yes, of course. Certainly." He started back toward the station, stopped to look at us, then continued on his way.

Ledsome turned to me. "Did Ms. Barcinski tell you we're here for Otto Bland?"

"Otto? Seriously?" I did my utmost to look shocked. "No, she didn't. What does Otto have to do with this?"

"That's what we plan to find out."

"She mentioned the gun. You found his gun?"

"Yep. We got a call about it, from someone who saw him there. The ballistics match the bullet taken from one of the victims."

"A call? A phone call? From who?"

"Yeah, a phone call. Is there any other kind?"

"No, sorry, I just . . . from who?"

"Anonymous. We're working on finding out, though."

"Okay, good." I shook my head slowly. "Otto," I said, "I just can't believe it."

We huddled around the hood of my car. Detective Ledsome had a map, and I stood back as she pointed out Otto's house. The plan was simple. A slicktop would drive down Porter Street and a detective in the backseat would hold his phone up, video app running, for a drive-by. They'd look at the video on the way back here to see if he was home, any little sign would do. Once back here, whether he was home or not, two more slicks would set off and block either end of the street. The SWAT vehicle would lead the way to Otto's, pulling up on the lawn and decamping in a matter of seconds to take down the door. SWAT would clear the place, the detectives would follow right behind.

Ledsome went to the trunk of her car. "You know Bland pretty well, don't you?"

"Acquaintance, I'd say." I kept my face blank.

"He worked at the DA's office, right?"

"He did."

"What can you tell me about him?"

"Not much. Nice guy. Nice enough, anyway."

"Why'd he get fired?"

"No clue. Probably spoke his mind and upset someone."

"When did you last see him?"

Why is she pushing me like this? "At the DA's office a month ago. Juvenile Justice Center. He's a witness in a case and I interviewed him. Burglary, or car theft, I can't remember the case, it's not mine."

"Okay." She started to turn away.

"Oh, wait," I said. "Jeez, I forgot. I was at his house, like, two weeks ago."

"His house."

"Yeah, it was weird. He called me after we'd met in the office. I guess for old times' sake or he thought we'd connected, or something. He and I, we'd always got on pretty well. I know, you wouldn't think, but I kind of liked him. Maybe I felt sorry for him. Anyway, he called me one evening, I was just heading out of the office and he was all upset, not making any sense. Not babbling, exactly, but he sounded truly miserable."

"Why would he call you?"

"From what he said, he didn't have anyone else. Anyway, he said he wanted to ask me about something, and when I asked what, he changed his mind and said he just wanted to talk. I didn't have anything planned, so I went over and drank a beer with him."

"What was his state of mind?"

"All over the place. I mean, I had one beer, he must have had five or six. Eventually he nodded off on the sofa and I left."

"Did you hear from him after that?"

"Nothing. Not a word."

"Okay, thanks," she said. "So, you're not one of those paper-pushing DAs, are you?"

"Meaning?"

She popped the trunk and handed me a bullet-proof vest. "Meaning, you're coming in with us, right?"

"Absolutely." She was testing me, not just to see if I'd be scared of running into the home of a murderer, but to see what kind of person I was. Some irony, there. I pulled the vest over my head, secured the Velcro straps, and turned to her. "So do I get a gun? AR-15 preferably, but I'll take a shotgun."

"Funny," she said, with the first hint of a real smile. "You can ride with me, I'll carry the gun."

Ledsome went over the plan one more time, and when the recon car drove off to scout Otto's house, the SWAT commander assigned specific roles to his men: who would breach the door, who would go in first, second, and third. The detectives and I would go in as soon as the place was secure.

The recon car returned within five minutes, and we took turns looking at the video, grainy and wobbling, but we all agreed that Otto's car in the driveway meant he was probably home. With a rumble of exhaust and a small crowd watching from the gas station, we headed out of the parking lot and set off north on Montopolis Drive. I rode in Ledsome's slicktop at the head of the convoy, saying nothing. I could tell she was nervous; she was checking her mirrors, licking her lips, and adjusting her radio every few seconds. I shifted about in my seat to give that same impression, but I wasn't feeling it. Nerves didn't come to me that way. My responses were physical, if any. My mind didn't seem able to torture itself with the what-ifs that empaths suffered in certain situations. Maybe he'd be there with a bazooka to blow us all away. Maybe he'd be on vacation in Hawaii and we'd find no evidence of anything. I knew Ledsome was considering all the options and her mind was teasing her with which it might be, and her body was responding accordingly. Like the robbery itself, I hoped she was too preoccupied with her own worries to notice my lack of them.

Ledsome signaled and turned right on Porter Street, and when she saw that her entire team had made the turn, she picked up her handset. "Charlie 501. Let's go." She gunned the engine and the car leaped forward, and I turned to see the snake-tail of vehicles surging after us, winding around the cars parked on the street and snapping back to the curb. A block away, Ledsome pulled to the side, and the car following us roared past. It was one of the detectives, who'd park his car across the street fifty yards on the other side of Otto's house. The armored truck went by next, aiming straight for Otto's lawn, bumping over the curb and coming to a halt across his front path. We followed at a crawl, giving them time to get into position and execute, watching them as they leaped from the back of the vehicle. Two men ran around either side of the house to cover the rear, while the rest went straight to the front door. A short battering ram made quick work of it, and as we pulled up opposite Otto's house, the door flew inward and the troops went in.

We got out of the car and Ledsome looked over. "Follow my lead," she said.

"Will do."

Her head turned toward the house and we waited for a minute. Then she put a hand to her earpiece. "We have the all-clear." She started moving toward the house.

"That was quick."

"Those guys are good. And being fast is part of being good."

We reached the front of the truck. "Not in my book."

She looked over like I was weird, but part of not being nervous was not recognizing when to make sexual jokes. And when not to. I just smiled and followed her through the front door, going in sideways as several of the SWAT officers filed out.

As we passed them, Ledsome stopped the team's second-in-command with a hand on his arm. His name patch read Shindler. He pulled off his helmet and looked like a Boy Scout, young and fresh-faced, like he wouldn't be ruthless enough to win an arm-wrestle with a preteen. Ledsome still had her hand on his arm and I felt a flash of jealousy.

"Greg," she said, "no one in there?"

"Yes and no." He grinned like a kid playing a prank on his mum. "It's safe, but I'll wait out here for you."

For you. Greg.

She let go of his arm, and we went inside.

"Detective, over here." The SWAT commander stood by Otto's dining table and pointed at the floor. From the entrance, his sofa blocked our view, but as we rounded it, we saw what he was pointing to. Otto's body lay face up, his eyes half closed and his mouth slack. The right side of his head sported a black hole the size of a dime. Blood had trickled from the wound, down into his ear, a dark line leading to a congealed dark pool on the floor. A gun lay under the table.

For ten long seconds we stood there looking at Otto Bland's body, all processing this apparent suicide in our own way. Ledsome's way was to lick her lips some more and slowly reach for her little notebook; the SWAT commander's was to stand in grim and respectful silence, Otto's personal honor guard. Me, I felt a warm wave of relief that started in my toes and washed upward, a relief so palpable I was sure these cops would feel it emanating from my body, or see the muscles of my face fighting the smile that every man smiles when he's told he no longer has to go to prison.

CHAPTER TWENTY-EIGHT

DEATH'S TWILIGHT KINGDOM

As Ledsome took notes, I moved forward to get a better look. I knew Otto was dead, but the best way to truly believe something is to see it with your own two eyes. Up close. But when I drew level with her, Ledsome put a hand on my chest.

"Let's let CSU do their thing," she said.

"Sure." I nodded and backed off. The crime-scene guys were thorough, and they'd almost certainly find my prints. They wouldn't be able to identify them, though. Even though all county employees gave prints for a criminal-background check, they weren't put into the automated fingerprint identification system, more commonly known as AFIS.

Ledsome wandered over to me. "So what you told me before. Looks like we'll need that in a formal statement."

"Yes, of course. Whatever you need."

"Thanks."

"I don't understand something, though," I said. I didn't understand a lot of things. Suicide, especially in this situation, was one of them. To me, there is no one as important on the planet as me. My world revolves around me, and I try to make other people's do the same. So the idea of ending my own life is incomprehensible, and that meant I had my doubts about Otto's demise. I didn't think Tristan was up to the task, but given Gus's odd disappearance and Otto's unpredictable nature, there was room for doubt.

"That's suicide for you," Ledsome was saying. "Although most people who blow their brains out don't have the cops about to descend on them."

"Can you tell when he did it?"

"No. The medical examiner is on his way. He'll give us an idea. Five or six hours ago, maybe, since the blood looks dried but there's no smell."

I grimaced. "Poor Otto."

"Unless he killed two men, in which case sympathy will be a little harder to come by."

"How did he know you were onto him?"

"That's what I want to find out. Being former law enforcement, my bet is someone tipped him off somehow. Or just called with a question about his gun that made him suspicious. I really don't know, but I sure as hell intend to find out."

"I can't believe he's really a suspect in a double murder."

"It'd explain his bizarre behavior with you the other week."

"Yeah," I said. "But his crappy, dead-end job and objectively miserable life would explain that too."

"And you just gave him a motive to commit those crimes."

"To commit murder? Why?"

She looked at me for a moment. "No harm in me telling you, I guess. We think one of the victims was basically a slum lord. Likely he had a few hundred, maybe a few thousand, bucks on him in cash."

"For real?" I processed the information for a moment. "How would Otto know that?"

"Not sure yet, but he did a lot of security-guard gigs, and that included one at the Crooked Creek trailer park. He'd just started and maybe he got the job there on purpose when he found out about the money."

"That's possible, I guess."

Ledsome looked back toward Otto's body. "It's also possible he had no idea we were coming and decided that killing people wasn't something he wanted to live with."

"He killed himself from guilt?" An image flashed in my mind, not of Otto but of the man who'd accused me of stealing his music. The image wasn't dissimilar to what I was seeing here, a gun and a body, but the body had a different face. The reason was similar: the bastard's guilt at ruining my music career in Austin.

"It's certainly possible. We'll look around once the body is gone, maybe find a note or something."

"Suicides usually leave one, I suppose?"

"No, in my experience that's a myth. More often than not they don't. You have to look for other, less obvious signs."

"Such as?"

"A glass of whisky. A sappy card to a relative. Evidence of private or business affairs being put in order. Sometimes there's nothing at all, no evidence whatsoever. If a sense of guilt hit him, it might have come like a tidal wave. People commit suicide very quickly, sometimes, when they see no way around what they've done."

"I didn't know that." I turned to look out the window and suppressed another smile. If he'd done this to assuage his guilt, and not because he wanted to avoid prison, then he was heaping irony on top of irony. If that's what happened, then a man with a conscience had seen the error of his ways and reaped his own soul, thereby saving a man who didn't have one.

It may have been that warm tickle of relief still, but oh, how I wanted to laugh.

O

The cops cleared out of the house when CSU arrived. In the front yard, neighbors peered over the yellow crime-scene tape and took photos with their camera phones, and we all knew that the media were minutes away.

With so much going on, it was easy for me to slide around the crime scene, listening in and watching but with no one paying much attention to me. I didn't know what I expected to learn, or hoped to hear, but I kept my eyes and ears at work for anything that might conceivably link me to this place or the dead Otto. At about three o'clock, Ledsome offered to have an officer drive me back to my car.

"We'll be here for hours, not much for you to do," she said. "And after the initial excitement, now come hours of tedious police work."

I felt like I was in the clear, and while I was reluctant to separate myself from a place that might incriminate me, to give up this illusion of control over a potentially dangerous situation, I was genuinely tired. I also told myself that if they'd not yet turned up a diary or some sort of written confession with my name in it, they were unlikely to. I accepted that offer of a ride.

The cop's name was Steven Constable, which was perfect of course. He was built slightly but moved like an athlete, graceful almost. He held the passenger door for me and went around to his side. As we drove down Porter Street, we talked.

"So you knew that guy?" he said.

"Yeah," I replied. "Decent chap, I'd always thought."

"Maybe he was. Couldn't live with what he'd done and ended it. Better than most assholes who try and get away with it."

"I suppose. I just couldn't see Otto doing a robbery like that. Always been a law man, one of the good guys."

"People change. Desperate circumstances, maybe. I heard he quit APD under a cloud and got fired from your office."

"Yeah, I don't know what for, though," I said, preempting the inevitable question. "And he was working some pretty shitty gigs, security-guard stuff."

He shook his head. "What a way for it all to end."

I was thinking the same thing, but from a slightly different perspective. Otto's death could also be the death of the investigation. If the cops went into this with no idea who was responsible, they'd be licking their chops at pinning the whole thing on a dead guy. Sure, one of the bullets they pulled from the bodies wouldn't match his gun, but the cops could reason that Otto had used two weapons and gotten rid of the one he used to shoot Silva. Unlikely, but so was a former APD officer being a double-murderer. The last thing the police would want, it seemed to me, was to admit there was another shooter out there, someone they couldn't begin to identify. With an unpopular victim in Silva, all the more reason to close up the file, call it a day, and pat each other on the back in the local bar.

At the gas-station parking lot I shook hands with Officer Constable and we peeled off in opposite directions, him back to the crime scene, me heading for home. I drove slowly, running my mind through Otto's house for the umpteenth time, wondering if there was anything there that might incriminate me. Any fingerprints were easily explained as coming from my prior recent visit there, and I simply couldn't think of a single other thing that might hurt me. Otto didn't seem the journaling type, and the lack of a suicide note ruled out another chance to drop my name into police hands.

As I pulled into my parking spot, I allowed myself a small smile and the thought that Otto was a loose end well and truly tied off.

Tristan, of course, took a while to see it that way. I sat on the couch in the living room as he paced back and forth in front of me.

"You're sure there's no note or written confession, absolutely sure?"

"I was there almost two hours. They found nothing."

"What if he hid it? They could be finding it right now."

"Nope." I shook my head, like I was explaining to a child. "Think about it. If he shot himself out of remorse and had written some sort of tell-all confession, then it would have been on the table. Or the floor. Or pinned to the fridge. He's not going to write a note like that and hide it, is he?"

"I guess not." Some color returned to his face as the good news sank in. It drained away as his brain latched onto another problem. "My fingerprints. From when we were there."

"Relax. Those prints are useless unless they have some to compare them to. You're not in the AFIS database, are you?"

"I don't think I am, no."

"Have you been convicted of a crime?"

"No."

"There you are then. Free and clear."

"Unless I become a suspect, in which case they can take them and—"

"If they ask your permission, just say no. Get all civil rights on them. But they won't, because they have no reason to. So like I said before, relax. I'm wondering if they'll even look for a second person."

"What do you mean?"

"They have Otto. They know he's guilty, but they have no idea if anyone else was involved, right?"

"I guess."

"Even if they did, they wouldn't know where to start. So it's easier for them just to lay it all at his door. A dead perp doesn't argue with you. And there'll be no trial, obviously, so there won't be a slimy defense lawyer trying to point the finger at someone else, haranguing the detectives on the witness stand about why they didn't look for the real killer, or the ringleader. Whatever."

He stopped pacing as he considered the theory. "All wrapped up, nice and tight for them."

"With a bow on top," I added.

"Jesus, poor Otto. You really think he was feeling that guilty about it?"

"Didn't seem like it to me. More likely he knew his gun had been found and took the easy way."

"Easy for us, anyway."

My phone buzzed in my pocket. It was Ledsome. "Detective," I said. I resisted the urge to make a joke about her not being able to stay away from me, and instead went with, "What's up?"

"Not much. We're wrapping up here. Just wanted to say thanks for your help today, and ask whether you're the point person on this for the DA's office, or whether Maureen is the person to call."

"Probably her. I think I was covering while she had a kid thing."

"Got it. Thanks again, Dominic."

"Wait, did you find anything?"

"Not much. Plenty of fingerprints that aren't his, but that's not surprising because the place hasn't been cleaned in a decade. Men are pigs, you know."

"We try to be. Nothing else?"

"Nothing to speak of."

"So that's it then? Case closed?"

"What do you mean?"

"The capital murder. Your suspect is dead, so I assumed you'd spend a few weeks writing a report and that's that." I kept my voice light, casual, like I didn't care either way.

She laughed. "I wish. Don't get me wrong, he's definitely our shooter. But he wasn't out there alone."

"How do you know?"

"We have two bodies with two different holes in them."

"Maybe he had two guns? For a former cop, that wouldn't be unusual."

"I agree. The thing is, we didn't find any money. If he did this alone, I would have found the money at his place."

"Not necessarily."

"We went through everything, Dom. No locker keys, no storage-facility contracts, nothing like that. And it looked like the guy hadn't spent a dollar in weeks. Not on his place, his wardrobe, or his car."

I clenched my jaw. "So what's your theory?"

"Someone else is keeping the money until the heat dies down. The leader of this little expedition."

"The real bad guy."

"Precisely. And something else crossed my mind."

"Go on."

"That Otto Bland didn't kill himself at all. That he was a risk, a liability to whoever planned the whole thing. And as a result, he found himself staring down the wrong end of a gun barrel."

CHAPTER TWENTY-NINE

WE WHISPER TOGETHER

I hung up the phone and looked at Tristan, who'd sat opposite and stared at me throughout the conversation. "Our pretty bow just came undone," I said.

"That was the lead detective?"

"Yeah, and she's overthinking this one."

"She knows Otto didn't act alone, doesn't she?" He stood up and ran a hand through his hair. "Dammit."

"Quite an irony, if you think about it. She didn't find the money, so she assumes he had someone else helping him. Or several someones, she didn't specify."

"Fuck."

"She's got no idea it's us, don't worry."

"Right, okay, I'll just stop worrying." He paced back and forth, making abrupt little turns like a toy soldier. "Otto's dead, and there's a smart detective breathing down our necks. How exactly do you suggest I relax? Drugs?"

I stood. "Hey, do what you gotta do."

"Don't you worry, I will."

An edge in his voice stopped me in my tracks. "What exactly do you mean by that?"

"I'm not going to prison for this. I'll do what Otto did if I have to, but no fucking way I'm going to prison."

I couldn't resist. "Technically you might not, you could get the death penalty since it's capital murder."

227

"So could you."

"Yeah," I agreed, "we both could. But we're not going to because we're keeping a low profile and I can keep an eye on the investigation."

Tristan stared at me for a few seconds, then sank back into the couch. "Okay. Do you believe in the perfect crime?"

More shades of Gus, I thought. "I don't know. You?"

"Maybe. If they'd blamed Otto for it, let it go when they found him, then I'd say we committed it."

"And now?"

"Now, not so much." He wiped a hand over his face. "This is really fucking stressful."

"I know. But we just need to hang in there, we'll be fine. And maybe this is the perfect crime. I'm starting to think that there aren't specific elements that bring a crime to perfection, just because every crime is so different, so unique. I mean, the one thing they can all have in common is that the criminals get away. And so far we've gotten away with it. So as stressful as this feels, we just need to ride it out. And then, in a few days or weeks, we can look back and realize that we did, after all, commit the perfect crime."

"No," Tristan said quietly. "It can't ever be perfect."

"Why not?"

"Because someone else has our money."

O

I went to my room and sat on the bed with my guitar. I was torn between wanting to think about where we were, what was happening, and losing myself for a few minutes. I chose the latter and began to play those simple songs that I'd learned as a kid. They were songs that used only the essential chords of A, C, D, Em, and G, songs like *Sweet Home Alabama* and Van Morrison's *Brown Eyed Girl*. I strummed each one slowly, the way I had done a million times before, the way I'd first done, hesitantly and haltingly, when I was eleven years old and learning.

The familiar chords brought back the smell of my school's music room, a wood-beamed loft at the top of the school, a place of refuge for me and the few of us who liked to play music. Our days were structured at prep school, even our free time was regimented and restricted, but on Wednesday afternoons and Sunday mornings, after church, Arthur "Artie" Halliwell and I used to meet up there and play music together. He was a quiet child, in my class but a year older than I was. He was reed-thin and timid, and on the rugby field he drifted around like the wind was blowing him from play to play, his spindly fingers constantly hitching up the shorts that sagged from his minuscule waist. He and I didn't speak the rest of the week, we had no cause to, but the one thing we had in common was the refuge of that attic room. He was good, too, better than I was, which is the reason I let him play when I was there. I learned things from him, and I liked the quick squeak of the chord changes he made, the songs that were one step ahead of the ones I was playing.

One afternoon, about six weeks into the summer term, the music teacher found us up there. Mr. Flowers. I didn't know his first name, same for all the teachers, and didn't find out what it was until his death about six months later, in the middle of the next term. He was a tall, thin man, and the only person I've ever met to wear an Adolf Hitler–style mustache. With his light Scottish brogue, he came across as gentle and a little creepy, and always wore perfume. Not aftershave or cologne, but women's perfume, a sickly sweet cloud following him around the school. When he taught the young boys guitar, he'd have them sit on his lap so he could "make sure they had perfect form."

That Sunday, he just watched us play. He made Artie nervous and, being in there with them both, I saw certain similarities between the two. The physical resemblance, the fragility of them both, the birdlike way they perched on their chairs. Flowers, though, was like a vulture, eyes pinned on Artie as he played, and though I was too young and naïve to understand what was happening, I knew instinctively something was wrong when he asked me to leave and come back later so he could give Artie some private lessons.

That day repeated itself the next weekend, but the weekend after that, Artie declined to go to the music room with me. When Flowers found us buying candy at the tuck shop that afternoon, he seemed put out.

"Have you boys given up the guitar?" he asked.

"No, sir," I said. "Just not practicing today."

Artie was staring at his feet.

"Why don't you both come to my study and practice?" he asked.

I narrowed my eyes and looked at him. As far as I knew, the headmaster was the only one to have a study at the ninety-person prep school. "Where's that, sir?"

"My cottage," he said. "I have a little music study set up, very conducive to practice and the understanding of music."

His cottage was at the end of the rear driveway, one of four that belonged to the school. They were stone houses, small but attractive, and allocated to the more senior teachers at the school, the ones who were single. Which most were.

"Right, then," he said. "Get your tuck and bring it to my place, with your guitars. See you both in a few minutes."

"Yes, sir," I said, and glanced at Artie. He was still staring at his shoes.

"He's a ponce," I said to Artie, when Flowers had wandered off.

"I don't want to go," said Artie.

"I don't think we have a choice," I said. And we didn't. All of us, even me, had been programmed at boarding school to obey the teachers unquestioningly. To do otherwise risked detention, hours of "hard labor" in the garden, or a beating.

We showed up at four o'clock, leaving it as late as we dared and knowing we had to be back in the main school for five o'clock tea. Flowers sat in a leather armchair and watched us as we played, his only interruption to tell us what to play next. When we left together at ten minutes to five, I could feel the relief coming off Artie in waves. We never talked about his "private lessons," but I think Artie told himself they were over, that the visit to Flowers's cottage meant he was safe.

He was wrong.

The next day, Mr. Flowers appeared at the front of my class and announced, in his soft voice, that he was taking over as our Latin teacher. I looked over at Artie, but he didn't seem bothered, because what could the man do in a classroom of kids?

Nothing, as it turned out. He talked about Socrates for forty minutes, then sent us to wash up for lunch. We began to file out of the classroom, and we all looked back when Flowers raised his voice loud enough to be heard over the shuffling of feet.

"Halliwell, stay behind, please."

I looked back and saw that the boy's face had turned pale, and his little body sagged as he retook his seat to wait for the empty classroom and Mr. Flowers's attention.

For the remainder of the summer term, I saw less and less of Artie. He sat quietly in class and didn't speak, on the few occasions I asked if he wanted to go to the music room, he just shook his head. I suspected he was still playing for Mr. Flowers, and on a couple of Sunday afternoons, I went looking for him. When he was nowhere to be seen, I assumed I was right.

I forgot about Artie and Mr. Flowers over the summer holidays, which I spent with my family in France. But when the winter term began in early September, Artie was nowhere to be seen. I asked around, and someone said he'd left the school for good, no idea why.

I had an idea, and I wasn't happy about it. Not so much because of what Flowers had done to Artie—I didn't fully understand it back then, and, if I had, I wouldn't have cared that much. No, I was mad about what he'd done to me. He'd taken away one of the few pleasurable interruptions in an existence that otherwise varied from mundane to miserable. I still went up to the music attic to play guitar, but Flowers never appeared. I was left alone up there with the smell of dust and floor wax, and the tunes I played by myself, to myself, for myself.

Flowers himself seemed angry, that term. He continued to teach music and Latin, and continued to smell like a woman, unaware or ignoring the wrinkled noses of the other boys. But he seemed intent on punishing me for Artie's absence, or perhaps for my unformed knowledge about what he'd done to the boy. Too often I found myself chided for messy handwriting, yelled at for fidgeting, punished for not listening. He was clever about it, too, not overtly bullying me but doing it incrementally, when no one else was there or when my misdeeds were real, and all he had to do was exaggerate them. Disproportionate punishments were common at the school, the severity of the crime depending on the whim or mood of the teacher. So to be ordered to scrub a bathroom floor with a toothbrush for taking too long to piss attracted no one's attention. Except mine.

Mr. Flowers died the day after my birthday, a birthday being the one day we were shown a modicum of humanity. Instead of whatever the sport was, we were allowed to go off on our own, or with up to two friends, for a walk in the Scottish highlands. My birthday always fell in cross-country season, which I hated, so I took full advantage of the custom and went walking. By myself. The second tradition was for the cook to make a large cake, which the birthday boy could share with his classmates. Often, a piece was delivered to friends outside one's class, maybe the captain of the football team as a way of sucking up, likewise to a favorite teacher. I took a piece to Mr. Flowers, catching him on his way out of the main school. He seemed surprised, but my downcast eyes and submissive tone made it clear it was a peace offering, or perhaps one of defeat, the way a vanquished soldier might give up his weapon to a captor.

He died that night, or in the morning. A heart attack was the word, and the headmaster gathered us all in the chapel to let us know. A tragedy, we were told, one that the school would recover from in due course. Stiff upper lip and carry on, we were told. John Flowers would have wanted it that way.

John Flowers. The first man I ever killed.

CHAPTER THIRTY

IN THIS HOLLOW VALLEY

Tuesday morning crawled by. I was in court scrolling through the docket case by case, the weekly procession of misdemeanors and juvenile delinquents pretending to be sorry. I'd never seen the appeal of tattoos, but so many of these kids, some as young as twelve, had them all over their bodies. Ugly, blotchy, homemade tattoos, of course, because no professional artist would work with a kid. One little punk, a repeat offender according to his probation officer, had his area code, *512*, tattooed under his eye. A gang thing, and an absolute guarantee of a thug life.

A rare cool front had blown through central Texas, so at lunchtime I walked to a taco truck half a mile away, a place that made its own salsa. I sat at a picnic bench to eat and felt someone behind me. I knew who it was immediately, that soft perfume and the uncanny knack of appearing out of nowhere. She slid onto the bench beside me.

"Hi, Dominic. Lunch looks good."

"Hungry? You want something?"

"No thanks. Ate already."

"Okay. Stalking me?"

"Kind of. I need to talk to you."

"About?"

"Bobby."

"What about him?"

"I need to know what to do. How to help him."

I looked at her. Her face was serious, that alabaster skin seemed to shimmer in the sun, and the openness in her eyes made me want to kiss her, hold her, help her. I sometimes wondered if my condition was absolute, if there was perhaps a continuum of psychopathy so that I could find in myself the occasional glimmer of humanity that might allow me to truly connect with another person. It wasn't something I wondered about often, just because I didn't really believe it was likely. But in rare moments like this, when I felt (or thought I felt) something more than physical sensations, I really did imagine it possible.

"I don't know what to tell you," I said. "He's in good hands with probation—they have all kinds of services set up. Drug treatment, gang awareness, family counseling if you want it."

"That's not enough," she said, her voice almost a whisper.

"I'm a prosecutor. I don't fix people, I just . . ." I struggled to boil down my role in the juvenile system. It wasn't to convict and punish, not like in adult court. "I prove up the case so the probation department can go to work. Treatment in the community . . . if that doesn't work, a residential treatment facility somewhere. I'm just the intake guy, basically."

She tilted her head and looked at me, like she was waiting for me to understand. It came slowly, like a tide creeping up a beach, and she waited patiently while I made the connections. I thought back to when she'd sought me out, always exhibiting a remoteness and calculation that made me wonder if she was like me. I'd understood at some level, even at the start, that she was looking to use me, and that was another count against, or for, her, another reason to think maybe she wasn't an empath. Even at my work, she'd showed up and played the sad sister to get me to help her little brother, manipulated me because she knew I'd do it, understood my compulsive and reckless nature. Exploited me the way I exploited others. And she knew I'd do it because she knew what I was, had recognized that in me. As she gazed at me with those lovely brown eyes, eyes so full of light and life, eyes so different from mine, I realized that she'd recognized me for what I was because she'd lived with the same curse, lived with it day in and day out, and had done for the last twelve years.

She wasn't the psychopath, her little brother was. Bobby, the hollow boy soon to be a hollow man.

The fact that she was there, asking for my help, confirmed it. She loved him despite his affliction. She cared enough to target and seduce me. She wanted to save him, and she would do whatever she could, and no sociopath has ever been that unselfish.

"There's no cure," I said. "I'm sorry, but there's nothing that you, I, or the system can do to change what he is."

"There has to be," she said.

"I'm sorry. He has to decide for himself what he wants to be, how he wants to deal with it."

"How did you decide?"

"I didn't, not initially. My parents sent me away to boarding schools, places remote enough that I couldn't do much harm."

"What do you mean?"

I smiled. "When you're in a small group in the middle of nowhere, it's hard to get away with bad things."

"I can't send him to boarding school," she said.

"I know. He'll have to figure it out for himself somehow. Maturity is his friend, so the issue is how much damage he'll do before he matures."

"At the rate he's going ... a lot." She paused, then asked, "He knows, right? I mean, you knew at some point?"

"Yeah, when I was about his age I suppose." I wanted to tell her, to explain, but this was weird. I'd never talked to anyone about it, never been open. Not because I was mortally opposed to the idea but because the situation had never arisen like this. The few people who'd suspected or said something saw my condition as a bad thing, a danger to them. Fair enough, too—it wasn't like I had a secret Santa Claus inside me itching to get out. But there, with her, it was a gift. A blessing. Something that she wanted to know about, not so she could judge or avoid me but because she wanted just to understand. And telling her, well, that gave me a little power over her, maybe just influence; but nonetheless it was a bridge between us, not a chasm. "It's not a sudden realization," I said. "You just know you're different, not sensitive like other people. You see people having emotions that you don't have and it makes you wonder."

"Makes you take advantage," she said. "He does that all the time, even with me. Does he . . . does he love me?"

"Not in the way you love him. He's not unfeeling toward you, but it's hard to describe."

"What if he saw a therapist?"

"Then he'd manipulate the therapist unless he saw an expert, someone who knows about this stuff."

"And then he'd get a formal diagnosis, and his life would be ruined."

"I don't think they diagnose psychopaths before the age of eighteen."

"Were you diagnosed?"

"I was. My parents never gave up hope I could be cured, so they spent a lot of money on me. Including a first-class ticket to America. Idiots."

"See, I don't want Bobby talking about me that way."

I smiled again. "Then don't be an idiot."

We both looked up as a slicktop police car pulled into the parking lot and stopped with a screech of brakes, its nose pointed at us. The first person out of the car was Megan Ledsome, and two large, plain-clothes cops stepped out behind her.

"Dominic, stand up, please."

"What's going on?" I asked.

"You need to come with us."

"'Please' would go a long way."

She didn't smile, and I suddenly got that this was serious. "No jokes, Dominic. We got some new information on our capital-murder case. Information that means you're coming downtown with me. Now."

CHAPTER THIRTY-ONE

OF EMPTY MEN

T ime stopped. I felt people watching me, the guys in the taco truck, the cops, and, of course, *her*. I stood, slowly, and moved away from the picnic table. I looked at Detective Ledsome and let a measure of bemusement drift into my eyes.

"I don't understand," I said. "You're joking, right?" But I didn't know her well enough for practical jokes.

"No. We really do need to talk."

I felt a hand take mine, and I looked down into those soft, brown eyes and saw fear. "It's fine, don't worry," I said.

"Capital murder?" she whispered.

"I promise," my voice was warm, unconcerned, "everything's fine. It's an investigation I'm helping them with." I turned to Ledsome. "Okay. So let's talk, we can go over—"

"Not here. The police station."

"Seriously?"

"Our little talk needs to be on tape."

"Why?"

"For the record. So when the prosecutor handling the case gets the file, everything is aboveboard and by the book. Same as we do for all witnesses and suspects."

"Which one am I?"

She didn't respond, just walked to the passenger side of her car and opened the door. "You can ride up front with me," Ledsome said.

I let go of the comforting hand that was gripping me and walked toward the car. I got in without saying anything, and Ledsome slammed the door a little too hard once I was in. As a reminder of my situation, the car rocked when the two burly detectives climbed into the backseat. Ledsome slid behind the wheel and locked the doors. She waited for me to buckle up before she put on her own seat belt.

As we bumped out of the parking lot, I looked at her profile and decided how I was going to play this. "Look, Megan, I didn't want to make a scene back there, frighten my girlfriend, but what the fuck is going on? You're acting like I'm a fucking suspect and I don't appreciate it."

"Your girlfriend, huh?"

"Seriously, I want to know what's going on."

Her voice softened and she glanced over as she spoke. "I know. But hang tight until we get to the station. I really do have to do this by the book, have the video camera capture everything."

"Fine, but tell me one thing. Do you seriously think I had anything to do with this?"

"That, Dominic, is what we're going to talk about."

When an innocent man is accused of a crime, his first reaction is outrage. If that doesn't work, he calms down and tries to explain why it's all a mistake. If the accusations persist, and graduate to chats at the police station, he starts to worry that maybe a series of unfortunate coincidences points to his guilt, and that he may not be able to make the cops understand that they are, in fact, just coincidences.

When a guilty man is accused of a crime, he often confesses. A combination of guilty conscience and a sense of inevitability, especially if he's in a police car, come together to crush any resistance and bring forth a confession. Alternatively, a guilty man will lawyer up, demonstrating that he's been through the system enough to know he can't trust his own mouth and won't help himself by talking. Sometimes, a guilty man will try to lie his way out of trouble, getting increasingly nervous and more fidgety the more his lies don't stick. The police are used to this, and if he keeps lying he'll be caught out and, eventually, confess.

When someone like me is accused of a crime, whether he's guilty or innocent, he'll lie. But he won't get nervous, and, because he's been lying his whole life, chances are they'll be good lies and they'll stick. This depends on the sociopath being smart, of course, there's always that caveat. Stupid men tell stupid lies, there's no way around that. But smart or not, a sociopath has no guilty conscience to provoke a confession.

So I sat there quietly for the ride, waiting to see what they had. I wasn't under arrest, which was a pretty damn good start, and despite the serious faces and muscular cops literally breathing down my neck, I knew I was free to leave. I couldn't do that, though, because if they thought I knew something and declined to help them, I'd be fired in a heartbeat. And if they knew that I knew something, they'd probably arrest me on the spot if I refused to cooperate. At the very least, they'd have me suspended without pay, which would be great for guitar practice, less great for paying the rent.

At the police station, Ledsome took me into one of the small interview rooms that I'd seen a thousand times on video tape. It smelled of stale body odor and some form of cheap cleaning solvent. She acted like she was used to the smell, didn't even wrinkle her nose. There were four of these rooms and each one had a camera high in the corner, and it was from that perspective I'd watched and listened to dozens and dozens of interviews with suspects and witnesses. Mostly suspects.

"I need to go to the control room and turn the camera on," she said. "Need anything? Coffee? Water?"

"No." I sat at the small, round table. "I'm fine."

"Be right back." The door swung closed with a whoosh, locking itself automatically. I'd been told this was an intentional design feature so the cops didn't have to manually lock the door when they left the room. That, the theory went, would undermine their attempts to play nice guy, appear all trusting and understanding.

She was gone a long time, but I'd expected that. Another one of their little tricks to soften up their suspect, if that's what I was. I checked my watch and realized I hadn't told anyone at work I'd be out.

Then I wondered if they already knew.

Ledsome came back after twenty minutes with a can of Diet Coke and a note pad. She sat opposite me and made a big show of settling in, which is tough for a petite lady. She gave the date and time aloud, looking at her watch, and said our names clearly for the camera. Then she said, "Dominic, I want to confirm that you are here voluntarily and know that you are in no way obligated to speak with me, and that you are free to leave at any time."

"Apart from the locked door, you mean."

That seemed to fluster her a little because she shouldn't have let it close on me before. Doing so meant I was detained against my will, which undermined this new statement that I was free to leave. And, as I knew and she might have been figuring out, if she ever wanted to use my statement against me, that could be a problem.

"I apologize for that," she said, "I didn't mean to close the door. You are free to leave now, if you like."

"No, it's fine. Although the door is closed again."

"Thank you. We appreciate your cooperation, and the door is closed purely for privacy. I can open it for you at any time." She looked up at me when I didn't respond. "Right, then, shall we start?"

"I'm just wondering if we should begin by letting people at my office know I'm here."

"No, actually. We'd rather not."

"You don't want anyone to know I'm here?"

"Not yet."

"I am really not understanding any of this."

"Dominic, I'm going to level with you. And the chances are, you're going to be mad at me and that's fine. But please remember that we have two dead people, two families who lost loved ones, and all I'm trying to do is get the guys who killed them."

"And sometimes you have to fuck with people to do that."

She cocked her head. "Yes, something like that. Just out of interest, how do you know I'm fucking with you?"

Wishful thinking. "Because you don't interview a suspect and start with an apology for making them mad. You do that to a witness you've lied to about something."

"Very astute." She took a deep breath. "I'll start with the minor deception and explain why after. First, no need to tell your boss you're here; she knows."

"Maureen?"

"Yes. In fact, I had her switch out with you yesterday, for the raid on Otto Bland's house, on purpose."

"Why?"

"Because I wanted you there when we arrested him. I wanted to see your reaction, and his reaction." She grimaced. "I guess I got to see yours, after all."

"Go on."

"That call, the phone tip about the gun. It wasn't just the location of the gun that we got. The caller gave us a make, model, and license plate for the car that drove out of the trailer park minutes after the shooting."

"It wasn't my car."

"No, it wasn't. It was your roommate's." She was staring at me intently, watching for any and every reaction. Just like she must have been doing at Otto's.

I let my mouth fall open, but snapped it shut when I thought maybe I was overdoing it. "You're fucking kidding me. Tristan?"

"Tristan Bell."

"That's not possible. It's . . . it's ridiculous." I looked up quickly. "Unless you mean someone stole his car . . . but he'd have said something to me."

"No one stole his car. He also fits the vague description we got from the caller."

"Who's the caller? Can he ID him in a lineup?"

"We don't know who it is. A woman. She called from a gas-station pay phone not far from the trailer park, so that backs up her claim that she lives there."

"You sure she wasn't involved?" I asked. "I mean, she's giving you a shitload of information. The gun, the license plate, the description."

"I guess it's possible, but if she's involved, why give us the gun?"

"Good point."

"Plus, she sounded scared, which also fits the way things go out there."

"Snitches get stitches, and all that."

"Right."

"So why the games with me?" She didn't respond, just stared until it sank in. "You thought I was involved, didn't you?"

"Not really. I mean, no. For one thing, the caller said there was only one person in the car."

Thank God for nighttime and poor people who can't afford glasses. "Then why give me the runaround?"

"This is a capital-murder case, Dom. We had to be sure."

"And are you?"

"Yes. We checked with your neighbor, and he gave you an alibi."

I frowned. "I didn't see my neighbor that night."

She smirked. "No, and he didn't see you. But he heard you. You and your girlfriend." She turned her face so the video camera wouldn't catch the wink she gave me. "And she seems so demure and sweet."

I liked the way this conversation was going, so I let the humor out of the bag. "Yeah, well, it's always the quiet ones, Detective. You seem jolly quiet yourself."

"We'll need a statement from your girlfriend confirming she was with you, of course."

"Of course."

"Without the sound effects." She suppressed a smile and cleared her throat. "Anyway, I need to know if you saw Mr. Bell that evening. If you saw him in the apartment, or if you noticed him leaving."

"I didn't. No, none of that. I was in my room the whole evening."

"So you can't say he was there, and you can't say he wasn't."

"Correct."

"Do you have any information about Bell that might help us? Has he been flashing cash or anything?"

"I don't think so, no. Nothing like that."

"Think about it and let me know if something occurs to you."

"Sure."

She sat very still for a moment, her eyes on her pad, like she was wondering what to say next. "There's one other thing."

"Oh?"

"Yeah, and I'm hesitant to tell you, but I kinda have to. Again, let me finish before you say anything."

"I'm intrigued."

"How well do you know Bell?"

"Not very. He keeps to himself and we don't hang out together or anything. Now I'm in juvie, I rarely see him at work as he's usually downtown."

"He may not be the mild-mannered computer geek you think." I raised an eyebrow and she continued. "We took a little look-see on his work computer. It's county property, so we didn't need a warrant or anything, and we saw he'd been on your computer."

"Oh?"

"Yeah, a couple of times. Looks like he connected remotely, which made tracking his activity harder, but from what we can see, he was searching that trailer park on your computer. And then deleted the searches."

"On my computer?"

"Yes. Dominic, we have reason to think that he killed those two men with Otto Bland as part of a robbery. And now he's trying to frame you."

CHAPTER THIRTY-TWO

FALLS THE SHADOW

Detective Ledsome stood and said, "I don't think we need the camera for this bit." She left the room, letting the door sweep shut again. I didn't know if it was intentional, but for the first time she had truly thrown me, because I had no idea what she was about to say. She was back in under a minute. She sat, put her pen down on top of her pad, and looked me in the eye. "We don't think you're in any danger. It just seems like he might be laying a few crumbs to turn suspicion on you."

I shook my head. "On me?"

"Yes. He's smart, very smart—and if he really killed those men, then he's also ruthless."

"I can't believe this," I said. "I mean, that he would be involved in something like this, and then that he'd try and frame me."

"I know, it's hard to grasp. But we have a good motive for the crime. He has a gambling addiction, and he's even used his work computer to place bets, which tells you how bad it is."

"So the murders, they were about robbery?"

"Right. Like I told you, Ambrosio Silva was a landlord who carried a lot of cash at the end of the month. Somehow Bell found out and robbed him."

"How would he know about that?"

"We aren't sure, but probably through Otto Bland."

"So three people are dead over money."

"The oldest motive in the book. And, by the way, another

reason we can exclude you. As far as we know, you've no gambling problems, debts, or drug addictions. In fact, I'm told you don't even drink."

"Wow, you really are thorough."

"Although . . ." She cocked her head. "You told me you went to Otto's and had a beer with him."

"Sorry, I was speaking figuratively. He had the beer, I had a Diet Coke." I cursed myself for being so loose with language, and suddenly wondered if they'd checked for empty soda cans. "Hang on, I don't think he had any. Now that I think about it, I just had water. Sorry to be so imprecise, I know little things like that matter."

"That's okay, we did check for cans and bottles to see if anyone else had been with him. Didn't see anything like that."

"As I said, impressively thorough."

"This is capital murder. We get real thorough for those."

"What else do you know about me?"

"Not much. You're good at your job, you're fair, and people like you. Oh, and I'm told you play guitar a little."

"A little?"

"Never heard you play, so I can't really judge, can I?"

"You could take my word for it." I gave her a little smile. "Or you could come watch me play."

"Maybe, after the case is closed, and if your girlfriend doesn't mind."

My mind went immediately to the Norman Pub and my permanent ban. I'd been so distracted, so consumed with getting away with double murder, that I'd not tried to get gigs elsewhere. As a result, I had no clue whether my name was mud in the Austin music scene. I had gotten as far as finding out who screwed me over, but I didn't know how bad the damage was. If it stopped me from sleeping with Detective Ledsome, it was very bad indeed.

"Yeah, that'd be nice. I don't think she'd mind at all—it's not like we're steady or anything." I looked up. "Don't you have a husband?"

She shrugged. "We don't do everything together."

"Then come hear me play; it'll be fun."

"It'll have to wait until the case is closed, now that you're a witness."

"Right, sure. About that, are you going to arrest him?"

"We're watching him right now. I want to get a few more things in place, then we'll draft the arrest affidavit. A couple of days, no more. We don't think he's a danger to anyone else, and since we're watching him, we'll know if he tries to run."

"This is crazy," I said. "You really think he's trying to frame me for this?" The idea that Tristan was smart enough to pin the crime on me was patently ridiculous, not something I'd ever consider or accept. But I wasn't averse to the police buying the theory.

"We do. I know it's bizarre but it's a fine way to get away with a crime."

"Yeah, sure, but the guy's a dork, not a double-murderer."

"People get desperate when they run out of money. Remember, he's not stealing just to pay off his debts, but also so he can keep gambling. It's an addiction and he'll do anything to support it."

"Even kill?"

"It's quite likely it was a stickup that went wrong."

"Maybe. And I guess he knew Otto through work."

"Right."

I shook my head slowly. "You think you know people."

"I know. I'm sorry." She reached over and put a hand on mine. "But please don't feel bad or beat yourself up. There are a lot of bad people out there, and they disguise themselves well. And I guess there are good people out there, people we know and like, who end up doing bad things. We see that all the time."

"True."

"If it makes you feel any better, like I said, they probably didn't go out there intending to hurt anyone, certainly not kill anyone. They were amateurs at this, and when things went wrong, they panicked and started shooting. It's not like they're evil geniuses who planned it all, fooling you, me, and everyone else they know into thinking they're sweet, little angels."

"I suppose not."

She let go of my hand and sat back. "Are you able to stay out of your apartment for a couple of days?"

"And go where?"

"We just don't want you to give anything away while we wrap things up." She gave me a sheepish grin. "We even thought about pretend-arresting you, to keep you out of harm's way and so that he'd think his plan was working."

"Seriously?"

"Yeah. But you can thank your boss that didn't happen. She said you'd crap your pants."

"Probably would have. I'm guessing the other inmates wouldn't be too happy sharing a cell with a prosecutor."

"We'd have kept you in solitary, don't worry."

"Splendid, much better."

"So can you? Stay somewhere else?" She smirked. "Your girl-friend's place, maybe?"

"Maybe. Of course, thanks to you I'll have to explain that I didn't actually commit a double murder for a few hundred bucks."

Her cell phone buzzed on her hip and she unclipped it. "Ledsome. Yeah, we're done. We'll be right there." She hung up and smiled at me. "One more favor to ask."

"Cavity search?"

"You wish. No, just a formality. The guys at the top of the food chain, they like to be sure we're satisfied internally when we rule out a potential suspect."

"'Satisfied internally.' What does that mean?"

"Like I said, it's another favor. So we can cross you off the list once and for all."

"My fingerprints?"

"I guess technically it's two favors, now that you mention it."

"You're welcome to my prints. What else?"

"We need you to take a polygraph exam."

"A lie detector? Are you serious?"

"Very."

"I don't know; those things aren't reliable. I mean, I want to help, of course, but you're kind of catching me by surprise here."

"Up to you, but that was the examiner who called. He's here now, set up and waiting for you. As I tell people, if you've nothing to hide, you've nothing to fear. Am I right?"

○

Lie detectors weren't admissible in any courtroom in Texas, but that wasn't the point. The Austin Police Department used them for their own reasons—two of them. One was so detectives could satisfy themselves they were correctly ruling out a potential suspect. Peace of mind, you might say. The second reason was that even though the results weren't admissible, people had cracked under the stress of taking the test. Knowing their lies were found out, they simply confessed.

I myself had handled a case in which the defense lawyer insisted his client was innocent of a burglary. He believed his client so much that he offered to have him take a lie-detector test. Not agreed to, but offered to. Not only did his client fail the test, but the guy broke down and spilled his guts halfway through the exam. The defense lawyer, a nice-enough fellow, was highly embarrassed and, I suspect, didn't suggest polygraphs to his clients after that.

The science is questionable, but in theory it's pretty simple. It's supposed to measure bodily responses to stress, things like skin conductivity and heart rate, stuff people can't control and that will give them away.

Only, I don't suffer from stress, which means that I'll flatline a polygraph in all the right places.

The examiner used by Detective Ledsome was named Tony Bentley, and I don't know if it was on purpose, but they picked an Englishman. He looked like a small-town GP, red-cheeked, soft-bodied, and full of smiles. He pumped my hand and chattered merrily to himself as he wired me up. Ledsome wasn't allowed in the room to watch, but I was pretty sure there was a camera on somewhere.

Bentley began by asking my name, date of birth, and job title; then he moved on to current events. He asked these as his preliminary questions, simple ones with answers that were obviously true or false, to establish a baseline against which he could compare the important answers.

"Is Barack Obama the president of the United States?"

"Yes."

"Do you know who won the Super Bowl last year?"

"No."

"Is the Pope a Roman Catholic?"

"Yes. And a bear shits in the woods."

"Sir, please just answer my questions."

"Sorry, I was anticipating. Go on."

"Were you born in England?"

"Yes."

"Were you involved in a murder-robbery two weeks ago?"

"No."

"Do you know Tristan Bell?"

"Yes."

"Was he involved in the murder-robbery two weeks ago?"

"I don't know."

"Do you currently work in the juvenile division of the district attorney's office?"

"Yes."

"Have you ever shot anyone?"

"No."

"Have you ever killed anyone?"

"No."

"Are you in any way familiar with a man by the name of Ambrosio Silva?"

"No."

"Are you in any way familiar with a man by the name of Dave Gass?"

The security guard? "No."

Bentley picked up a list of questions written by, I assumed, Detective Ledsome and worked them in. The whole thing took twenty-five minutes, and when we were done, he left me there, hooked up, while he consulted with Ledsome.

They both appeared about five minutes later and Bentley, wordlessly, unhooked me. When he was done, he stuck out a hand.

"Jolly good show. Thanks for the cooperation."

"Most welcome," I said.

"You need a ride to your girlfriend's house?" Ledsome asked. "You know where she lives?"

"Yeah, I know where she lives." I stood and stretched my back. "Cute little cottage on the wrong side of the tracks."

"You want a ride there, or to your car?"

"My car, but I need to go home to get some stuff first."

She shook her head. "That's not a good idea."

I moved out into the hallway and Ledsome stepped out with me. I leaned against the wall, as close to her as I dared. "Why not? Cos the big, bad Tristan is there?"

"He killed two people."

"Probably just one, if we're getting technical."

"That makes a difference to you?"

"Been living with him for a couple of months now. He's not killed me yet."

"No, he's got your best interests at heart. He's merely setting you up to take the fall for his 'just one' murder."

"If he is, then all the more reason he won't kill me. A dead patsy isn't much of a patsy."

"Maybe. And then his patsy shows up acting weird and gathering his belongings, looking nervously out the window for the cops."

"None of which I'll do," I said. "Look, it'll take me five minutes. I'll shove some stuff in a bag and be out of there before you know it."

"And tell him what?"

"That I'm spending a few nights with my girlfriend. You know, the truth."

She thought about it for a moment. "I don't know, letting you go back into a closed environment with—"

"Look, if he's that dangerous, why don't you just arrest him?"

"We're not there yet. We have enough for a search warrant, but I'm not ready to arrest him."

"So execute the search warrant. While you guys are in there, I'll pack and go."

She looked at her watch. "It's being prepared as we speak. Funnily enough, we're having trouble getting hold of a prosecutor to review it before we show it to a judge. And no, Dominic, you're a witness for this case, not a prosecutor, so you can't review it."

"So what, a couple more hours?"

"Yep, no more than that."

"We could go hang out at your place."

"Jesus, you don't quit, do you?"

"Then take me back. I'm not in danger and I'm not hanging around here until you've finished your bloody paperwork."

She acquiesced with a tilt of her head, and I followed her down the hallway and out of the building.

As we got into her car, she said, "But I'm waiting until you come out. And I'll give you my number, just text '911' to me, or call me, if he so much as looks at you funny."

"If he's not there, can I call you in for a cup of tea?"

CHAPTER THIRTY-THREE

WIND IN DRY GRASS

I walked into the apartment to find Tristan locked in his room, as usual. I heard him moving about, the sound of music seeping into the living room, and I stood there for a moment, watching his door. He had no idea I was there, no clue that the police were lining up all the right paperwork so they could kick their way in and help themselves to his stuff. He had no idea, either, that the cops had concluded that he was trying to frame me.

I went into my room and looked through my things. One final check before the cops nosed through them, just to make sure everything was where it should be. I looked at my gun, my lovely Smith & Wesson that I'd tucked at the back of my bottom dresser drawer. I wanted to take it out, touch it, because I missed carrying. I knew I couldn't, not yet, anyway. I tidied a little and took out a piece of paper I didn't want anymore, crumpling it into my pocket for later disposal. I packed a couple of days' clothing, work and home stuff, then slung the bag over my shoulder.

I knocked on Tristan's door and called his name. He opened the door.

"Oh, hey," he said.

"Hey. Going to head out in a few, just checking in. All okay?"

"Yeah. I guess."

I saw the trashcan just inside his door and pulled out the scrunched-up ball of paper. "You mind? Mine's full."

He shrugged. "Go ahead."

I tossed it in and then headed down the hall to the living room.

He must have noticed my bag because he followed me and asked, "Going somewhere?"

"Yep. Gonna spend a few days with my special lady."

"Ah." I could tell he wasn't sure whether to believe me. For my part, I was deciding whether to give him one last chance to make it. He was so clueless and in so much danger, like a blind man standing near the edge of a cliff, enjoying the air. Maybe a baby antelope wandering under a leopard's tree. Looking at him, I remembered another lesson from my childhood, one about giving our targets a sporting chance, and I resisted a smile as I mentally transposed his head onto the body of a low-flying pheasant. Giving him an option seemed like the decent thing to do.

"You should pack a bag, too," I said.

"Why?"

"I just spent the afternoon with the police. They know you're involved in the murders."

His eyes widened. "What? You're joking. Fuck, Dom, that's not fun—"

"I'm not joking. They're preparing a search warrant right now. You probably have an hour or two."

"What? How's that possible?"

"They're the police. It's what they do. And they know you're responsible."

"Me? You, too."

"No. Just you, actually. So you might want to pack that bag pretty quickly, assuming you can avoid the cops in the parking lot who're watching this place."

He stared at me for a moment. "You cut a deal?"

"No, not at all. I just had nothing to do with it, and the cops know that. They also know, by the way, that you're trying to frame me."

"What?" he gasped. His face was a kaleidoscope of confusion, his head shaking, eyes wide one minute, narrowed the next, and his cheeks coloring and then blanching by the second. He felt his way to the sofa and perched on the arm.

"Yeah, I'm afraid so. They got a call, someone saw you and your car at the scene and called it in. 'Anonymous tipster,' I think they call them."

"But . . . but . . . you were there, too. It was *your* car."

"Nope, they saw one person and even gave the license plate."

"How's that possible?" He shook his head, still trying to figure it out. "Who? Who called?"

"Like I said, an anonymous tipster."

"That doesn't make any sense."

"I'm just saying." I cleared my throat and hoped he was catching up. I wanted him to get there while I was explaining why he was going to prison, why he deserved to go to prison. And not for the murder. "Your secret little drawer in there. The one you keep locked."

His head snapped up, but he said nothing.

"Things aren't looking good, and maybe it won't make any difference, but you might want to do a better job of hiding that shit. I'm told pedophiles don't do well in prison, though it's possible things are different on death row. And by different, I mean there are more murderers around."

"I'm not a pedophile."

"Yes, you are. I saw your stash of pictures, and I may not have any kids, but I recognize children when I see them. Especially when some of them are in diapers."

"That's not . . . I'm not . . ."

"Things happen in threes, Tristan. You're the third pedophile I've known, and you might want to bear in mind that the other two wound up dead." I shrugged. "You might too, of course, but you're white and middle-class, so I doubt it. Especially in Austin."

"You turned me in because I'm . . . because of those pictures?" He was getting there and his eyes flicked from side to side as he put the pieces together. "Otto?"

"Otto's still dead."

"Jesus. You killed him." I didn't respond to that. "Are they really coming here?" he asked.

"The police? Yes. They've been watching you since they connected your car to the crime scene. One car is out there now, plus the cop who brought me here from the police station. You can probably make it out the back way, through the laundry room."

"There's no back door in the laundry room."

"Come on, Tristan, you're a fucking idiot. The police are coming to arrest you for capital murder. Which you committed, by the way. The laundry room has a big fucking window, so you can pack your shit and squeeze your skinny body through that. Use your imagination."

For an empath, he wasn't as freaked out as I expected him to be, and it was pissing me off. Of course, maybe he was so freaked out he was paralyzed. Either way, his self-preservation instincts were crap.

"If they catch me," he said. "I'll just turn you in, you know that, right?"

Ah, he still thinks we're in this together. "Dear chap, listen to me. The cops know I didn't have anything to do with it. They believe you've been trying to frame me. So if you start telling them I'm involved, that just strengthens their theory. The more you protest that I had something to do with it, the more in the clear I am."

"How? How did you—?"

"Plus I have an alibi."

"An alibi?"

"You don't recall all the wild, kinky sex I was having that night?"

He nodded slowly as he remembered. "Yeah. But that was later, after we got back."

"Two things about that. First, neither the police nor our neighbor have a good timeline. Second, I have a witness who says she was with me all evening, as well as all night, doing rude things to each other. You remember our neighbor, how mad he was?"

He stared at me. "Why are you doing this? This is evil."

"Right, and fucking kids is a harmless pastime."

"I didn't do anything to you. I gave you a room, a place to live." Tears welled in his eyes. "I treated you like a friend, I never did anything to you. Now I'm going to die, in prison or in . . . in an execution chamber. A fucking needle in my arm. All because of you."

"Grow up, Tristan. You'd fuck a little baby if you had the chance. And you're the one who pushed yourself into this thing. You remember that?"

"But I never wanted anyone to get hurt." He rose. "You, you're the one who shot someone. I'll tell them that. I'll fucking tell them everything, and yeah, maybe I'll go to prison, but so will you. No way you're getting away with this, no fucking way."

"Relax, you're sounding like a Scooby Doo movie. I already got away with it."

His mouth opened and closed and I knew he was looking for something, some tiny foothold, not even so he could get himself out of trouble. So he could get one up on me.

"The money," he said. "All this, all this shit, this killing, this planning, you evil fucker, and someone else stole your money." He smiled and his eyes gleamed like a crazy person's. "The fucking money. You think you're so smart, but some asshole took your money, and you've done all this for nothing. I may rot in prison, but you'll have that on your conscience and not a penny of that money."

I hesitated because I realized at that moment that he was right about something, that after all, the money was the fulcrum of this little jaunt. Not just the motivation, that's obvious. But even afterward, when two people had been killed, the money was what we focused on. We even made a risky trip to get it, placing ourselves in huge danger. The excitement, the terror, the death, the risks, all revolved around our desire for the money. And if he knew that I had it, he'd lose his mind.

So I told him.

"You ever see the movie *The Sting*?"

His eyes narrowed for the tenth time that afternoon. "What?"

"The movie with Robert Redford."

"What the fuck are you talking about?"

"It's a very old trick, Tristan. And I'm telling you because I don't want you to think all this was for nothing."

"Telling me what?"

"You remember how I put the bags of money in the trunk? Then I went back and took them out, and buried them. Remember that?" He nodded so I went on. "You never looked in the trunk, did you?"

"Why would I?"

"Right, why would you? Great point. But if you had, you'd have seen *four* camo bags. The two I brought to the trailer park stuffed with paper, and the two with money. Now, guess which ones I took out to the woods?"

"Oh, no. Oh my God."

"And guess which ones were in the trunk of the car when we came back here?"

"The money," he whispered.

"So yeah, I have the money. All of it."

I could see the wheels turning in his head, the cogs clicking into place as he searched for a hole in my plan and didn't find one. His breathing quickened as the panic rose in him, but then he looked at me, a glimmer of hope, or at least doubt, in his eyes. "The camera from the woods. Was there ever really a camera?"

"Yes, actually, I had to do the surveillance. That was my one risk, an unavoidable one. When I left the bags, I took it down and threw it into the trees, after wiping my prints off it, of course. Someone must have found it and sold it, like we saw." I gave him a cold smile. "Of course, that whole business following the schmuck who was selling it, that was just for show. A fun expedition with no downside and a good way to keep you guys busy."

"That guy never had the money, any of it."

"Nope. I did. All of it."

Tristan looked at me and his spine seemed to stiffen. The air between us crackled for a second, and then he rushed me. He covered the five feet between us in a flash, and I barely had time to hit the right button on my phone. I'd planned on him losing it, so I had "911" typed in. When that anger flashed in his eyes and his skinny little body flexed taut and hurtled toward me, I pressed *Send*. He hit me head on and we both went to the ground. My phone skittered away but I didn't care. I was too busy trying to stop him hitting me. He was a man possessed, swinging his fists at my face and my body, spittle streaming from his mouth and spattering me as he cursed and yelled, a hatred so intense that I was caught off guard. My rages burn cold and lingering, my revenge is always deliberate and emotionless, whereas this was a passion I'd not seen in any human, ever. For a moment, the sparest of seconds, I felt envy that one man could feel so much, so deeply and, even though it was anger, I resented him for it because I knew I'd never feel it, that my body would never explode with the passion of rage, horror, agony. Or love. This scrawny little fucker about to spend the rest of his life getting raped and bullied by inmate thugs had something I'd never had, and never would have. And to punish myself for that, I let him hit me, my forearms acting like shields but letting in his fierce punches, softening but not ending the pain from his sharp little fists.

And then Ledsome and two detectives were there, pulling him off me, screaming at him that he was under arrest, driving him to the floor with knees in his back and his wrists pinned between his shoulder blades. He was in pain now, wailing and crying, his feet kicking at the floor, but in despair, not in any real attempt to be free. He knew it was over, and I wiped the blood from my nose as I watched him, knowing why he'd chosen to attack me instead of escape, to hurt me rather than save himself. Because of the money.

In seconds he was handcuffed and lying still on the floor, crying quietly and moaning the occasional phrase that neither the cops nor I listened to. Ledsome still had one knee in the small of his back.

"Are you okay?" she asked me.

"Yeah, fine. I'm fine."

"What the fuck happened?"

"Nothing. I mean, everything was fine, I was getting my stuff, then he came out. I think, I don't know, but I think he knew you guys were coming. He must have."

"How could he know that?"

"I have no idea. I mean, he works at the DA's office and is a computer geek; maybe he hacked into something. I don't know. Maybe he saw these guys out in the parking lot and guessed. Anyway, I was getting my stuff together, and I opened my bottom drawer to get some trousers. In the back corner was my gun."

"Your gun? So what?"

I took a deep breath. "What I mean is, it used to be my gun. My Smith and Wesson. But a week or so before all this happened, I sold it to him."

"You sold him your gun?"

"I should have mentioned it when we were at the station, but I didn't think of it."

Tristan kicked and wriggled. "No, no, he's lying!"

"I'm not fucking lying, you gave me a check for it." I turned to Ledsome. "I didn't get it back from the bank yet, but when I do you can see. The memo line says 'Smith & W'; it's for two hundred dollars."

Tristan howled again, but Ledsome ground her knee into him to shut him up. "You done?" she snapped and, when he went limp, she stood. The two detectives moved forward, bent over Tristan, and pulled him to his feet. "Take him to the car and read him his rights," Ledsome said. "Make sure he understands them, and that the in-car video records you."

"Yes, ma'am," they said in unison.

She pulled the radio from her belt and connected with dispatch. "I'm going to need EMS to my location. No emergency but get them started this way, please." She helped me to my feet. "Quite a terrier, that guy. He got you good."

"Yes," I said, pinching my bloody nose. "He sure did."

CHAPTER THIRTY-FOUR

NOT WITH A BANG
BUT WITH A WHIMPER

I kept out of the way as they searched the apartment. They found my Smith & Wesson in the dresser's bottom drawer, just as I'd said. I knew they'd test it for prints and find his, and not mine, because the night of the murder I'd worn gloves and he hadn't. After the shooting, I'd handed him my gun to hold for a moment. When he gave it back, I handled it carefully, not wiping it clean. I hadn't cleaned it since, nor touched it with my bare hands.

They found the crumpled-up map, too, right there in the trashcan by his bedroom door. They wouldn't get any prints off that, but they wouldn't need to. A thorough hand-writing comparison would show he'd drawn the map and written on it. No prints needed to show it was his.

I hated to part with any of the money—that was the hardest thing for me. But for authenticity, I just had to. My special girl, as I'd started calling her, had helped with that. In fact, now that I think about it, *that* was the hardest part: her using his bathroom, having his spidery little hands on her naked skin. That was sickening. But it'd bought her time to put some of the money in the space above his ceiling tiles in the bathroom, a place I couldn't get to. If he talked to the police, he'd have to admit that I couldn't get into his room because he always kept his goddam door locked. I consoled myself over the loss of a few hundred dollars by reminding myself that the money the cops found had blood on it, yet more evidence of his guilt. And I congratulated myself for that touch, the kneeling beside a dying man to feel his pulse, to touch him as life left, and to dip my fingers in his blood and smear it on the bills that I knew I'd be leaving for the police to find.

Of course, the child porn in the little drawer helped. Not to connect Tristan to the crime but to paint him as a horrible human being. If there's one thing cops, prosecutors, and juries hate, it's a pedophile. And the media made sure everyone knew. He'd put that particular nail in his own coffin, of course; that wasn't my doing at all. But even sociopaths deserve a little luck now and again.

O

I saw Gus's wife, Michelle, a few times after Tristan's arrest, but I decided not to pursue her, an assertion of self-control that I was quite proud of. As for Gus, he's gone. He won't be found, by her or the police. Ever. He'd hate that, too, the permanent, unexplained disappearance, because he'd be much happier as a victim—all that drama and pathos, the adulation and adoration that comes when your faults are no longer around to annoy people.

As for why he's gone, well, it was his name I saw on Marley's computer. It was Gus who'd complained about me stealing one of his songs, and that's the real reason Marley didn't want him playing that night. Not a show of solidarity at all, so he'd lied to me about that. I should have figured it out. As for the song, sure, I'd heard him play it, early versions, stop-start versions in his den and my apartment. My version, the one I played and that he called "stolen" just wasn't. A few chords are similar, and I concede a similarity in rhythm and pacing, but that's all. Stolen? Hardly. If I write the words, "I'm not sure I want to be a killer," am I stealing from Shakespeare because I used the words "to be"?

Like writers, musicians feed off each other's work and gain inspiration. If he really thought I'd stolen it, he should have said so to my face. Going to Marley behind my back, sneaking around like that, well, it's the kind of stunt I'd pull. He really shouldn't have done that. I was supposed to be his friend, and he was supposed to be mine.

And speaking of that, it's not like I formed some devious plan to do away with him. Friends argue and fight. Well, anyway. You don't need to know that part of the story. It's not like you'd have good cause to believe me.

I split some of the money with my girl in green. After all, she'd put those bloody bills over Tristan's tub and made those anonymous calls to the police for me. Somehow her brother had found out about it all, though we weren't sure what or how much. Seemed like putting some money his way was a good move. I'd also come to trust her. Maybe it was because she'd sealed herself into this crime with me. If that seal broke, we'd both be done for and we knew it. But it was more than that. I told her stuff about me that I'd never talked about with anyone. Once she realized that I was empathy-challenged, there didn't seem much point hiding anything. It was, and always had been, the biggest and meanest skeleton in my closet, and she'd opened the door, seen my bare bones, and not run away screaming. I suppose I was too much like her brother to scare her and, of course, she wanted my help in helping him. To understand him, she needed to understand me because I represented one possible future for him. She didn't judge me; she just asked questions with her head cocked in that adorable way, her soft, wet eyes drinking me in as she listened. And I do love a captive audience.

She continued to try to understand me, and asked repeatedly about the reason I was in America in the first place. She didn't swallow the story everyone else seemed to take so easily. She knew there was more to it, and so I told her.

I told her about Mr. Flowers, the first pedophile I'd encountered, about his picking on my friend and then on me. I left out the details, but she got the picture of his sickness. I left out the details of his death too, the monkshood that I picked on my birthday walk, the poisonous leaves I covered the plate with, and the fact that he died the same way Agrippina killed Emperor Claudius. I so wanted to tell her about that, the wonderful irony of a perverted Latin teacher dying in agony like a Roman king. But I didn't think she'd appreciate it; she wasn't ready for that.

I did tell her about the second pedophile I knew, Gary Glasscock. His name would be funny if he'd been anything but a child molester. He was the gamekeeper on our estate. A short, red-faced man who waddled from side to side when he walked. I always wondered, with all that walking he did for his job, how he stayed fat. To everyone else, he was a jolly fellow, and his penchant for littering the woods with empty bottles of Navy rum was overlooked because he managed such fine pheasant shoots.

When I was fourteen, he took an interest in me. He showed me the tracks that the game followed and showed me how to build a quick but good hide for shooting pigeons. He taught me that the best time for pigeon shooting was the evening, during a snow storm. I went out three times in those conditions, and he was right, the birds would swoop into the trees and flee when I fired, but turn back immediately because of the wind and snow. I could just shoot and reload, shoot and reload, until the barrels got too hot to touch.

It was in one of those hides that he made his move. One minute I was looking out over the decoys we'd set up, the next he was behind me, panting. I looked back and saw his trousers around his knees, his face redder than usual and his tiny dick standing to attention. I was fourteen and had only a dim awareness of what he might be doing, but my secondhand experience with Mr. Flowers was still fresh. For some unknown reason, gamekeeper Gary had been unable to contain himself any longer and threw his body on top of mine. He weighed a hundred pounds more than I did, and I crumpled under him, face down. His fetid breath pumped into my ear, my cheek, as his hips ground against me, and the more I fought to get away, the louder he grunted, as if my squirming was for his benefit. I would never forget the sweet stench of rum on his breath and his bulging eyes that shone with desperation and lust. It took me a full minute to elbow and kick him off, and I wanted to shoot him right there and then. I probably should have, but I didn't know what the ramifications would be. More than that, I'd been lying a lot to my parents—and been found out a lot—and I simply didn't think they'd believe me. And if they didn't believe me, the police wouldn't. The oldest son of landed gentry could get away with a lot, but not cold-blooded murder.

No, his murder needed to be accidental.

Glasscock's role in the pheasant shoots was as the backstop, the flag man. He'd stand on the edge of the wood and try to change the mind of any pheasant that didn't want to fly forward, flapping and shouting to turn it around. Which put him about twenty yards from whichever gun was stationed on the flank. His last outing was when I was sixteen. I'd wanted it to be the year before, but the situation had never been quite right, the timing and positioning not close enough for an accident.

But on December 26, a snowy Boxing Day a few months after my sixteenth birthday, the beaters were pressing through Box Wood, with me on the flank and Gary in his place. We were at the mid-point, and so far all the birds had taken off and flown straight and true. Then I heard the familiar flap and squawk of a pheasant closer to me, the crack and rustle as it headed out of the trees, this one sideways instead of forward. Almost immediately it banked toward me, like it was trying to sneak back into the safety of the woods. Gary Glasscock raised his flag and started waving to deter that turn, but the pheasant stayed low and ignored him. I'd waited long enough, buried the image of that man on top of me for too long, and the threads of planning and impulse wound together in an instant, pulling my gun up, swinging it across, and putting a deadly dose of lead shot right into his fat, leering face.

I left out the colorful descriptions when I told this story, but I don't think she bought the mock regret. She knew better.

In the days and weeks that followed Tristan's arrest, I gave several statements to the police and to my boss about what happened and couldn't foresee any problems upsetting Tristan's upcoming trial. Except one Monday afternoon, when I walked past Maureen's office and saw Detective Ledsome inside.

"Hi, Dominic." She spoke quietly because Maureen was on the phone with someone else.

"Detective. I meant to call you."

"I told you, I'm married."

"Funny. It's about my gun. I was hoping to get it back."

"It's evidence; you can have it after the trial."

"Why can't you just use photos in the trial? I've done that a million times; you don't need the actual gun."

"Not my call. Speak to the prosecutor."

"I will. So, you ever find that money?"

"No. We did find a couple of bags that we think they used to transport the money, though."

"Oh?"

"Yeah, the victim, Ambrosio Silva, used a couple of camouflage bags to carry it in. We found two just like them."

"Where?"

"Did you know Tristan had a storage unit?"

I thought for a moment. "You know, maybe he mentioned it when I moved in. I'm not sure."

"Well, he does. We found the bags in a filing cabinet, along with a laptop we're processing. And a little box of child porn, to match the sick stuff in his room."

"Seriously?"

"Yep. Locked in a little gun safe, again inside the filing cabinets in his unit."

I shook my head in disbelief. I'd planted the former, not the latter. Just for the record.

"You know," she said, "one thing struck me. About the gun." The timber of her voice changed and set me on edge. "You said in your statement that Bell was trying to get past you, so he could get the gun and shoot you. That's why you were fighting."

"Right. He threatened to shoot me, yeah."

"Thing is, when we found it, the gun was unloaded. He put it in your dresser, so he would have known it was empty."

"I guess."

"Yeah. Just weird."

"Maybe he was going to grab it, load it, and shoot me."

"Seems a slightly drawn out process given the circumstances, plus we didn't find ammo for it in the apartment. None at all."

"Maybe you didn't look hard enough." I shrugged and started back to my office. "Or maybe he used it all up on that guy he shot."

"That's cold, Dominic," she called after me. "Just plain cold."

O

There is such a thing as the perfect crime, and I'll tell you what it is. The perfect crime is one where you get to keep the proceeds. It's one where you get to watch the press and police go into a frenzy because they can't catch you. And it's one where the police eventually get their man. Of course, to be the perfect crime, the man they get has to be (a) guilty and (b) not you. I learned that lesson at a small boarding school in the highlands of Scotland, a simple lesson that played itself out for the first time when I dreamed up a scheme to short-sheet another kid's bed, and my accomplices shouldered all the blame. It was a lesson that stuck.

Just like at my boarding school, once the police and press had their teeth sunk deep into Tristan and the dead Otto, I was all but ignored. The idea of a district attorney's employee and a former cop killing two people in a stagecoach-style robbery was too much for the press. They slathered over every detail, of which I was one. Naturally, I overplayed my hand a few times, but the general impression stuck: I was the guy who'd almost been framed but who'd gone undercover to snare the mastermind behind the plan and captured him in a fight to the death in our apartment. Detective Ledsome never corrected the details I put out there, and occasionally I wondered whether she had a few doubts and was hoping I'd open my mouth a little too wide one day.

The result of my media appearances, which featured the reluctant but always-available-for-an-interview hero, meant that getting gigs in Austin was a cinch. The fact that Gus wasn't around seemed to help on that score because there was no one to complain about the stolen songs I was playing. I had club owners begging me to play and, in fact, they were so desperate they offered to pay me an appearance fee. Once the first had done that, the others had to follow and I, quite literally, laughed all the way to the bank. Even Marley called and, timidly, asked if I could play at his place. I wanted to tell him to go fuck himself, of course, but instead I said "Sure" and doubled my appearance fee. I hadn't forgiven him, it wasn't that. No, I just hadn't decided on the appropriate punishment for him and, until I did, I figured I should keep him close, nice and grateful and trusting.

The cash from the heist came to slightly under $96,000. When I supplemented it with the music money, I was able to go part-time at the DA's office. I could have gone back to trial court, but I hung on to my gig in the juvenile division because I wanted to keep an eye out for Bobby. Not just because I wanted to keep my hands on his sister, no it was more than that. Bobby and I knew a thing or two about each other, and that knowledge had fostered a mutual, unspoken détente. I liked to remind him of my usefulness by scrubbing his cases, and he was always polite and outwardly grateful. It was in my own interests, of course, not his, that I took risks to keep his record clear, because it's an absolute truth that if you cross paths with a psychopath, you have two choices: either get out of the way entirely, or stay on his good side.

And that lesson, I'm very well aware, applies as much to me as it does to anyone else.

ACKNOWLEDGMENTS

Several people inspired me to write this book, and plenty more helped me put it together. To Juan de Kruyff for the true story that sparked my imagination, a tale told during a wonderful ski vacation several years ago. And to the real girl in a green dress, I don't recall your name and you have no idea that I, or this book, even exist but I hope your life turned around and you are in a better place.

My thanks to Dr. Stephen Thorne and to M. E. Thomas for all the help on the matter of sociopathy and psychopathy, which was absolutely invaluable. To Doug Skolaut and Tim Hoppock of the Austin Police Department for their assistance, filling in the gaps of my knowledge on police procedure and criminal investigations. And thanks to Michelle Pierce and Kevin Lance for their tips on music and how the music business works.

Thanks as always to the publishing professionals in my life, especially Dan Mayer and Jill Maxick, and my agent, Ann Collette. And finally to my wife, Sarah, and the three beautiful people who make us so happy, Nicola, Henry, and Natalie.

ABOUT THE AUTHOR

Mark Pryor is a former newspaper reporter from England and now a prosecutor with the Travis County District Attorney's Office, in Austin, Texas.

He is the author of five novels in the Hugo Marston series, which are set in Paris, London, and Barcelona. The first, *The Bookseller*, was a *Library Journal* Debut of the Month and was called "unputdownable" by Oprah.com. The sixth is due to be released in 2016. Mark is also the creator of the nationally recognized true-crime blog *D. A. Confidential* and has appeared on CBS News's *48 Hours* and Discovery Channel's *Discovery ID: Cold Blood*.